TIE THE DINGO DOWN, MATE!

AN AUSTRALIAN VETERINARIAN'S WORK EXPERIENCE IN AFRICA

Nicole O'Connor

Nicole O'Connor
WELLINGTON, NEW ZEALAND

Dear Reader

WELCOME!

I'm excited to have you on board. I wrote these stories with you in mind. Although many veterinary memoirs have been written; mine are unique because they are written from a veterinary wife's perspective.

Be warned, if you LOVE James Herriot's delightful veterinary tales; then you will be disappointed with these. Trust me; this is not for you, so put the book down.

A vet's life is a dog's life.

Disagree?
Snap off.

Yours truly
*Yappity-yapper Stoepkakker **CRaP**per*

ILLUSTRATIONS: Nicole O'Connor

Lightning never strikes twice in the same place.
Really?
Ask Satan.
RIP
dark horse.

To my esteemed family and pets:

*

Kangaroo Keith
--Thanks for hopping up with your valued contribution--
*
Caracal Colin
--For watching quietly from a safe distance--
*
Secretary bird Sean
--for technical support--
*

Fat Chops
Furry Felix
Muffin Puffin
Rastkin-Wingnut
Bounty Scrounty the
Dingo Dog
Ruby
&
Stoepkakkers International

Contents

Business as Usual

ANGUS BULLOCK

1981

SYDNEY, AUSTRALIA.

Barbeque weather. Warm social Saturdays never failed to procure lines of vaccination candidates and traumatic business. Casualties rolled in with conveyer-belt-style efficiency, delivering canines with bones stuck in throats to stitch-ups after brawls. Angus Bullock, better known as Gus to friends, manned the busy veterinary clinic single-handedly. As he prepared to leave, yet another emergency arrived. He placed the shivering, wounded poodle on the table for examination. Deep bite wounds punctured its body. He pulled the stethoscope out from his ears and considered options. "Miss Sinclair, I am afraid it's serious. Bella has a punctured lung and a ruptured bowel. She requires intravenous fluids and emergency surgery—I must start immediately."

The woman bursts into tears. "Please save my Bella! She's like a child to me. She's all I have."

Gus considered the ageing, childless woman kindly. "There, there, Miss Sinclair, I'll certainly do my best, but I can't guarantee success. Please stay calm. Hopefully, Bella will need you later. In the meanwhile, I suggest you go home and try to relax. I will keep you informed of any changes right after Bella's surgery."

A couple of hours later after surgery, true to his word, Gus phoned Miss Sinclair. "Bella made it, but she'll have to stay in the hospital for a few days."

"Thank you, Dr Bullock! Thank you so much." Miss Sinclair sobbed tears of joy as she hung-up.

Gus was relieved to have a survivor and a happy customer. However, the extra three hours would make him late getting home. And, considering he had promised his fiance, Sheila, that he would be early for a change, he knew she would be disgruntled.

As he drove home, his mind drifted back to 1980, the year before, when success had come after studying for five and a half years. Back then, his heart had almost burst with pride and joy as he strode up the red carpet towards the podium to receive his Veterinary graduation certificate from Sydney University. It had been the pinnacle of student success. Euphoria had surged through his veins as his mind explored infinite possibilities crammed with splendid prospects. Surely, a secure future lay ahead while doing the work he loved best—treating sick animals.

No more exams. No more financial worries. A good life.

He envisioned himself driving a glitzy Mercedes-Benz. The smell and feel of the leather upholstery were almost tangible. He would propose to his girlfriend, Sheila Sparks, a smoking hot brassiere model, and together they might breed a colony of cute, clever kids. God willing, that was the plan.

But months later, reality had struck. Money was tight. The Mercedes-Benz concept got placed on ice as a second-hand Toyota Corolla tootled along in its place. Balancing the costs of exorbitant Sydney living while paying off student debt was a challenge. Night-duty and weekend call-outs governed his time instead of hot steamy nights with Sheila. *Sigh.* That was the price for being the most junior vet.

Later, when he returned home, Sheila cast her eyes downward. The weight of her sexy, black false eyelashes made her lids droop as she sat cross-legged on the sofa, filing her red fingernails. "You work appalling hours." It was an accusation. Her full lips pouted. "I hardly see you when you're awake. In fact, we don't go out anymore. In my opinion, you might as well be a *monkey.*"

"*A what?*"

"You earn peanuts dancing to your profession."

Gus groaned. "I've just qualified! I'm the youngest at work. Hang in there. My hours will improve; they can't last forever—you'll see."

Sheila saw nothing as she buried her face in her slender hands. "How do you expect to support a family on your pathetic salary?"

"Other vets manage. Give me a chance—I'll get there."

"I doubt it." Her mouth tightened.

Gus touched her chin gently and tilted it up. "I love you, honey. We'll make it."

"No—we won't!" She pulled back, pushing his hand away. "It's over! I'm leaving."

Gus reeled. "But why?"

"I don't love you anymore! It's that simple."

He shook his head. "I don't understand."

"I've found someone else—a hotel owner. He's mature; twenty years older, and *wealthy.*"

Gus stared in disbelief as the awful truth hit. "Don't tell me you're running off with that scumbag--what's his name? Ah, Cecil Flounders from that poncy hotel, Preston Heights, from across the road where I took you to dinner last month." Gus paused as he rubbed his chin. "I thought that creepy manager was over-attentive at the time."

She snorted. "You're sharper than you let on."

His heart plummeted like a ship's anchor into stormy waters. "You cheated on me while I worked!" He raged. "That Cecil guy--looks as though he's hung like a mosquito! What's the attraction? Does he *sew* like a machine? *I know those rutting fox terrier types.*"

Her averted gaze and stony silence aggravated his fears.

Gus folded his muscular forearms against his chest. Every hair on his body bristled. "You're a gold-digger!"

Sheila's eyes blazed. "Well, at least he doesn't stink of dog and cat muck! And I won't have to wash filthy clothes and cook budget meals."

Gus stood rigid. "I thought you loved animals and wanted to be a stay-at-home mum one day."

"I love sexy beasts who make decent money--enough to keep a woman satisfied."

"But you knew I was a vet when we began dating. I can't change my profession now."

She guffawed. "Don't bother! As I said, I'm leaving."

His jaw muscles flinched. "Thanks for your brutal honesty. At least you woke up before we married. And what about that extravagant engagement ring I gave you? You know—the one bought with my *peanuts*."

"Work, work, work!" she mocked as she twisted the diamond ring off her finger in a fluid movement. She dashed to the toilet and flushed it away. "There!" She slapped her palms together as if dusting filthy soil from her hands. "Go back to your worker-treadmill and grind your nuts."

"Sheila!" Gus winced. That hurt. Her vicious words cut his heart more than her careless action scorched his pocket. It was the ultimate rejection. Furious, his hands became fists that he quickly thrust deep into his pockets, as if they were independent madmen in need of restraint. He spoke from between gritted teeth. "Get out!" A jerk of his head indicated the way.

"Goodbye, loser!" She slammed the door and disappeared with a suitcase in each hand.

"What a fool I've been!" Gus fumed. *The woman's feral!* He stared out the window. His large, square fists remained planted deep inside his trouser pockets. Bleak thoughts obstructed his ability to visualise good prospects. Repetitive thoughts whirled. *What can I do? What now? Where can I go?* His Adam's apple bobbed as he swallowed. Emotional pain seared his throat. An idea began to form.

CHAPTER TWO

A Fresh Start

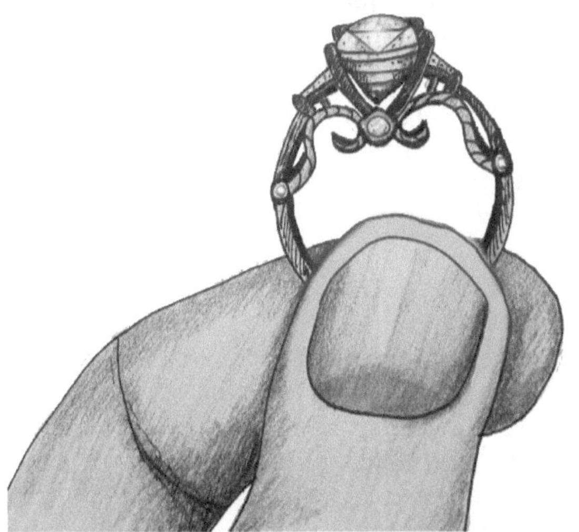

G us felt like throttling her, but she wasn't worth going to jail over. Such a foolish act would incriminate him unnecessarily, and he would be struck off the Veterinary Register. Self-control and sanity were paramount. He pulled himself together by starting with a pragmatic approach. First, he went to the bathroom and peered into the toilet.

In her haste, Sheila had knocked the toilet roll sitting on top of the cistern into the bowl when she had flushed. He shuddered with disgust as he bent down and retrieved the sodden mass, placing it into a bucket. A glimmer of hope emerged, so he fetched a wire coat hanger and bent it into his desired shape. Carefully, he lowered the coat hanger down into the bowl and dragged it around inside the S-bend. Nothing. Then he put his hand down as far as he could, but still nothing. His fingers explored the toilet bowl, discovering the siphonic jet hole. He made a small hook with the tip of the coat hanger and fished around inside the opening. Voila! Out came the ring. The toilet roll must have prevented the ring from going down. Such a stroke of good luck could only mean fortune was now in his favour.

To sterilise it, Gus placed the diamond ring into a glass jar filled with bleach and water. He planned to take it to a pawn shop and salvage his losses.

Next, he opened a can of beer and put his feet up. He reflected upon his failed relationship and grimaced. Sheila had been engaged three times before; that should have been a warning. She had probably run off with a divorced man, possibly a notorious philanderer. They might be good medicine for each other. Of one thing he was certain, they were over.

***

The following week at work Gus made his important announcement.

After it, his boss clicked his tongue in disbelief. "I can't believe you're leaving." He marvelled that a young veterinarian would leave his practice and the wonderful city of Sydney, for the sake of transitioning to politically unstable South Africa. "Where about are you heading?"

Gus grinned. "There's a practice near Phalaborwa that wants a locum to start next month. It's situated next to the Kruger National Park."

They shook hands. His boss said, "Good luck, mate. I reckon you'll need it."

***

The size and sophistication of the Johannesburg Airport and the magnitude of the surrounding city left Gus wondering if any African wildlife remained. Johannesburg, as seen from the air, was a sprawling mass of highways and houses. After one night's stay at an airport hotel, he caught a connecting flight in a twin-engine plane to the town of Phalaborwa, an arid mining town on the north-eastern border.

As viewed when coming into land, Phalaborwa's dry, dusty, compact red soils had similarities to places in Australia. From a bright, cloudless sky, the baking sun scorched the airport's short, tawny grass runway. His eyes watered as he squinted down and noted it was fenced off from surrounding bush, probably to stop animals crossing. Flat-topped acacia thorn trees sparsely dotted the outer boundaries. Gus braced himself as the plane touched the bumpy runway and taxied to a halt outside the small, terminal building.

Once disembarked, Gus grabbed his suitcase and sat on a chair, feeling grateful for shade. Flies sought moisture as they buzzed towards his perspiring face. He shooed them away.

A tall, bronze-skinned man approached Gus. "Good-day! Are you Angus Bullock?"

"Yeah, mate. Pleased to meet you. Just call me, Gus."

"I'm the guy you'll be working with—Steve Prinsloo."

"Hi, Steve!" A firm handshake ensued followed by casual conversation as they strolled towards the parking lot. Steve put Gus's bag in the back of his truck and started the engine. As Steve's truck turned the corner onto the main street, he jammed on brakes.

"Whoa!" Wide-eyed, Gus froze in his seat.

Steve's lips twitched as they watched the large bull elephant crossing the road in front of the truck. Its large head looked weighted by the magnificent ivory tusks it supported only inches from the ground. Its long trunk swayed and twirled as it explored new smells. Most intimidating of all was its gigantic penis that scraped the road as it ambled forwards.

Gus let out a low, quiet whistle. "Wow, he's a big fella."

"Sure is," Steve replied. "Elephants often escape from the park. One swipe from that beast could flip this truck, leaving us like scrambled eggs on the tarmac."

Gus winced.

"It's best to drive slow or stop. *Never* blow your horn—that can upset them."

A bare-footed, black man jogged towards the elephant with a small branch, shouting in his native lingo as he herded it, not unlike a prodigal cow, back towards the park's gateway.

"He's brave," Gus remarked.

Steve slapped Gus's shoulder. "Welcome to Africa, Ozzy friend!"

That evening, Steve and Gus chilled off with cans of ice-cold Castle Lager Beer while cooking meat outdoors. The cooker was fashioned from an old, charcoal-filled drum with a wire mesh top upon which the meat was placed.

Gus sighed and licked his lips. "I've always enjoyed a good barbeque."

Steve laughed. "*Barbie-Cue!* That sounds like a Barbie doll thing. In South Africa, men enjoy cooking meat outdoors. We give it a decent name, *braaivleis; (pronounced: br-eye-flays)* that means roast meat."

"Cheers to braaivleis!" Gus raised his beer can.

"Now, you're learning. Hey, see that?" Steve pointed to a mozzy on his arm. "That's an Anopheles mosquito. See how it sits with its butt pointing straight up?"

"Yes."

Splat! Steve slapped it dead. "That particular species is responsible for transmitting Malaria."

Gus raised his brows. "Should I take anti-Malaria tablets?"

Steve shook his head. "The people who live here don't. It's a hazard in certain places inside the National Park. Sleep under a mosquito net and be mindful of symptoms that are similar to the onset of influenza; fever and stiff neck. Most doctors know to check for it." Steve grabbed the meat with wire tongs and served it.

"Delicious," Gus said between mouthfuls of succulent, juicy beef.

High-pitched, eerie calls drifted across the still, warm night.

"What's that weird, eerie noise?" Gus inquired.

"Jackals and hyenas."

"They sound weird."

"Some nights we hear lions too; you'll know when you do—they're extremely loud. Have you had any anti-rabies shots yet?" Steve asked.

"No."

"Okay, I'll organise a course for you. Best not take a risk."

"Thanks."

***

"What the hell ... ?" Gus exclaimed as he entered his bedroom and switched on his bedroom light. A mass of seething, crawling, small black ants covered the wall.

Steve peered over his shoulder and returned with a can of fly spray. "Here, use this. Tomorrow morning we'll vacuum the dead ones. It must be time to get the foundations sprayed against ants again. One has to do it every ten years or so. For now, the best thing is to stand each bed leg in a small bowl of water. The ants drown before they climb up the legs."

After helping Gus do that, Steve said, "Goodnight, see you in the morning."

Gus pulled his bed away from the wall and brushed ants off the pillow. Being weary, he slept well until first bird fart; only to be awoken by competing roosters in a crowing chorus. An array of raucous birds soon joined in the fracas. Gus pushed back his sheet, stretched and staggered to the window where he abruptly flicked the skimpy curtains open.

"Crikey!" He was face to face with a yawning baboon perched on a tree branch outside the window. It was busy scratching its brightly coloured blue and red scrotum. Shocked by the sudden drapery jerk, the unfortunate creature screamed in terror and fell over backwards. It landed on the hard soil below with a dull thud before scrambling away with its shrieking companions in hot pursuit.

CHAPTER THREE

Foot and Mouth

Steve's veterinary clinic was an extension built onto the side of his roughcast brick and tile house. Inside, it sported modern veterinary facilities.

Over the next few days, a constant stream of small animals were brought in by worried pet owners. Treatments could range from routine desexing, vaccinations, deworming and snake-bites, to trauma resulting from wildlife encounters, accidental poisonings, and parasite-triggered diseases.

At tea break, Steve asked, "Do you hunt?"

Gus shook his head. "I save lives."

"Sometimes it's necessary. Anyway, I received a call from an army vet, David Swanepoel, stationed at Metz Hospital. Tribesmen spotted a lone bull buffalo running with cattle. Last seen between Trichardtsdal and Ga-Sekororo. He wants me to shoot it."

"Why kill it?"

"Buffalo are natural carriers of Foot and Mouth. Outside of their natural environment, they must be separated from cattle to avoid transmission. Meat exports could be jeopardised, and it's not safe for herdsmen to drive cattle to dip tanks with a buffalo in their midst."

"Can't you dart it?"

"M99, the tranquilizer, is lethal to humans. It requires careful handling. And, buffalo are not sufficiently endangered to warrant rescue and capture for one animal. It would cost a fortune that nobody would pay."

"Why can't David shoot it?"

Steve shook his head. "Buffalo are treacherous. If a hunter isn't accurate, it could turn and kill him. It's best to go with two or three guys for backup. Can we count on you?"

Excitement beckoned. "Yes."

"We'll pack after lunch. It's a two-hour drive. We might sleep rough for a night or two."

Their journey began on a tar road until Trichardtsdal where they turned off onto dirt that soon narrowed into a bumpy bush track. Steve swerved as he negotiated around trees, anthills, and boulders, heading towards the foothills of the northern Drakensberg Mountains. The road widened as it traversed through a small township and then on towards Metz Hospital.

"Beautiful countryside," Gus murmured, gazing through the open window as hot air fanned his perspiring face.

From between trees, a trio of thatched rondavels loomed ahead. Steve parked his truck causing a motley crew of stringy-looking, free-range chickens to scatter. David appeared. Introductions were made as they shook hands.

"Nice hut," Gus said, surveying David's abode.

"Thanks. It's a *rondavel*—that's the name given to traditional, round dwellings with thatched rooves."

"Neat! I can't wait to see inside."

"Come." David led the way. He jerked to a halt.

Gus and Steve's eyes darted in the direction of David's pointing finger. A huge brown snake slithered ahead and into the doorway.

Steve chuckled. "Hunting's just begun!"

David peered in through the window and saw it slide behind the kitchen door. "Judging by the colour and size, I reckon it's a cobra."

"Crikey, mate!" Gus exclaimed. "That's poisonous!"

"Hell, yeah," David answered. "A bite from one that size will cause death unless seven or eight ampules of anti-venom are used, and I only ever keep two with me."

"Why only two?"

"It's expensive and has a short expiry."

Steve loaded his rifle. "I'll shoot it before we lose sight."

"Let me flush it out." David offered.

"Don't get too close," Steve warned.

Gus kept a safe distance.

"That hunting rifle's too powerful," David cautioned. "A shotgun would be better."

"It's all I have with me."

"The bullet might ricochet."

"I know."

"Wait. First, I'll try to drive it out with this stick." David waved a long, thin branch above his head as he poked it in through the window and rattled it towards the snake. The snake's hood went up as it swivelled, making three quick consecutive strikes.

"Now he's angry," Steve said. "Careful! You're not a snake handler."

"Stand back and take cover." Steve raised the rifle.

"CRACK!"

An ear-splitting blast. They peered in through the window. Only splinters remained of the lower bathroom door. The snake was shot in two; the front half writhed madly with snapping jaws. Steve said, "Get back." He raised his gun delivering the second shot. The snake's head blew off, leaving a gouge in the concrete floor. Afterwards, they carried out squirming snake coils on the end of two sticks. David swept the floor with a broom and retrieved all snake fragments onto a piece of newspaper. Gus offered to take it from him. "Careful, Gus. Don't touch any part. The fangs remain toxic after death, that's why tribesmen burn dead snakes."

Bare-footed African children came running. A feared inyoka was dead. They shouted and danced joyfully while maintaining a safe distance. One of the elders lit a small fire to incinerate the remains as the curious villagers babbled and gawked.

"It's a pity it died," Gus said. "Maybe it could have been relocated."

Steve shook his head. "If a snake comes into human territory—I shoot it. Cobras are territorial; you'll not chase them away. They are not endangered. When you see the results of snakebite, you'll understand. Once I helped a doctor revive a woman who stepped on a cobra while picking pumpkins in a field. It took eight ampoules of antivenom and eleven hours of manual Ambu-bagging to revive her to the point where she could breathe unassisted. There's no life-support equipment out here; most victims die. It's a terrible, painful death. Victims foam at the mouth and endure encroaching muscle spasms and paralysis. They vomit, defecate, urinate and convulse until their last breath."

Gus shuddered.

"Enough!" David intervened. "I have beers and boerewors!"

"*Boerewors*?"

David grinned. "Farmers' sausage."

After dinner, Steve said, "Early start tomorrow. Let's hit the sack."

"Where shall I sleep?" Gus asked.

Steve threw him a sleeping bag. "On the floor."

Gus caught it with one hand.

"Watch out for scorpions and snakes creeping under the door."

"Thanks."

The men rose before daybreak, climbing into Steve's two-seater, 4 x 4 truck. Steve and David sat in front while Gus parked his butt on a rolled up sleeping bag at the back, gripping onto the sides of the truck as it trundled along. Dawn glowed orange along the horizon, silhouetting trees and squawking birds. His keen eyes surveyed the African bushveld, drinking in the grace of agile, leaping Impala as the noisy vehicle startled them. Overhead, curious, black-faced, vervet monkeys shrieked and peeked out from behind leafy foliage. Their keen, beady amber eyes, glinting mischievously in the early sunrise. A terrified black-faced baby Vervet monkey raced, screaming towards its mother, slipping from a branch. The mother grabbed it by the tail, hauling it towards her breast, where it clung fiercely with wide-eyed alarm.

Farther along the road, Steve pulled the truck up under a flat-topped acacia tree. A pair of duiker dived into the undergrowth, vanishing from sight.

Steve and David carried their rifles while tracking. Gus followed, unarmed. Clear, bright skies warmed noisy insects and flies to life.

A group of black and white spotted Nguni cattle grazed ahead. No sign of a buffalo. Steve spotted a child-herdsman and went to speak with him. The barefooted lad nodded his head, speaking his own lingo while pointing in another direction.

Steve returned. "His brother saw it a few days ago, moving towards the Selati River."

They returned to the truck and drove towards the river's sandbanks.

Steve parked the vehicle. "The bush is too thick here. Let's walk."

Gus carried the heaviest backpack as they headed out.

David cast his eyes along the sand. "That's buffalo spoor."

"How can you tell?" Gus asked.

"The imprints are larger than cattle's. See, the prints embed deeper? That's because they are heavier." David picked his way along the waters' edge. "See here—that's cattle spoor. It's smaller and shallower."

Steve pushed his hat back and mopped his brow. Humidity had increased. "Good, we're on track. Let's cross the river." He glanced towards Gus. "Don't get your feet wet. Bilharzia's rife around here."

"What's that?"

"It's an illness transmitted from waterborne parasites that breed in stagnant and slow-moving water. The microscopic organisms burrow through the human skin on contact. Snails feeding on these reeds form part of the parasitic life cycle."

By midday, away from the water, the tracks were harder to follow.

"I reckon that's buffalo droppings," David said, looking ahead. "See there? The texture is coarser. And look here, there's the same large spoor with a longer toe on the front left."

"How fresh is it?" Gus asked.

"Today. Keep going."

Another two hours of trudging came to an abrupt halt when David stopped and raised his binoculars to his eyes. "I see it."

Steve let out a slow whistle and cocked his rifle. "Yeah, that's him. He's a big fella."

The buffalo stopped grazing and lifted its head.

"Damn. It heard us."

All eyes followed as the buffalo stepped into the dappled shade of an acacia tree, swishing its tail.

"Listen," Steve said. "Gus, climb a tree and hang on. David, keep me covered with your rifle."

The buffalo bellowed, pawing the ground as Steve crouched, inching closer. Steve lifted his rifle. Its horns were too thick for a head-shot, so he positioned a side-shot, aiming at its heart. CRACK! The explosion rang out. The buffalo charged. Steve fired again, but the beast continued advancing.

David lifted his gun and fired two shots, hitting the beast twice, neither stopped it.

Steve shot again. This time the buffalo collapsed, skidding onto its side like a ten-ton lorry careening into an embankment as it plunged headlong, twisting sideways into the dust.

Not trusting appearances, Steve approached with caution until he was twenty metres from the beast. His advance caused a twig to snap. The buffalo lifted its head and turned to look. Things happened fast. It rose to its feet and charged. David lifted his rifle to shoot but Steve was between him and the beast—he couldn't shoot.

In the face of adversity and imminent death, Steve raised his rifle and fired into the beast's face. Too low. Maddened and unstoppable, it advanced until it was four strides away. Unflinching, Steve fired the last possible shot. Kill or be killed. The buffalo fell, stone dead, at Steve's feet.

Gus mopped his brow. "Wow, that was awesome, mate! You nearly died—I can't believe you had the balls to stand your ground for that last shot."

"I had no choice. It was shoot or get gored."

"Phew!" David exclaimed. "If that last shot had failed, we'd be taking your corpse home in your own meat bags."

Steve swigged from his water bottle. "Let's sharpen the knives."

***

Swarms of blue-bodied meat flies honed-in as Dave began skinning the carcass. Steve sliced off thick layers of rump, placing them into plastic bags. Chattering African children and young men gathered around, all smiling and joking.

The gathering crowd astounded Gus.

Steve chuckled. "Word's out—free meat. It would be a shame to see good meat go to waste. I prefer seeing people helping themselves and eating well. When they're finished, there'll be nothing left. They use offal--everything."

"What about the risk of Foot and Mouth and other diseases?" Gus asked.

"Don't worry," David said. "They regularly snare wild animals that don't pass through inspection anyway. They know to cook meat well. Foot and Mouth only affects cloven-hooved animals. If the meat's cooked, it's okay."

"I'm keen to taste some," Gus said grabbing a knife and slashing off a chunk.

"Ow--ee!"

All eyes fixated on Gus who dropped the knife and clenched his left thumb with his right hand as he danced a maddened jig of pain with blood pulsating from his hand.

"Oooh! That's bad." David bent and rescued the tip of Gus's left thumb off the ground before a village dog ate it. He placed it into a small plastic meat bag and handed it to Gus. "You might need this."

<u>CHAPTER FOUR</u>

Thumbs-Up!

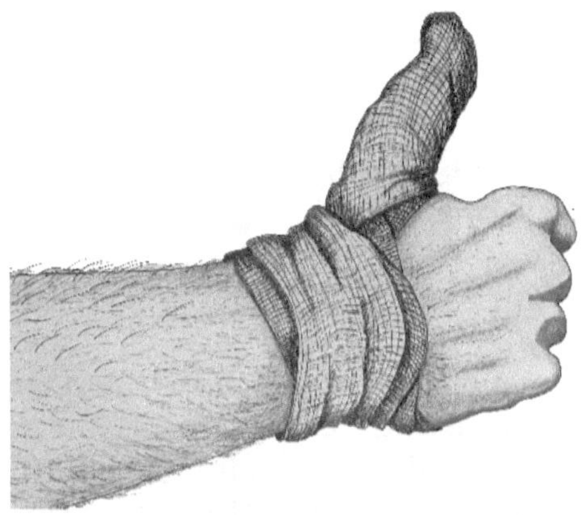

From his medical bag, David produced a sterile gauze swab and crepe bandage, binding Gus's thumb with just enough firm pressure to staunch blood loss.

Steve glanced at his wrist watch. "Thanks, David. Gus and I better pack and drive to Tzaneen hospital. Hopefully, there's a doctor who can do something."

David helped load some meat and the equipment. Gus grabbed his own bag with one hand and jumped into the truck. They bade Dave farewell. Steve headed his truck at a steady pace towards the small town, Tzaneen. Upon reaching the twenty-two-bed hospital, he parked his truck. Tranquil gardens surrounded the parking lot with established indigenous trees and rolling lawns. He ventured inside with Gus.

They were met by an attractive young nurse who had a long, blonde plait down her back. "Good afternoon, gentlemen. How may I help you?"

Steve spoke, "Good-day. My friend cut off the top of his thumb. I reckon we need a doctor."

Gus ogled the fair-haired nurse with approval. Her clear skin and soft lips were a pleasure to behold. He held up the clear, plastic bag containing his thumb part with his bandaged hand.

Her pretty face softened as she made sympathetic noises. "Oh! You, poor man." She took Gus's hand and examined it. "The bleeding is under control. I'll put the top of your thumb in the fridge until the doctor arrives."

Gus smiled as he read her name tag. "Thank you, Miranda Mostert."

Miranda blushed and smiled as she considered ailing, handsome Gus with his mop of dark hair and droopy moustache.

Right then, a stout woman entered the hallway. "Nurse Miranda! What's happening?"

"Matron, this poor man cut off the top of his thumb. I'm heading to the fridge to store it in a cool place."

"Let me see," Matron barked. She snatched the bag and held it up to the light. "Bah! It's old and dirty. How careless. The doctor can't use this dead flesh--discard it."

Miranda countered, "But he might wish to try ..."

"Nurse, Miranda! Don't argue. Do as you're told and dispose of it in the *dirty* bin. You can't put that filthy thing in my clean fridge."

Miranda's cheeks flamed. "Yes, Matron." She cast Gus a sympathetic glance as she headed towards the yellow dustbin to trash it. Soon after, a hospital cleaner arrived and emptied the bin into her trolley before continuing her rounds.

Gus and David waited for fifteen minutes for Dr van der Westhuizen to arrive.

"Come this way, gentlemen." Dr van der Westhuizen beckoned with his finger. "Please, take a seat and tell me what happened."

Gus relayed the story as the doctor unwound the bandage. He peered closely into the stump of the severed thumb. "Mmm ..." was all he said as he poked and probed.

Gus mopped the perspiration from his brow with a limp handkerchief as he willed himself to sit still and not cry out loud.

The doctor said, "You must be in pain."

Gus grimaced. "Yes, but I'm coping."

Dr van der Westhuizen frowned as he set about preparing a syringe filled with a local anaesthetic. "Fortunately, the bone is intact, but there's a considerable amount of flesh missing that includes part of your nail and thumb pad."

Gus nodded.

"Do you still have the part?" The doctor asked.

Steve glanced towards Gus with a smirk. "We saved it in a plastic bag," Steve said. "But Matron *Moron* insisted nurse Miranda discard it."

The doctor scowled as he rang the bell. Nurse Miranda appeared. "Yes, doctor?"

"Nurse--fetch me the tip of this man's thumb."

Her eyes widened. "Doctor, I threw it away."

"Please find it; fast."

"Yes, sir." She turned and sped down the corridor.

"Nurse Miranda!" Matron called. "Slow down. Where are you going?"

"Matron, I have to find that thumb tip. Doctor wants it."

"Oh." Matron rolled her eyes. "Well, hurry up and find it!"

Nurse Miranda hunted through the dustbin, but it wasn't there, so she looked in all the other bins. Nothing. She headed back to the Matron, close to tears. "Matron, I can't find it!"

Matron stood square, hands on hips, and bawled, "Ask the cleaner! I saw her emptying the bins."

"Yes, Matron." Miranda rushed away.

Five minutes later, Miranda reappeared bearing the prized trophy, held high, for all to see.

"Congratulations!" Doctor exclaimed.

Gus smiled with relief. The young nurse blushed, fluttering her eyelashes as she attempted to avoid his welcome, penetrating gaze of approval.

The doctor rinsed the body part in sterile saline solution before reattaching it. Afterwards, he sat back admiring his handiwork. Black stitches, in a small neat ring, connected the thumb tip in place. He administered light padding and bandaging to protect the thumb from dirt and injury. Next, he prescribed some antibiotic and checked that Gus's anti-tetanus shot was up-to-date.

Dr van der Westhuizen had a confession to make. "I'm not sure if the piece will reconnect or not; it's the best I can do. It's better to try than not to try."

Gus smiled, giving him the thumbs-up with his bandaged paw.

***

Over the weekend, Gus bought beer, while Steve prepared the buffalo meat that had been curing in the fridge for three days to help relax its fibres.

"How do you want yours?" Steve asked.

Gus licked his lips and held up his bandaged thumb. "Ultra-rare, thanks."

Steve grimaced. "Yuck. I only eat well-done meat."

"Why?"

"I was weaned on it—that's the way most Africans eat it. Blackened on the outside and cooked right through the middle."

"That kills flavour!" Gus argued as he tucked into his rare steak. "Mmm ...! Man, this is so good." He munched salad in between mouthfuls of succulent buffalo steak, drooling with pleasure. Then he eyed Steve's dry, charcoaled piece. "How's yours, mate?"

"All good—just the way I like it."

That night they went to bed with full stomachs and slept like bloated hyenas until the phone rang.

Gus fumbled to turn on his bedside lamp. He got out of bed and walked down the hallway where he heard Steve talking into the receiver. "Well, I don't know ... don't usually treat humans. Yeah, I understand—it's an emergency. Okay. Bring him along. I'll try to help."

<u>CHAPTER FIVE</u>

Cock and Bull

Yawning, Gus rubbed his eyes. "What's up?"

"Some American campers with a sick teenager. They can't locate a doctor, so they're bringing him here."

"What's wrong with him?"

Steve frowned. "Not sure, and neither are they. The background sounded chaotic. I hope it's not a snakebite or malaria. Anyway, they're on their way."

"I'll make coffee," Gus volunteered.

"Good idea."

Twenty minutes later a camper van drove by; reversed at an alarming rate and then turned into their driveway where it came to an abrupt halt. Its doors burst open, regurgitating a group of dishevelled youths. Two supported a weak lad by the arms, half dragging him indoors. Steve led them straight through to his consulting room where he seated the ailing teen. The kid's face was red. Snot and tears flowed, wetting the front of his T-shirt.

Gus handed him roller towel. "Here, wipe your face. What's your name?"

"Jason Squires," answered the squirming patient, still writhing in a half-crouched stance.

"Are you in pain?" Gus asked.

Jason nodded vigorously.

"Where does it hurt?"

Although already flushed, Jason's face turned a darker shade of crimson. He emitted a guttural cry of pain and shook his head.

Steve gripped him by the shoulders. "Jason. Listen to me, I must know—were you bitten by something?"

The young man shook his head. Gasping, he had the appearance of a dying fish.

"Are you sure? You're struggling to breathe."

The young fellow was squinting with pain. "Not snakebite," he gasped.

"Well, what happened?"

Jason moaned and turned away, gripping onto the windowsill with whitened knuckles desperately trying to support himself.

"Show us where it hurts," Gus demanded.

Jason took a deep breath as he burst into fresh agonised sobs and then pointed towards his crotch.

"We must see," Steve said.

The young fellow sank to the floor, clutching his balls while shaking his head.

Steve scowled as his eyes surveyed the group. "Who the hell knows what happened? Speak now—it's an emergency."

The boys shoved one guy forward. "Go on, Karl. You're his brother--tell him."

Jason cringed and closed his eyes as he continued to writhe in pain.

Steve escorted Karl into an adjacent room. "Please speak. It looks serious. Jason needs help."

Karl's face went scarlet. "We went on a day trip where the tour guide told us of an alleged African tradition. He showed us some Bushmen paintings--all the men had erections. The guide reckoned they had big cocks that never went down. He said the Bushmen used a particular plant juice that enhanced penis size." Karl cleared his throat before continuing, "Anyway, we were lucky enough to find the plant on a walk, so we dared Jason to try it first."

"Ah..." Steve's lips compressed into a straight line as he hid humour. "What is the name of the plant?"

"Euphorbia tirucalli."

Steve groaned, "Oh, no!" The other name for that plant was *Fire Sticks*. He shot back into the consulting room. "Guys, please go outside—except for Jason. Karl, you're his brother--stay."

The others made a shuffling exodus.

Steve turned to Jason. "So, you rubbed Euphorbia tirucalli sap on your penis?"

The young man nodded. Tears of shame and humiliation oozed.

"Right, if you wish to save your marital prospects—get those jeans off *now*."

Jason unzipped his fly and dropped his pants. Everyone in the room winced and shuddered.

"Good grief, mate!" Gus's eyes watered. "Talk about cock-rot."

Sympathy entered the eyes of the beholders as they surveyed the lad's inflamed genitals, now swollen to alarming proportions. White patches had formed, in between, serous fluid leaked from split crevasses in the engorged, red skin.

Steve clicked his tongue. "This is serious. Your penis is covered in second-degree burns. I hope it doesn't continue to deteriorate."

Jason rolled his bloodshot eyes heavenwards. "Will I lose it, Doc?"

"To be honest, son, I'm not sure. I hope not. I'm a vet—not a human doctor. All I can I can do is to administer first aid. You need a hospital with a burns unit."

Gus and Steve wore latex gloves as they attempted to wash the hardened sap off Jason's penis with soapy gauze swabs. The wilted lad sat on the toilet while they worked. It was important not to let any of the run-off water contaminate his good skin.

Some dribbled onto his testicles. Afterwards, they rinsed his genitalia with copious amounts of cold water. Finally, Jason's family jewels were swathed in a thick layer of Flamazine, sterile gauze swabs and padded with generous wads of cotton wool.

"Dr, it hurts! May I have a painkiller?"

Gus handed him two Paracetamol tablets with a glass of water.

"Is that all?"

"That's all we're permitted to give you."

Steve released a slow whistle. "Karl, please use my phone and make arrangements for Jason to be flown to the Johannesburg Hospital as soon as possible." He gave Karl a list of contact numbers. "I hope matters turn out well."

Afterwards, Steve and Gus watched the subdued group depart with their comrade.

"It's almost sunrise," Steve said. "Let's have another coffee and early breakfast."

"Great idea," Gus said.

Over breakfast, Gus helped himself to seconds and then went to the kitchen and made another large sandwich. In between mouthfuls of bread and cheese, he said, "I sure hope that kid never trusts another cock and bull story."

C H A P T E R   S I X

Mink and Manure

Steve pulled a wry face. "Yeah." Then he pushed his coffee cup away. "There's something I must ask you."

"Yes?"

"I wish to open another veterinary clinic. Are you interested in starting it?"

"Yeah. Where about?"

"In a small town named Magoebaskloof. It's about two hours' drive away."

"When?"

Steve smiled. "Soon as possible."

"Tell me more."

"It's situated in the north of the Drakensberg Mountains, about twenty minutes' drive from Tzaneen. I reckon you'll enjoy it. The weather's cooler. There are forest walks, waterfalls and spectacular views. The fast-flowing streams are safe for swimming; they're bilharzia free. And, unlike

Tzaneen's dam, there aren't any crocs and hippopotamuses because it's cool and steep."

"It sounds fantastic!"

"Good. It's too far away for me to manage. It's a lucrative town with good potential. You'll have to do surgery and farm calls."

"Okay."

Steve glanced at Gus's thumb. "How's it healing?"

"Steadily," Gus lied, dismissing further questions. He longed for the opportunity. "When do I start?"

"Next week. I bought a piece of land up there with a simple rondavel on it."

"Ready when you say *go*."

***

Ten days later, Gus found himself driving towards his new abode. As he drove through the town of Tzaneen, his mind flittered back to the charming young nurse at the hospital. *Ah, she was a pretty one; but too young and innocent.*

As he headed out of Tzaneen and onto the dual carriageway that crossed the Fanie Botha Dam, he looked down upon the sandbanks and spotted a herd of hippo wallowing. He pulled his VW Beetle over and got out, leaning over the railings to admire his lucky find. Hot humidity caused his skin to perspire. Hippo made strange noises. A baby hippo floated close to its enormous mother while a much bigger one, possibly a male, climbed out the water, swishing its short fat tail as it expelled a spray of dark, mud-coloured excrement. His gaze travelled further along the bank. A crocodile lay with its mouth wide open as a small white bird darted in and out of its mouth, picking food from the reptile's jagged teeth. A wave of pleasure filled his heart as he observed the raw beauty of natural Africa. After ten minutes of admiring the pod, the sun seared his skin. It was with reluctance that he began to continue his journey.

A few kilometres down the road he turned left towards Magoebaskloof and then drove past a tea plantation. He wound his way up the steep forested road that snaked higher until he could see down into luscious valleys. Behind him, a mere twenty kilometres below was the Lowveld, and in front of him lay a completely different climate and forested, misty world.

In comparison, Magoebaskloof was cooler and more pleasant than Phalaborwa's dry, scorching heat. Gus parked his VW Beetle under a massive, thick-trunked tree. He strode across to his thatched hut with its whitewashed walls. His abode overlooked a wide, sweeping, forested valley teaming with bright butterflies and exotic bird calls. The sounds of a fresh, bubbling stream drifted up as it gurgled over moss-covered boulders. He peered down and saw its banks were lined with emerald green tree ferns, fronds of vegetation and large tree roots. Overhead, brightly coloured butterflies flitted while birds squawked and called.

That night, Gus retired early to bed, but pain disturbed his rest. More fidgety than a flea-infested ferret, he awoke at 5:00 am, feeling tired and hungry. He switched on his bedside lamp to survey his pulsating thumb. Carefully, he unwound the bandage to stare balefully at the black, cold, dry tip of his failed graft. The stitched-on part was dead and needed removal before infection set in.

He located his medical supplies and removed the stitches. The blackened flesh peeled away, leaving a slimy surface below. He rinsed his thumb with diluted peroxide and then saline. Afterwards, he bound his thumb with a moist Flamazine pad and took oral antibiotics.

***

Gus spent his first week exploring the local area for cottage furnishings. Next, he set up his clinic with basic equipment and supplies. His bedroom was separated from the clinic by a door.

Over the following week, his thumb healed well to the point where he reduced its dressing to a simple plaster. It was all good, only shorter.

***

An archaic Veterinary Council law prohibited vets from advertising, resulting in slow business. Gus arranged for postal flyers to be printed and delivered but with little result. His salary depended on commission. Initial euphoria over his exotic African location soon gave way to anxiety regarding personal finances. All that changed when ginger-haired Gretchen Blundell arrived carrying a basketful of kittens.

"Good-day. What have we here?"

"Oh, doctor Bullock...."

"Please, Mrs Blundell, call me Gus."

The middle-aged woman smiled. "Okay, Gus. I found these kittens in the hotel barn. They need homes."

Gus frowned. "Must I put them to sleep?"

Her eyes widened. "No! I can't do that. Look at them. They need homes, and where else to find a good home than at a veterinary clinic?"

Gus backed off, holding his hands up, signalling a *stop*. "I'm really sorry, but I can't give them a home. Perhaps you should contact the SPCA."

"No, I won't take them there because they'll be euthanised. Just vaccinate and deworm them. Then we can leave them here at the counter and clients will give them homes."

Gus's eyes filled with sorrow. "Gretchen, they are cute, but I can't keep them here. I've hardly got any clients."

Her tongue tut-tuttered. "Where's your assistant?"

"I don't have one."

"Please let me work here. I'll find homes for them--I promise."

"I'm not in a financial position to employ anyone."

"I want to work here. I love animals--I'll work for free. Call it volunteer service."

"He shook his head. "I can't."

"Why not?"

Gus shrugged. "You should be rewarded in some way."

"If you treat my animals for free, I'll help you get customers. I know everyone in this area. Trust me. Once your business is going well, you can start paying me."

He shifted uncomfortably. "Well, I don't know ...."

"Nonsense! You need help, and I'm it. Now, get me a phone and a desk. I'll show you what I can do."

Gus surveyed the woman's ageing green eyes and saw a rare kind of honest sincerity. She was worth a risk. "Okay. You've got one week to show me what you can achieve."

***

Although Gretchen lived on the phone, she obtained clients. Within five days, all the stray kittens found homes with advanced bookings for de-sexing and follow up vaccinations. She ordered in pet products, proving herself to be a wonderful salesperson.

One day, Gretchen arrived carrying a canary cage. "Meet Sonny and Cher," she declared.

Gus peered into the cage and spied two bent, crooked canaries sitting on the floor. They didn't look normal. "What's wrong with them?"

"Nothing. They're just old. I've had this pair for fifteen years."

He peered closer, spying their swollen arthritic joints and scrunched up claws, no longer able to grip onto perches.

"I can't do anything for them," Gus said.

"I don't expect you to. They're perfectly happy--just like old people. They still eat, drink and sing. I reckon they'll die when nature's ready to take them home."

"Do you have other pets?"

"Yes. I have nineteen cats and two dogs."

"*Nineteen*?"

She nodded.

He hadn't thought to ask her how many pets she had before signing her up for free treatments. So far, she had proved her weight in gold. She knew most people, causing his clientele to rise.

***

Gus awoke to a beautiful Saturday morning with clear blue skies. Today was the local annual gymkhana, a series of speed games on horseback, to be held at the Magoebaskloof Hotel. Gretchen had arranged for Gus, as the local vet, to make a social appearance. She would do the rounds and introduce him to people.

Several acres of freshly mown lawn ran alongside the old stone hotel building. It was lined with fragrant, old English pink roses and beautiful mature trees. Trucks and horse boxes filled the parking lot. Picnic baskets and children dotted the sidelines. At the entrance to the grounds, stood a long table decked with a crisp white cloth, bearing drinks and eats. Uniformed waiters proffered champagne to adults and orange juice to children.

Well-dressed women, dripping with expensive jewellery, had turned up for the occasion. Gretchen walked around, introducing Gus as the local vet, to everyone including the hotel owners. Everything ran smoothly. As the competition began, Gus helped himself to his second champagne. His gut churned. He felt hungry, and the food invited. While he stood at the table, he noticed a shapely arse in tight white jodhpurs in front. The young girl turned around almost bumping into him. He looked straight into the beautiful, sloping eyes of the nurse, Miranda Mostert.

She beamed. "Oh, you're the poor man who cut his thumb."

"Gus is my name."

"How's it healing?"

Gus grinned and held up his plastered thumb. "Okay, thanks, Miranda."

"Good!" The corners of her mouth dimpled. "Please, excuse me. It's my turn to ride." She brushed past him; her bosom touched his arm. She blushed with coquettish pleasure as their eyes locked. He felt a stirring in his loins. *No*, he told himself. *She's too young. She's jail bait.*

As he watched her departing figure, he fought the sudden urge to run his fingers through his hair and straighten his collar. He flexed his well-muscled arms as he rolled up his shirt sleeves and strode towards a shady spot where he planned to sit and watch.

Her presence made him feel image-conscious. It couldn't be denied; she was gorgeous. With champagne glass held elegantly in one hand, Gus sat down onto the grass. *Squish!* A terrible smell assailed his nostrils. He had sat right on top of a large, soft dog turd. *Urgh. What now?* His grin turned to a vexed grimace as he fought to extricate himself with the utmost discretion and stood.

Two small boys ran past, pointing and laughing. They pinched their noses, sprinting towards a group of other children chanting, "He pooped his pants! He pooped his pants!"

A wave of hot embarrassment torched his body. The champagne glass fell from his paralysed hand as he slipped backwards behind a tree and into shadow. He kept walking backwards away from the terrifying crowd. He had to reach his car. Two old women stood in his path. He smiled, facing them, as he continued his back-trot.

"Are you okay, Dr Bullock?"

"Yes, thank you. There's an emergency--I must leave."

The old duck smiled. "Nice meeting you. Gosh, there's a terrible smell ...."

Gus ran backwards while attempting to avoid trees and rose bushes en-route to his vehicle. He reached it. But only then he realised he couldn't sit on the seat with filthy pants. He looked around with furtive intent; nobody nearby. He quickly whipped off his trousers and underpants, throwing them in the boot. Next, he dived into the driver's seat and slammed the door. In a desperate, panicky attempt to extricate himself from further humiliation, he flooded the car engine. It wouldn't start. With head bent low, he readjusted the foot pedals and checked the choke. Gretchen strode up to the side of the car.

Gus stifled a curse.

"Surely, you're not leaving?"

Gus nodded. "Yeah. Emergency."

"I'll come with you."

"No! Don't worry."

Too late. Gretchen opened the passenger door and got seated.

Gus covered his crotch with his hands.

Her eyes bulged. "Well, excuse me. Sorry, I didn't mean to intrude ..."

"Gretchen! I'm no pervert. I sat in a dog turd. My trousers are dirty, and now my car won't start."

She roared with mirth, reached onto the backseat and threw him a hat. "Here's a fig leaf!"

He snatched it and covered his crotch.

She climbed out. "I'll push the car while you try restarting."

Gretchen heaved, her face suffused with blood as she made a great effort, leaning all her weight and everything she could muster into forward propulsion.

Right then, Miranda appeared. "That's not very gentlemanly to make an old woman do all the work!"

Her eyes challenged him.

Gus squirmed as Miranda encroached to the point where she could see straight into the car. Her eyes widened. The engine chugged to life. Breathless and exhausted Gretchen jumped in. Gus shook his head. "Look, I swear it's not what you think. I can explain ..."

Miranda averted her gaze, turned and sauntered away.

<u>CHAPTER SEVEN</u>

Kitchen Surgery

On Monday morning, Gretchen arrived early to work. "Look what I made especially for you!" she said, holding up a large platter bearing a decadent-looking chocolate cake.

"Wow! Thank you! Especially for me? What's the occasion?"

"I thought you might need cheering up after the weekend. It won't harm you to put on some extra weight--you're starting to look skinny."

"It looks scrumptious. I'll put the kettle on, and we'll start the day with chocolate."

"Great idea."

Gus scraped his plate clean and helped himself to seconds, thirds and then a fourth piece. "It's yummy, Gretchen. I just can't get enough. Please feel free to feed me anytime."

She tossed her head back, laughing. "My pleasure. I'm glad you like it. My late husband couldn't eat sweet things; he was a diabetic."

"What a pity. He missed out on your brilliant expertise."

A wistful sigh escaped her lips. "Oh, well, that's life. Now, if you'll excuse me, I have plenty phoning to do."

Gretchen spent the morning phoning people, telling them in a conversational style, about Gus's mishap at the gymkhana. Her ploy, based on *bad publicity* is better than *no publicity*, turned out to be a good one. The hilarity of the situation spread like wildfire. Anybody who hadn't heard there was a vet in town, now knew there was. Business rolled in with ever increasing interest as merry clients came to meet the new Australian animal doctor.

Gus hoped Miranda heard the true story via the village network. If not, there was nothing he could do.

Over the following week, Gus received a few call outs to horses in need of tooth rasping, deworming and vaccinations. He also went to a dairy farm that specialised in organic cheeses, to test their cows for Tuberculosis and later returned armed with an assortment of cheese that he shared with Gretchen. Several dogs came in for vaccinations and skin treatments. Things were running smooth and calm until the phone rang.

Gretchen hollered, "Mr Smit has an emergency and he's coming in now. He drove over a kitten. It sounds serious."

"Surely, there can't be much left of it," Gus replied.

"He reckons it's still alive and he'll be here within minutes."

"Okay, I'll get things ready."

A car roared into the drive. The driver jumped out and ran inside carrying a limp ginger kitten wrapped in a blood-soaked towel followed by a howling child. Gretchen pulled the young girl aside and offered her sweets from inside her drawer. "Let the doctor help kitty. Stay here with me and look at my old canaries. You can feed them. Here give them this ..."

Gus placed the kitten on an old kitchen table that served as a consulting counter and unwrapped the towel. His brow furrowed as he winced with sympathy. One hind leg was completely crushed--pulverised to the bone. Dangling by a thread of skin it was clear to see there was little hope.

"Please save it. It's my daughter's kitten. We only got it yesterday. I feel so bad--I didn't mean to drive over it. I never saw it--it's terrible. I feel like a monster. I'll pay anything--if you can just make it right. I beg you ... do something, *please*."

The kitten was already going into shock. Its body began slowing down as a weak, drowsy look came over its shivering form. Gus bit his bottom lip and shook his head. "I've never seen such an injury before. The hind leg is virtually severed. I don't think a cat can manage without a hind leg--it's too high up."

Mr Smit swallowed. "Please, doctor, please try. You *must* try."

Gus shook his head. "Sorry. I can't save its leg--it's impossible."

Speechless, Mr Smit bent his head forward, pinching his eyes between thumb and forefinger.

Gus said, "You can put it out of its misery right now, or I can try an amputation, but I'm not sure that it will survive the surgery. The chances are that it may never cope with one hind leg even if it survives."

"No, I won't put it down. Please try an amputation. We'll never know if we don't try."

Gus nodded. "What's its name?"

"It doesn't have one yet."

Gus began setting up intravenous fluids and getting things ready. "Leave it with me, Mr Smit. I'll give you a call as soon as I know whether it's going to make it or not."

"Thank you, doctor."

***

Gus treated the kitten for shock while he waited for its respiration to stabilise. After careful monitoring over a few hours, he decided to operate.

Anxiety threatened to swamp him as he set about preparing for an amputation without an anaesthetic machine. His equipment was basic, and that meant using intravenous anaesthetic and getting the balance right between sleep and possible overdose. He hoped its vein wouldn't collapse. He looked down at the ginger fluff ball. Its soft, blue eyes stared deeply into his with such complete, desperate trust. It tried purring, but the vain attempt ended in a feeble cough. He loved kittens--they were cute, and this was no exception. He had to try his best. The lengthy operation strained his eyes and back, but it was nothing compared to what the kitten had endured. Now and then Gretchen passed him materials needed.

Finally, the mangled leg was successfully separated from the kitten's tiny body. A sad feeling filled Gus as he dropped the limb into the dustbin. With head bent low, he set about tying off blood vessels and made sure the nerve endings were severed straight and clean to avoid unnecessary complications. What a relief to finish. Gus mopped his brow, stretched his back and washed his hands. This was where the waiting game began. He wrapped the kitten up warmly into a soft woollen blanket and placed it in a protected cage. Slowly it came around from the anaesthetic but remained weak. It was hard to know if it would survive the night.

The following morning, a strange sound woke Gus. He blinked his eyes and listened. *Oh, what joy!* It came from the cat cage. Gus looked down into it. The kitten stood on three legs, mewing. It was a rather hoarse kind of meow, but it was a demand for food. He opened the cage door allowing it to amble out, plodding squarely on two front legs and a hind. It followed him into the kitchenette with an erect tail, purring as it rubbed its whiskers against his ankles while he prepared breakfast. He felt happy and very hungry. A six-egg omelette, two tomatoes and several sausages would get him through until tea time.

Gus phoned Mr Smit and told him the kitten had made it and could go home if they promised to look after it carefully.

Absolute joy and relief shone from Mr Smit's face as he cradled the kitten in his arms. "My daughter will be so pleased to see it again. I can't thank you enough."

"Bring it back in two days' time, so I can check on that suture line."

"I will, thank you."

Two days later, Mr Smit and his daughter arrived with the ginger kitten. As they opened the cage door, it bounded out and sprang up onto Gus's chair. Everyone's eyes shone with incredibility at the sight of its surprising dexterity.

On day ten, when Gus removed the kitten's stitches, differences between animals and people came to light. He realised animals have an advantage with more legs and they don't have the same psychological issues with disability. An animal's priority was to get mobile and return to enjoying life. He would remember this when assessing future injuries.

"Hey, kitty--you're a survivor."

Mr Smit laughed. "We've named him, *Tripod*."

Gus grinned. "And I reckon Tripod has another eight good lives left to enjoy."

<u>CHAPTER EIGHT</u>

Tea and Cake

Business thrived as Gretchen began receiving her well-deserved income. As a measure of gratitude, she always baked something tasty to bring to work on Monday mornings. Feeding Gus was an extension of appeasing her latent nurturing instincts that were usually reserved for pets. She stopped typing accounts and peered at Gus over horn-rimmed spectacles. "You don't look well."

He smirked. "I'm fine. Fit as a ferret and hungry as a horse."

She frowned. "I can't believe the volume of food you tuck away, and yet you stay so slim."

"I work hard while pining for love."

She chuckled. "Your appetite astounds me. If I ate what you did, I'd be larger than a lolly larder. If I didn't know better, I'd swear you had tapeworms."

Gus chuckled. "No chance."

The phone jangled. Gretchen answered, spoke and then hung-up. Turning to Gus, she rolled her eyes skyward. "May God help you."

"What's up?"

"That was Mrs Batty from that la-di-da farm up on the hill, *Howl at the Moon*. She needs a vet to see her sheep."

"I don't recall meeting her."

"No, you haven't. Watch out; she's quite mad."

"What do you mean, *mad*?"

Gretchen clicked her tongue and pointed towards her head. "She has more nuts upstairs than an army of squirrels can hoard for an ice age."

"Sounds crackers."

"Beware, she's extremely wealthy with friends in high places. Years ago, she was an excellent artist until she fell off a horse and was injured. She's never ridden or painted since."

"What put her off?"

"It's hard to tell," Gretchen replied. Then she lowered her voice to a whisper. "Sometimes she appears normal; other times she's gone barking. I suspect she takes too many painkillers. Be patient and treat her well; she's an important key to being accepted into prosperous society."

"Okay, got it. Scouts' honour," Gus said with a flippant salute. "I solemnly do declare that I shall not sit on her lawn."

She laughed and threw a cushion at him. "Go on, get out!"

He ducked and ran *quacking* with his hands tucked under his armpits all the way to the car.

***

Going up the two-kilometre driveway to Howl at the Moon challenged his VW Beetle. Good driving skills helped negotiate around large boulders and puddles that had appeared after heavy rain. He chugged through a dense section of Jacaranda trees that arched luxuriously over the muddied track. Their fallen pinkish-mauve buds made a thick, rich, virgin carpet on the road. They snapped, crackled and popped as he drove, forming a double track of crushed, bruised blossoms behind. Hydrangea bushes nestled at the base of the Jacarandas' gnarled trunks.

The track ended in a circular gravel driveway. Architecturally designed, the sprawling house consisted of a series of stone constructions that backed onto a rocky outcrop. Gus followed a moss-covered footpath that ran alongside a brick retaining wall to his right as he headed towards the front.

"Yee-ow!" A wild cat attacked. It landed squarely on his head. Its needle-sharp claws dug into his scalp and face. "What the...?" The huge tabby flew into a nearby shrub where it squatted with flattened ears, hissing. Its gargoyle-like eyes glinted reddish-black as its tail swished from side to side. His heart beat with fright as he mopped his face with a handkerchief, trying to staunch bleeding.

He took a deep breath and strode up to the imposing entrance. He lifted the weighty loop hanging from the shiny brass lion-head knocker and tapped. A servant dressed in a starched white uniform opened the heavy ebony door.

"I'm coming," hollered a voice. Mrs Batty appeared. "Good day, Dr Bullock."

"Good day, Mrs Batty. Please call me, Gus."

"What happened to you?" She squinted at his face.

"I was attacked by a wildcat, possibly rabid, coming up your garden path."

She chortled. "Oh, that's my pussy, Bouncer. He only attacks people he dislikes."

Gus scowled. "I see."

Already armed with a carved walking stick, Mrs Batty donned gumboots and jacket. "Follow me; I'll show you the sheep."

Alongside, trotted an overweight pug.

"What's your doggie's name?" Gus asked, attempting to win favour.

"Muffin." Mrs Batty smiled. "She enjoys rounding up sheep but doesn't always get it right."

Herdsmen and Muffin headed the sheep into a rustic stick and fence enclosure. Gus cast a knowledgeable eye over the flock. "Mrs Batty, they need deworming and hoof care."

"Well, do whatever you think right and then come back to my house for tea."

"Thank you, Mrs Batty, but I'd rather finish up here and head back."

A stern look crossed her face. "Dare you decline my invitation?"

"Oh, no, not at all," Gus replied. "I don't want you going to any unnecessary trouble on my account."

She beamed. "Don't be modest. You must come in for a cuppa."

Muffin leapt forward with a yap, startling the sheep. Three broke out and began trotting down the hill. The chubby pug scrambled after them, pursuing them farther and farther away. Its little white pug tail bobbed up and down with every mischievous bounding stride.

"Oh, no," Gus groaned. "I need them here for treatment."

Mrs Batty's face turned scarlet with rage. "Muffin! Muffy! Come, Muffy! Come."

The bratty pug appeared deaf.

"Urgh!" she growled. "Muffin always does this. It's so annoying."

"Muffin!" Gus called. It made no difference.

"TEA AND CAKE!" Mrs Batty screeched at the top of her voice. "Tea and cake!"

Muffin jammed on brakes, made a U-turn and headed back at full throttle.

The puffing pug chugged its way back to Mrs Batty. It stood at her feet with its pink tongue lolling out, waiting with bulgy-eyed expectation.

"It's a miracle," Gus said. "I thought she was deaf."

Mrs Batty laughed. "She has selective hearing. Muffin's a little pig. No matter where she goes or what she does, she always hears *tea and cake*." She began hobbling back to the house with wheezing Muffin at her side, begging for food. "See you later," she called.

***

After treating the sheep, Gus headed over to her house. The servant met him at the door and directed him to the guest bathroom where he cleaned up with soap and water and dried his hands on a plush lavender-scented towel.

As Gus entered the lounge for tea, his impression was one of opulence. His eyes drifted up to the high moulded ceiling with its impressive, sparkling crystal chandelier. Fragrant rose blooms mixed with Jasmine overflowed their huge crystal vase that stood on the coffee table. A deep red Persian carpet lay central on the stone floor. In front of the hearth, a luxurious leopard skin lay draped with the head still attached. Rich, scenic oil paintings mounted in curvaceous gilt frames adorned the walls and well-placed plumped up tapestry cushions rested on dark leather furniture.

"Those paintings are spectacular," Gus ventured.

"Thank you. I painted them years ago."

The chime of a mahogany grandfather clock sounded in the hallway, sounding out the hour: 3:00 pm. A maid entered bearing a tray laden with fine china, a silver teapot and a dainty array of fairy cakes. Gus's eyes lit up. Cake. He and Muffin waited with silent hope. The maid placed the tray on the edge of the square coffee table before returning to the kitchen.

A noisy fly buzzed against a window pane, struggling for freedom.

"Oh, bother," Mrs Batty said. "I despise flies." She reached down beside her chair and retrieved an old wire gauze flyswatter, already encrusted with fly corpses. She lumbered towards the window. *Slam!* The old woman struck lightning-fast. In an instant, the fly was squashed flat. She held up the swatter with triumph, displaying yet another gooey corpse stuck to it, and then she hobbled back to the tray.

"How do you like your tea?" she enquired.

Gus smiled. The afternoon was going well. "Strong, please, with a dash of milk and one sugar."

"Certainly." She was about to pour it. "Bother it! The maid forgot to bring the tea strainer, and now she's gone for her own break. Never mind."

She proceeded to pour the steaming tea through the fly-smeared swatter before handing him his cup and saucer.

Gus froze. There was no way he would drink the insect-blood-contaminated tea. Flies ate poop and then regurgitated it. No way on God's earth would it pass his lips. Perspiration broke out on his scalp as he endeavoured to make small talk while pretending to drink.

Mrs Batty rambled on in her posh, pretentious English accent, striving to impress her less fortunate visitor. "This precious tea set is Royal Albert China. I inherited it from my dear English mother, the Duchess of Bogville. You must know, I can trace our family lineage back to King Arthur. I hope you realise I only use this set for special guests."

Gus shifted uncomfortably but had to keep a straight face. As far as he knew, King Arthur was a legendary English king. "Thank you, Mrs Batty. I appreciate your generous hospitality."

She helped herself to a second cup. "Would you like another?"

"No, thank you. I'm still busy."

"You're a slow drinker."

Gus found himself resisting the urge to mop his perspiring brow with a handkerchief. Not to drink the tea would be to offend her, but to drink it would cause him to spew.

The phone rang.

"Excuse me, I must answer that," Mrs Batty said, rising with difficulty.

"Sure," Gus replied, realising a godsend opportunity.

After she had hobbled down the hallway, Gus leapt to his feet and strode across to the lounge window and opened it. He threw the tea outside with a deft flick of his wrist.

CRACK!

The teacup broke. He stood foolishly with one prized *Royal Albert China* handle in hand while his eyes stared stupidly at the cup lying upside-down on the lawn. He heard her say, "Mildred, I'll call you back. I have a guest now…"

He jumped through the window to retrieve the cup, only managing to wiggle back inside seconds before she returned. Hopefully, no servants saw.

She smiled. "Are you ready for that second cuppa?"

"No, thank you. Honestly, Mrs Batty, you've gone to much trouble today. I can't thank you enough…"

"No trouble at all."

He glanced at his watch. "Oh! Time's flown. I have other calls to make. Please excuse me--I must leave."

He placed the cup and saucer down behind the vase of flowers, with the broken side facing away. He moved towards the front door as fast as diplomacy permitted.

"Good-day, Mrs Batty. Till we meet again." He bowed. "Cheerio!"

From behind the closing door, he heard her muttering to Muffin, "What a pleasant gentleman that was.…"

He sprinted towards his car, ducking down alongside the garden wall, avoiding another potential side-swipe from Bouncer, the gargoyle cat.

The VW engine roared to life. He drove with urgency, pedal to the metal, and prayed never to return.

CHAPTER NINE

Sad Socks

As the first rays of sharp sunshine streaked through a crack in the bedroom curtains, Gus stirred. He lay in bed trying to snatch another five minutes rest before the day began, but it was not to be so because his arse itched. Suddenly, he was more awake than a tree full of owls. Nature beckoned, and he felt a need to answer her call with notable urgency. He rose, stumbling with fair speed through to the bathroom where he plonked himself down on the toilet seat and let rip. *Crikey*! Something wasn't right. If he were a dog, he would be scooting on his butt by now trying to alleviate that itchy-snitchy sensation.

PLOP! Something fell from the bottom of his world, and it wasn't excrement. Still blurry eyed and half asleep, he peered into the toilet bowl. *Shit*! His eyes widened with shock. Then his legs snapped shut as his arse clamped tight. He sat bolt upright. Awake. He knew tapeworm segments when he saw them. Fear fought logic. *But, how can I? Where could I have...? Huh?*

He cleaned up and washed his hands. A busy schedule lay ahead for the day, in fact, for the foreseeable week. No time to see a doctor now. He scratched his head, pondering *how* he got infected. Remembrance dawned as he recalled tucking into an ultra-rare, succulent, juicy buffalo steak that he had happily munched his way through at Steve's house.

After that *'Ah-ha'* moment, he hurried through to the dispensary cupboard and reached up for the Large Dog de-wormer bottle. He decided that he was a very large dog indeed, so he worked out the dosage versus his weight ratio accordingly and swallowed the pills with a gigantic glass of milk. *Urgh*! They tasted awful. Over the next few hours, every time he burped, the taste refreshed itself.

***

Miss Butcher, a young, thin woman with dreadlocks, was the first customer of the day. She brought in a sick cat, named Socks, placing it carefully on Gus's consultation table.

Gus examined the black cat and found nothing obvious, but something was wrong.

"He often vomits," Miss Butcher complained. "And continually demands food."

Gus stroked Socks' hair along his back; it felt stiff and dry. It appeared to be falling out in places, and there was a faded look to its colour. Socks appeared weak as Gus palpated unusually prominent rib bones.

"I suspect it's a case of worms," Gus said, thinking of similarities alongside his own symptoms.

"But I dewormed him myself last month," Miss Butcher replied.

"He's certainly underweight, and his coat feels rough. Maybe you under-dosed him, or he might not have swallowed it all. I reckon we should do it again and see what happens."

Socks was well behaved as Gus dosed him.

"What food do you feed him?" Gus asked.

"A varied diet."

"Okay, but what does he actually eat?"

Miss Butcher shrugged and said, "Mainly mince, I suppose."

"Okay. Let's see how Socks goes. If he doesn't improve, please bring him back."

"Thank you, Dr Bullock, I will."

***

Later that evening, Gus didn't feel hungry, so he ate a light meal and went to bed.

The next morning, nature called, so he ran to his throne room and let rip. Evidence proved a successful treatment. Afterwards, he vowed not to eat rare buffalo steaks ever again, and he would give the sight of stringy pasta a miss for a while too.

***

A week later, Miss Butcher returned to the clinic with Socks tucked under her arm. On examination, the cat appeared weaker than before. Gus re-examined sad-looking Socks but still couldn't pinpoint anything specific, so he said, "Please leave Socks with me for a week. I will watch closely and feed him. This is a peculiar case; I feel I'm missing something but don't know what."

"All right," Miss Butcher agreed. "See you next Monday."

Over the following week, sad Socks rallied, and his health improved. He ate and drank well, and a soft shine returned to his pelt. By the time Miss Butcher arrived to collect him, Socks was purring and doing flick-flacks with cat toys in his cage.

"Oh, my goodness me!" Miss Butcher exclaimed. "I can't believe the difference in Socks. What did you do to make him well?"

"Nothing," Gus said. "All I did was feed him and make sure he had plenty of clean water available."

"He gets clean water at home too."

"Good, but what do you feed him?" Gus asked, hoping for a new clue.

"Minced meat."

"What kind of minced meat?"

"You know--minced meat."

Gus sighed and tried again. "Pork mince? Beef mince? Fish mince? Mutton mince? What sort? It's possible he has an allergy."

"Soya mince."

Gus's eyes widened. "You feed your cat soya?"

"Yes. I'm a vegetarian. We share food. And, I keep him in the house so that he doesn't kill birds."

Gus's head jerked up, he folded his arms across his chest and proceeded to lecture her, as kindly as possible, regarding cats' dietary requirements. "Cats are carnivores. Eating meat is essential for their survival. Nature designed them that way."

"Yes, but Socks eats carrots and other vegetables that I feed him."

Gus drew a long, slow breath. Polite patience was vital. "Socks could eventually become ill and die. He must get the right food."

"Oh, I didn't realise...."

"If you keep him locked up in your house, essentially, he's a prisoner. He's forced to eat what you give him. A hungry cat will eat anything, but its body only processes meat protein."

She stared, agog; ready to hear more.

Gus went on to explain that a cat must have a balanced diet, suggesting some suitable brands and a few economical ideas for her to try.

Eventually, her eyes lit up with understanding. "Thank you, Dr Bullock, for explaining all this--I honestly didn't know."

Gus smiled with satisfaction, having discovered the solution to Socks' problem. "That's okay. If sad Socks starts eating right, he'll turn into a happy Socks real soon."

She smiled sheepishly. "Thank you. In future, I'll make sure Socks gets good food." She put Socks in her cat cage and proceeded to head out the door.

A mischievous grin tugged at the corners of Gus's mouth. "Oh, Miss Butcher, there's one more thing I wish to mention ...."

"Yes?"

"You're the first vegetarian Butcher I've ever met."

CHAPTER TEN

Night Call

After checking out the last customer at 6:00 pm on Friday night, Gretchen grabbed her bag. Armed with her canary cage and car keys, she called out, "Goodbye!" to Gus.

"Cheers, Gretch. See you Monday."

"Sure thing. Be good!"

"Always." Gus feigned Scouts' Honour as she left.

It was good to finish, and it was still early enough to visit the Magoebaskloof Hotel pub for a beer and social. After that, he would order a decent meal.

Rrring! Rrring!

"Darn," Gus muttered, glaring towards the phone. "I've worked all day--I just want to go out and relax." Momentarily, he hesitated as he considered ignoring the call. It might be an emergency. With a click of his tongue, he grabbed the receiver and answered.

"Good evening. Veterinary clinic. Gus Bullock is speaking."

"Good evening, Dr Bullock," a female voice crooned softly down the line. "I'm so sorry to worry you on a Friday night, but I have a very sick doggie. Please, may I bring him in now?"

"Okay." Gus rolled his eyes. "How long will it take you to arrive?"

"Fifteen to twenty minutes."

"All right," he said politely. "See you then." He hung up and waited.

Sunset came and went, leaving the yard in darkness, only tree-top silhouettes were visible on the horizon. He switched on the outside light. Half an hour later, a deep rumble of a large engine sounded as it trundled down his driveway and came to a halt. An exceptionally well-heeled woman carried a miniature Dachshund under one arm as she sauntered in through the door that Gus held open. A sweet-smelling perfume fog trailed in her wake, causing sex-starved Gus to conjure up exotic images of eastern brothels.

After introductions, Amour van der Skiet placed her ageing Dachshund on Gus's consultation table. Her shiny brunette hair dangled in soft, luxurious curls about her slim shoulders. She had a Vogue Model figure and was made up to the nines. Her V-neck, cocktail dress, displayed a plunging neckline that went right down to her bejewelled navel. Every time she bent to pat her dog, Sossie, Gus glimpsed a full view of her braless chest with its dark, pointed areolas.

"Doctor, my little Sossie is in pain. Sometimes he struggles to walk up the stairs, and I have to help him." She bent forward again, providing yet another sexy glimpse.

He tried hard not to smile as other things hardened. His male anatomy responded in a noteworthy and most biological manner, causing him intense embarrassment. Attempting to hide his bulging crotch behind the table top was futile because of his great height. Her cool gaze graced his trousers, noting his predicament, and she smiled. Gus smiled. He felt hot and awkward. Shaking his head, he tried not to visualise her tanned breasts dangling every time she bent forward. It occurred to him she enjoyed topless tanning because her rich, delicious, golden skin tone went right down to the very tips of her silky, swollen nipples.

Trying to refocus, Gus took a deep breath and said, "Sorry, please repeat that. What did you say?"

"Do you know what the problem is?"

"Yes. No. Well, yes. It's a ...."

Her eyes widened as they gazed into his. "Yes?" It came as a whisper.

Gus screwed up his eyes for a moment and thought hard. "It's definitely a back problem."

She leant closer. Her harem aroma intoxicated. "What should I do?"

Gus pulled back, standing erect, with hands clasped in front of his bulging groin as he tried to explain treatment that would help alleviate symptoms and hopefully avoid a possible future spinal disc prolapse.

He handed over painkillers and recommended that Sossie went on a stricter diet to reduce weight. As he spoke, her eyes caressed his physique, and her lips parted. Perspiration beads began sprouting all over his taut body.

She touched his hand; causing him to overheat. Sexual tension mounted. Sweat beads rolled down his back, threatening to transform him into a pissing water sprite. "Thank you, Doctor. You've been so helpful." She hesitated, as she wavered on the brink of fragile hope. He got the distinct impression this was supposed to be his cue to accept her sultry advances.

She continued smiling as her eyes flicked back to the front of his trousers and then up to his face.

He blushed and turned away. "Good night, Miss van der Skiet."

Only when she picked up her bag and dog did he dare to turn around again. She smiled coquettishly and left.

***

On Monday morning, Gretchen went through the paperwork looking for new accounts to write up. "I see you had van der Skiet's dog here on Friday after I left."

"Yes," Gus replied. "Miss Amour van der Skiet brought in a Dachshund with a sore back."

"Correction, that's Mrs, not Miss."

"Oh, what a pity," Gus said with a grin. "She's an attractive woman."

Gretchen snorted. "Yes, she is. Just don't look too closely. Those van der Skiets are a strange lot."

"What do you mean?"

"Well," Gretchen said. "She is Bruno van der Skiet's second wife. Just be warned, he's a dangerous man."

His interest perked. "Oh, yeah?"

"Bruno is a notorious poacher who claims hunting rights stretching from the Limpopo River to the Olifants' River and has many court cases pending. He's banned from local pubs for drunken brawling, and he beat up his ex-wife to near pulp."

"Ouch," Gus said. "He sounds violent."

Gretchen nodded. "But that's not all. His previous wife sued him for fifty percent of assets when they divorced, and do you know what he did?"

Wide-eyed, Gus shook his head.

"Every household item the court ordered him to deliver to her house, he sawed in half!"

"No way!"

"Oh, yes. Including her car."

Gus swallowed.

Gretchen wagged her finger. "Remember this; nobody messes with Bruno van der Skiet's wife."

<u>CHAPTER ELEVEN</u>

A Day's Work

The following Thursday Gus travelled over 80 km to a farm in the Lowveld outside of Mooketsi where 300 cow pregnancy tests awaited him. This amounted to nearly a full day's work. Doing all the cows together on one day meant the farmer only had to pay for one veterinary trip. Bringing the cows into the enclosure hampered their natural foraging time; therefore, efficient processing was essential.

Carrying a non-pregnant cow over a drought-prone African winter was too costly. The natural foraging tends to become limited in dry months. Cows that do not produce a calf every year are considered economically redundant and are sent to market. If a cow skips a season and is carried over until it calves again, that starts breeding low-fertility rate into the herd. Farmers who breed cows for meat and milk, use expensive and carefully selected bulls with proven genetic capabilities, to mate with their cows.

On the horizon, scorching heat waves shimmered across the wide expanse of flat land with its arid, dry bush and sandy soil, causing mirages of water to appear. Crooked, rusty barbed wire fences lined the road. Flat-topped acacia thorn trees were interspersed with low-lying scrub; and in between, loomed the large, weird shapes of red-sand, sun-baked termite mounds. Clumps of stiff, dry, half-eaten, sun-bleached grass sprouted upwards at sporadic intervals, creating shady spots for the possibility of puffadders to hide.

From the outset, Gus knew his day was to be jammed with intense physical labour. With 300 cows queued, he was to do a rectal examination on each one. About 20 cows where brought into the crush at a time. The crush was a narrow walkway that the cows were funnelled into so that they could not turn around. First, he manually cleared the cow's rectum by scraping out dung. Next, he must stick his arm, right up to his armpit, into that dark passage. It was only then that he could palpate her uterus and ovaries sufficiently well enough to make a diagnosis. This procedure would be repeated 300 times, once for each cow. It enabled him to establish the stage of pregnancy by feeling the size of the animal's womb. If the cow was not pregnant, he felt around for other problems. Did she have ovarian cysts? Or was there any sign of a corpus luteum? If so, it meant the cow was cycling or in the very early stages of pregnancy, and that could not be confirmed by mere uterine palpation.

The long-sleeved, plastic, orange glove he was supposed to wear for pregnancy testing proved futile. After a few rectal examinations, it always tore at the fingers. Also, his skin could not breathe inside the glove, causing profuse perspiration, therefore, he preferred testing without gloves. He kept a bottle of water at hand for frequent self-rehydration, and by 10:00 am the water was hot from the sun's rays, but he had to keep drinking. Now and then he took a few short pee-breaks, relieving himself behind a lucky bush.

At the end of his cow work, Gus's right arm was stained dark green. The colour spread from his fingernails to his armpit hairs, where they hung like slimy green, sulphurous stalactites like something inside a Martian grotto. A herdsman brought a tin bucket filled with water for him to wash. Gus felt exhausted, parched and sunburnt. The thought of driving 80km home in baking heat inside an unairconditioned VW Beetle was the last punishment of the day, requiring fortitude to stay awake at the wheel.

***

Gretchen heard the distinctive sound of Gus's VW putt-putting down the drive. She ran out to greet him with waving arms.

"Emergency!" she cried. "I'm so pleased to see you. A lady brought in a box of feral kittens that have been mauled by a dog. They're in a terrible state. Come quick!"

Fatigued, Gus turned his dust-gritted, blood-shot eyes towards her. "First, please, fetch me a big glass of cold water."

"Okay. Come inside. They're in a box on the floor under your consulting table."

Gus stooped to lift the box, placing it on the table. From within, tiny mew sounds wafted, begging release and respite from their dark, friendless box.

Gretchen handed Gus water and he downed it gratefully. Then he turned his attention back to the kittens. Two survivors. The one had no tail. A raw stump was the only indication of where its tail should have been. The tiny kitten mewed soft, squeaking cries as it nuzzled its tabby face into Gus's open-neck shirt seeking milk inside his chest hair.

"Oh, just look at it," Gretchen cried. "Can you believe it?" She dabbed the corners of her eyes with a tissue, fighting back tears as she took it from him.

Gus delved into the box removing the other survivor, a fluffy black kitten with one popped eyeball. It surveyed him with its good eye as it nestled down into the crook of his arm for comfort. Clearly, it was weaker than its sibling.

Gus sighed. "Who owns them?"

"Nobody. The lady who brought them here said they are strays she found."

"Does she want them back?"

"No, definitely not. She rescued them but didn't have the heart to kill them herself, so she brought them here for euthanasia."

Gus's shoulders drooped. A hard day's work followed by a grisly task. How could he put two cute kittens to sleep? They had already endured such suffering; the thought jarred his nerves. He looked down at *one-eye* in his arm, while *stumpy-tail* me-owed, appealing to Gretchen. They seemed to be saying, *"Me-ow! Help! Please, please, help us. We're still babies. The world has been cruel, but we promise to be good kitties."* Gus placed them back in the box and closed the lid. Their pathetic mews disturbed him. This was a detestable part of his work.

Gretchen's eyes searched his soul as a frown crossed her forehead. "What will you do with them?"

Gus shrugged. "I can't keep every abandoned animal that comes in through my door."

"Okay, I'll have them," Gretchen replied.

Gus folded his arms across his chest, summing her up. "You already have twenty-something cats."

"I don't care. If you fix them, I'll take them home."
Gus shook his head. "No."
"What do you mean, *no*? I want them."
"Well," Gus said, "Don't be greedy. I want one too!"
After surgery and treatment, the kittens rallied. Two days later, the pair were eating well and playing with a soft rubber ball. Every now and then they chased one another up Gus's curtains, ripping at the fabric with their tiny claws, causing threads to hang out.
"Look at them!" Gretchen exclaimed. "They're happy to be alive."
"They're causing bedlam here," Gus said. "I reckon it's time to strike an agreement. You take *Bonsai* home, and I keep *Spy*."
"Deal!" They shook hands.

CHAPTER TWELVE

Karl Kaalvoet

On Friday morning, the first patient of the day arrived in the back of a pick-up truck. The tan dog was carried in by a barefooted man wearing khaki shorts, a cotton shirt and a robust stainless-steel Omega wrist watch.

Gretchen poked her head in through Gus's door. "Do you have time to see Karl and his dog?"

"Sure."

Bare-footed Karl carried his dog in and placed it on the consultation table.

"What have we here?" Gus asked, trying to focus on the dog and not Karl's huge, dirty, ugly feet with their grey chipped nails and dry, cracked heels.

"There's a problem with Jack's head."

Gus took a closer view.

Sure enough, he spotted a small puncture wound above the dog's left eye. Gus wiped it with a cotton wool swab and analysed the foul, yellow-brown pus discharge.

"When did Jack's problem start?"

Karl scratched his head as he rolled his eyes upwards trying to remember. "Not sure, but I noticed it several weeks ago, so that's when I took him to another vet who gave Jack antibiotics. It never improved, so I used various lotions on the wound, but none helped. It's getting worse."

Gus felt no lumps, only a slight swelling. He listened to Jack's heart with his stethoscope. All good. Gus spoke, "It might be a sinus from an upper tooth abscess. Or a foreign body, like a stick or thorn, might be stuck there. Leave Jack with me, and I'll give him an anaesthetic. Then I will examine his teeth and possibly cut down into this tissue to look for something that might be lodged there."

"Thank you, Doctor," Karl said. "By the way, I have a horse that needs de-worming and vaccinating. Could you do it tomorrow?"

"Yes, I'll bring Jack with me when I'm finished. It'll save you a trip."

Karl smiled. "Thanks, Doc. See you."

After he left, Gus turned to Gretchen. "Whereabout does Karl live?"

Her eyes lit up. "Ah, that Karl Kaalvoet--he's such a nice man." Her colour heightened. "I feel sorry for him--His wife died only last year. He's now staying near Houtbosdorp Drive."

"Kaalvoet?" Gus repeated. "It's an odd name."

Gretchen laughed. "It's a nickname. Everyone calls him Karl *Kaalvoet* because he never wears shoes."

Gus looked blank. "Sorry, I can't connect the dots."

She smiled. "*Kaalvoet* is an Afrikaans word meaning barefoot. *Kaal* means naked, and *voet* means foot, so everyone calls him Karl Kaalvoet."

"Ah!" I thought there was something odd. "Can't he afford shoes?"

"Yes, he most certainly can! He's very wealthy and owns two farms. One here and the other is a huge citrus plantation down in the Letsitele Valley. Since he was a kid, he's always gone barefooted. He used to roam barefoot alongside Sotho children in the bush and now speaks their Sepedi language fluently--as good as one of them."

"Impressive."

***

When Gus had Jack on the operating table, he examined his teeth--they were all good. Cutting down into the weeping sinus would cause the wound to bleed, and then he would not be able to see exactly where the track led. Fortunately, Gus had managed to purchase an old x-ray machine from a small rural hospital that had upgraded. Gus injected some barium paste into the sinus and then took an x-ray. The x-ray revealed a long path that travelled between the dog's cranial muscles, coming to a distinct end several inches away from the left eye. With Jack under anaesthetic, Gus cut down, following the barium paste track until he hit his target. His forceps touched something hard; he made them latch onto it, and then he tugged. Voila! Out came a 4cm piece of a porcupine quill.

***

The following afternoon, Gus drove to Karl Kaalvoet's home to deliver Jack and to vaccinate his horse.

"Helloo-oo-oo!" Karl howled as Jack bounded towards him. Happy to be home the dog nuzzled Karl's hand with a lolling tongue and a wagging tail.

Gus held up the remnants of a porcupine quill. "This was the culprit."

Illumination dawned. "Oh, yes, now I remember. Jack tried to catch a porcupine, but it got away. Well, I never thought of that. Congratulations, Doc! Great job." Karl slapped Gus's back. "Now come this way. I'll show you the horse."

As they walked down to the stables, Gus saw the shapely backside of a young girl as she stood brushing the long tail of a fine-looking steed.

Karl smiled genially. "Doctor, meet my daughter, Miranda."

Their eyes locked. Gus smiled. "Yeah, I think we've met."

<u>CHAPTER THIRTEEN</u>

Entertainment

Only now Gus realised Gretchen had not told him Karl Kaalvoet's real surname. She had explained what Karl's nickname meant and of how to get to his house, but that was it. Today, caught off guard, he had to gather his wits.

Miranda sidled up to him, delivering a playful shove on his shoulder. "Pa, this is the same guy who sat in dog poo at the Gymkhana up at the hotel some time ago. Remember?"

Karl cackled with mirth. "Oh, yes! I remember hearing how Gretchen push-started your car because you wore no pants."

Gus smiled. "I'm glad you heard the truth. It wasn't a great kick start towards making a good impression."

Marinda giggled. "No, it wasn't but you certainly created a lasting one--and that was funny! I'm sorry that... I thought that..."

"Stop." Gus chipped in, raising his hand. "No apology is needed; I'm sure others thought worse."

She smiled and turned to her horse, leading it by a blue headcollar, she wheeled it around to stand facing him.

"He's a beaut," Gus said while stroking the animal's velvet-soft chestnut coat.

"His name's Ruby."

Ruby stood at ease while Gus vaccinated and dewormed him. Gus patted Ruby's neck. The horse nodded with approval and then nibbled Gus's hairy arm with its soft, thick, rubber-like lips.

"He likes you," Miranda crooned.

"A horse with good taste," Gus replied.

She smiled. "Yes." Her eyes raked over Gus with frank approval. "Seeing it's Saturday afternoon, I must invite you to come inside for a cup of tea."

Gus hesitated. "I don't have a good track record with tea-drinking. Perhaps not, thank you."

"Please?" Her eyes implored.

"I have a better idea," he said. "How about I take you to dinner at the Magoebaskloof Hotel tonight?"

She beamed. "Okay! What time should I be ready?"

"I'll collect you at 7:00 pm."

***

Gus hurried home and cleaned his car. Then he took a shower, donned some aftershave and wore his best clothes--a jacket, long trousers and a wallaby tie.

After collecting Miranda and entering in through the hotel entrance, that was adorned with fresh flowers, he stopped, turned and faced her. "Let me see you. Wow, you look gorgeous," he said, taking in her figure-hugging olive-green dress with its black lace trim. Her golden hair danced and bobbed about her shoulders, brimming with vitality.

"Thank you." The colour on her cheekbones blossomed into a delightful rose shade.

The Hotel offered affordable fine dining at its best. Smart, uniformed waiters strode to and fro, taking orders and delivering drinks to guests who sat at dainty candlelit tables. The tables were draped with white cloths and set with shiny, silver cutlery. A waiter stooped to light the single candle on their table that stood next to a small vase of flowers. Gus thanked him and conveyed their orders.

White wine arrived first, delivered in a silver ice bucket that was placed on a smaller table next to theirs. The waiter poured a sample, allowing Gus to taste first. After Gus had nodded approval, he filled both glasses.

"Thank you."

"Cheers." Gus raised his glass, clinking hers.

Their evening went by in a whirl of animated conversation, jam-packed with weird medical story exchanges. They laughed until they cried. Afterwards, Miranda said, "Thank you for a lovely evening. I've enjoyed myself--and I love your Aussie accent."

"Maybe we can do this again?" Gus offered.

Her eyes twinkled. "I'd love to."

On the way home, their conversation dwindled as, ruefully, they considered their beautiful evening was at an end.

Gus drove into Karl's driveway and parked outside the house entrance. He walked around the car to the passenger side and opened Miranda's door.

"Thank you." She climbed out and lifted her head for a kiss. Gus obliged. She latched on as the kiss fast turned into something intensely deeper than a mere peck on the cheek.

Old Karl Kaalvoet opened his front door. Feigning innocence, the kissing couple separated. Gus walked Miranda up to the entrance and said, "Goodnight."

Karl asked a few farming questions, and after that, Gus got into his VW, cranked the engine and proceeded to drive sedately down the drive. To his right, something pale flashed between the trees. He slowed down, half expecting an animal to jump out. The pale form darted into his headlights forcing him to brake.

He rolled down his window. "Miranda! What are you doing out here?"

Giggling, she opened the passenger door and hopped in. "I told my Dad I was going to bed. I locked my bedroom and jumped out the window."

Gus was incredulous.

"B-but why?"

"Because I want to be with you."

"Yes, but..."

"Shush!" she commanded, grinning impishly. "Turn left over there." She pointed ahead. "Park under the boughs of that tree. Nobody will find us here."

CHAPTER FOURTEEN

Fishing

Gus did as he was told, parking his car in the darkest shadows. "We must talk."

"Sure." She wiggled closer.

"How old are you?"

"Old enough to know what I want, and to do what I like."

"Yes, I see that," Gus replied, "but that's not a trustworthy answer."

She wagged her finger. "It's rude to ask a lady her age."

Gus smiled. "Exactly my point. Are you a lady or a child?"

"A lady of course! Don't talk to me like a child."

"Now, now. Calm down. I'm not treating you badly, but I can't afford to be caught with underage jail-bait."

"Huh! Do I look like jail-bait to you?"

"No." Gus tried keeping his face straight. "Tell me--what is your age?"

She snapped her fingers. "Eighteen!"

"Okay. Can you prove it?"

She grabbed her purse, whipping out her State Identification. "Here--see for yourself."

Gus switched on the interior light and checked it. He nodded and handed it back. "Thanks."

She stuffed it in her bag, and said, "The South African legal age for consensual sex is 16. I passed that two years ago."

"Whoa!" Gus exclaimed. "Who said anything about sex?"

"I did because that's what I want."

"Why did you sneak out of your bedroom window? What would your father say?"

"It's none of his business. I'm eighteen."

"What if you fell pregnant?"

"Don't be ridiculous--I'm a nurse--I take the pill."

Gus shook his head, "No, I'm sorry but...." Her dress was off. Argument ceased.

***

Sunday morning dawned warm and bright. Gus lay in bed with eyes closed, savouring delicious snap-shot memories from his previous night's excursion. Miranda, the little vixen, had made him feel all fine and frisky. Life in Magoebaskloof certainly had its perks.

Before long, a vehicle rumbled down his driveway followed by a knock on his door.

"Coming!" he yelled as he whipped on trousers, a shirt and a pair of shoes. He yanked the door open. Amour van der Skiet's scantily-clad twin perks faced him. His eyes traversed down to her tight denim shorts, revealing shapely, tanned legs.

"Good morning, Mrs van der Skiet."

"Morning, Gus. Call me Amour." Her lips curved.

Gus swallowed. "Sure. What can I do for you?"

"It's my little dog, Sossie, again. He has itchy ears." She placed the dog on the table. A heady perfume wafted from her body.

Gus examined Sossie, peering into his ear canals with an otoscope. He kept his eyes averted from Amour's braless chest as he conducted the consultation with a determined professionalism.

"Ear mites; but only a few," Gus said. "I'll give you this to use."

Her eyes assessed every inch of his body as he explained the medication usage.

Another car trundled down the drive. Gretchen strolled in, calling, "Good morning, everyone!"

Gus felt relieved. "Morning, Gretch."

Mrs van der Skiet took Sossie and his medicine back to her car and drove off.

"Thank goodness you arrived," Gus said.

Gretchen giggled. "Did Amour give you a hard time?"

"No, but I've noticed she always comes after hours. I don't want her husband, Bruno, getting wrong ideas."

"People!" Gretchen said. "They're tricky. You have to watch your back."

"Yeah, I guess so. Now, how can I help you?"

"I need cat food. Sorry to hassle you, but I thought I had enough."

Gus handed her a bag. "Here, take this."

"Thanks. By the way, how was your date with Miranda?"

Gus shuffled. "How do you know about that?"

Gretchen chuckled. "Don't think you can visit the Magoebaskloof Hotel and not be seen. News gets around."

"Indeed. It went well, thank you."

"Miranda's an attractive girl," Gretchen said. "But be careful. She's supposed to be going out with a wealthy citrus baron's son."

"Oh? What's his name?"

"I'm not too sure, but they've been dating since high school." Gretchen smiled. "Anyway, I must go. See you tomorrow. 'Bye!"

***

Outside, Gus stared up into the clear blue sky. It appeared to be a beautiful day to go fishing. He packed bottled water, apples and his fishing gear into his VW and was about to set off when a smart red car came down the drive and parked. Miranda got out. "Hi!"

"Hi!" Gus's eyes lit up. "Do you have a sick animal?"

"No, I came to visit you. Where are you heading?"

"I'm going fishing at the Tzaneen dam."

"That sounds like fun. May I come along?"

He grinned. "Sure. Good company's always welcome."

"I know a great fishing spot; I'll show you where."

"Okay, let's get out of here before anyone else arrives. I need relaxation time."

***

Miranda took him to the quiet side of the dam, showing him the nature reserve and camping grounds, and then further along where it became reedy and isolated.

"This is a good place to come. People catch carp in this dam. Sometimes you see hippo and crocodiles here, but they make for dangerous night fishing. Keep your eyes open and check behind you often. Crocs are sneaky. Oh, yeah, and be alert for snakes too."

"There's not much shade in this part," Gus said looking around. His eyes took in the murky grey-green depths. Suddenly they lit on several dark dots far out on the dam's horizon.

Miranda followed his gaze. "It's hippo. Only their eyes and nostrils are sticking out."

As they negotiated their way along the rough shoreline, stepping carefully over boulders and walking around thorny shrubs, an unusual, penetrating bird cry came from above.

"That's a fish eagle," Miranda said. "They love it here."

Gus squinted up into the hot, bright sky as a large bird flew overhead. "Magnificent."

They walked further. Gus stopped. "Hey, did you hear that?"

Miranda halted and listened. A splashing sound came from the water's edge. Something thrashed around. Questioningly, they looked at each other before venturing closer.

Gus's eyes widened.

"Oh, no! It's a Nile Monitor," Miranda said. "Something's wrong."

Gus tiptoed nearer. "It's caught in fishing line."

"You *must* free it," Miranda demanded.

"Do they bite?"

"Yes, and their claws give nasty, deep scratches."

Gus braced himself as he straddled the writhing 1.7 metre lizard before pouncing on it and grabbing it behind its head and back. A thick fish hook was embedded in the side of its mouth, and the line was attached to a log.

"Somebody's been fishing for barbel."

"What's that?"

"A type of catfish. I reckon they've left a handline here and are planning to check it later."

"Miranda, look in my fishing box and pass me the pliers."

She opened the box and rummaged around. "Here," she said, handing them over.

"I'm holding him," Gus said. "You cut the hook."

She backed off. "No way! *You* cut the hook."

The lizard fought furiously until its energy abated, and then it lay spent. Gus continued to grip it by the back of its neck as his other hand struggled to cut the metal. It took a while to sever it and remove the tangled line. The fatigued lizard lay helpless and passive on its back while Gus cut the remaining nylon from its claws.

Miranda beamed approval. Gus displayed courage. But the fearful monitor had one last self-defence mechanism to offer.

SQUIRT!

A massive fountain of foul-smelling, dark excretion ejected with rocket-like speed from its cloaca, narrowly missing them both. Gus set the offending reptile free by flinging it headlong into the muddy water. He reeled back spluttering with disgusted shock.

Miranda burst into peals of laughter, holding her sides until tears streamed. Her finger pointed to Gus as she continued laughing. Her hysteria was irresistibly contagious, and soon Gus joined in. Finally, she wiped her eyes and said, "Gus Bullock, you're the bravest man I know. I love you!" She flung her arms around his neck and kissed him.

Afterwards, Gus held her at arm's length and looked into her eyes. "As you saw; I take no shit."

CHAPTER FIFTEEN

Dirty Dog

The day had run smoothly, but all that changed when a car careered down the driveway, coming to a screeching halt. A young man sprang out carrying a bloodied bull terrier. "Doctor! Doctor, please help. My dog's dying."

Gus rushed to see. "Put him up here on the table. What happened?"

"Baboon bites."

"How?" Gus asked as his eyes quickly assessed the dog's level of consciousness.

The young man choked up as he spoke. "My farm backs onto the Wolkberg Mountains where baboon roam. And my dog, Jaws, just hates them. I can't stop him from chasing them. Today, they got him. Luckily, I had my shotgun at hand. I fired into the air and scared them off before they killed him. Please save him! I've never seen a dog bleed so much." The guy's eyes glistened with moisture as he fought back tears. His fists clutched his hair as he paced up and down in front of the table.

Gus knew of incidents where dogs had been torn apart by troops of baboon who used their long powerful fangs to eviscerate attackers. Due to blood loss, Jaws was going into shock. Gus worked fast to set up an intravenous infusion to help elevate Jaw's declining blood pressure.

"Gretchen," Gus called. "Please make this fellow a cup of hot coffee and give him some biscuits. Take him outside and make him comfortable. He's got a long wait. This could take an hour or two--if Jaws survives."

The lacerations were covered in a putrid mix of blood and faeces. First, Gus shaved the hair and muck away from the edge of the wounds with a razor. Then he scrubbed them clean with disinfectant. Each wound required copious irrigation with a warm saline solution before being stitched. Gus concentrated his attention on his patient. Scrubbing the wounds, monitoring anaesthetic and respiration while doing surgery all at once was a stressful challenge. If he topped up the intravenous anaesthetic too much, his patient would die. If he gave too little, it would wake up and start moving. Maintaining the delicate balance was stressful as the dog's stability was already compromised. It was paramount to stitch up as fast as possible to minimise risk during a prolonged anaesthetic.

An hour and a quarter later, Gus finished the surgery. He pulled off his gloves and administered antibiotic injections as Jaws awoke. Lastly, he disconnected the intravenous infusion and asked Gretchen to call the young man.

"His name's Eugene," Gretchen offered. Up until then, there had been no time for formalities.

Bright-eyed, Eugene hurried in through the door. "Doctor, is he okay?"

Jaws struggled to lift his head when he heard his master's voice. His tail wagged.

Eugene bent and hugged Jaws gently. Jaws whined, and his eyes opened.

"He's going to make it," Gus said.

"Thank you, doctor--I can never thank you enough."

"Try to keep him away from baboons. I'm not sure if he'll be lucky next time."

"Thank you, doctor; I'll try."

"Bring him back in two days' time, so I can check his wounds. I'll remove stitches in ten days' time."

"Okay, doc." Eugene beamed as he carried his buddy, Jaws, back to his car.

***

Gretchen popped her head in through the door. "Gus, there's another young man to see you. His name's Sarel Venter but he hasn't brought an animal."

"Okay, let him through."

Sarel, a tall, handsome man in his early twenties, entered.

"Good afternoon," Gus said. "How may I help?"

The young fellow cast a furtive glance back over his shoulder towards Gretchen before lowering his voice to a gruff whisper. "Doctor, *ek soek bul pille*."

Gus stared blankly. "Pardon?"

"Ek soek bul pille."

Gus shook his head. "Sorry, mate. I'm an Aussie. I don't understand Afrikaans. You'll have to tell me in English."

Sarel took a deep breath and tried again. "I don't know the English name, but I want *bul pille*."

Gus scratched his head. It had been a long day and his brain felt tired. No understanding sprang to mind. "Hang on. Gretchen is bilingual--she can translate. *Gretchen!*"

Sarel's face turned crimson. "No! No! Don't ask Gretchen."

Gretchen came in, causing Sarel to fidget with unease.

"Ask her," Gus said.

"Tannie," Sarel said. "Ek soek bul pille."

Gretchen smiled. "He says; *auntie, I'm looking for bull pills*."

"Bull pills?" Gus repeated stupidly. "Never heard of them. What would you use them for?"

An Afrikaans confab took place making Gretchen's face flush with illumination. She cleared her throat and said, "He and his friends are going camping with their girlfriends next weekend, and they want *bull pills* to enhance their sexual performance."

"Ah..." Gus said. "So, you want me to give you testosterone tablets to enhance your sexual performance?"

Sarel's face burnt scarlet.

"Sorry," Gus said. "I can't do that."

"No, no, no. That's not what I mean," Sarel replied. "Us guys are okay. We need the *bull pills* for our girls--you know--just to get them feeling horny."

"Well," Gretchen said. "I'll leave you to finish this conversation."

Gus fought to keep a straight face as he watched Gretchen's hurried exit. Then he said, "Sarel, I don't believe such a thing exists. And if it did, as a vet, I would not sell it. Sorry, I can't help you. Best wishes for a fun weekend." Then he showed Sarel the door.

Afterwards, Gus shook his head and turned to Gretchen with a cheeky grin. "Well, that was a dirty dog."

She laughed.

<u>CHAPTER SIXTEEN</u>

Joe Varella Onions

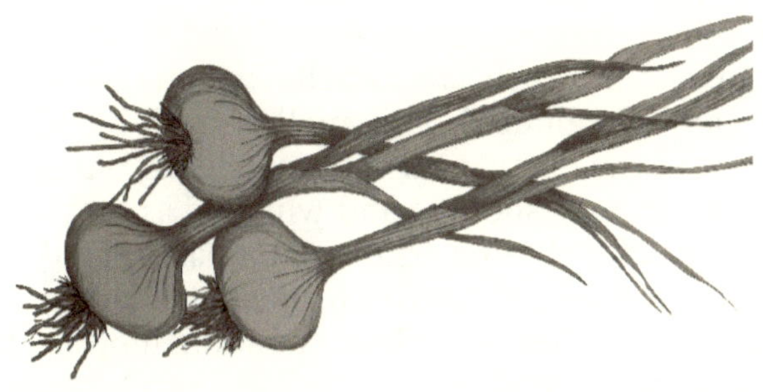

That evening Gus sat on his veranda drinking a beer while watching the sunset. Spy, his one-eyed cat jumped onto his lap, purred and rubbed its whiskers against his face. Gus stroked the kitten gently, and it responded with friendly nips to his fingers. His thoughts turned to Miranda, the little vixen was growing on him, but could he trust her? Gretchen had warned that Miranda was going out with someone else. Maybe it was time to find out who it was. A relationship with a two-timing hussy was not something he wanted. He made up his mind there and then to talk to her the following week when she came off night-duty.

The following day Gus awoke early to pack his car. Joe Varella, a Portuguese man, owned a cattle ranch near Modjadjiskloof and had booked Gus for a full day's herd work that included 120 pregnancy tests, 240 TB tests and about 50 for de-horning.

Gus knew the morning's bright clear blue sky would make for hot work later. As he drove down the mountain, heading towards the flat land of the Lowveld, he passed a dairy on the left with cattle grazing green pasture. He slowed down as a strange sight caught his attention. A dairy cow stood idly masticating a brightly coloured umbrella. *Good Lord*, he thought. *That's trouble, but I can't stop now.* He made a mental note of it and drove on towards Modjadjiskloof.

By 8:00 am the outdoor heat seared. Humidity escalated. Gus drank plenty of water; the heat was unbearable. He worked all day, not stopping for lunch. Sweat beaded his brow and trickled down inside his overalls and gumboots. The herdsmen and facilities available were not highly efficient; causing the cattle change-overs to be slow.

By 4:00 pm a strong wind arose causing dark storm clouds to gather. Inside the crush, steers bellowed and became restless as anxiety mounted. The smell of fresh blood from de-horning hung in the dusty, swirling air, causing unease. Barefooted herdsmen, shouted and whistled as they ran, armed with crooked sticks, chasing errant cattle back. Hand-rolled newspaper and tobacco cigarettes projected at jaunty angles from the corners of their toothless, coughing mouths. Despite fatigue, Gus knew they all participated in a race against the weather. Work must be finished before the storm began.

A roll of distant thunder sounded as he finished the last de-horning. The herdsmen whooped and shouted with relief as they set about directing cattle back to their paddocks. Nobody wished to be caught in a treacherous lightning storm.

Joe Varella came up to Gus and slapped him on the back. "Well done, man! Good work."

"Thanks."

"I insist you come to my house for a clean-up," Joe said. "And then drink a beer with me."

"Okay, I'd appreciate that."

Joe Varella turned out to be not only hospitable but also an excellent onion farmer. Gus savoured his beer slowly as Joe explained the intricacies of onion farming. He told of how his onions had become the best in the country since he and his family had fled Mozambique, with a few possessions in an old Mini, only a few years previously. As they spoke, lightning cracked, thunder rolled and rain poured down onto the old farmstead's tin roof.

"Stay for dinner," Joe invited. "The rain's too heavy for you to leave now."

"Are you sure?"

"Yes, there's plenty to eat. My wife has cooked a roast. Please, stay and be our guest."

Afterwards, Joe offered cheese and biscuits around, accompanied with thin slices of fresh onion.

"Ooh!" Gus said with approval. "They make my eyes water."

Joe beamed with pride.

"My tongue is on fire! I swear to you, mate, forever after this I'll call all hot onions *Joe Varellas*."

At 9:00 pm Gus left Joe's house laden with huge bunches of pungent onions. They were the fattest, freshest green onions Gus had ever seen--enough to make his eyes water.

As Gus trundled along the road in his VW, heading towards Magoebaskloof, the rain intensified to the point where his windscreen wipers could no longer cope, making visibility impossible.

SKID-DUNK!

His car slid into a steep storm water gully off the edge of the road, coming to a halt at an awkward angle.

Darn! Gus thought. *Now what?*

He climbed out in the bucketing rain to inspect his car for damage. Although intact, it was firmly wedged into the muddy trench. He tried to push it out but no go.

Already soaked through, the thought of sleeping in wet clothes in a car at the side of the road was unappealing. He looked around--no sign of traffic. All quiet. *I might as well walk.* He locked the doors, pocketed the keys and began to walk, following the power lines, which offered a shorter route up the mountain.

Rain continued to pelt his body as he walked. CRACK! Gus cursed and ducked. The ear-splitting sound seemed as loud as a rifle shot. He looked up. The sound had come from the overhead power lines. They cracked, hissed and popped with each lightning strike. He walked and walked. Eventually, the mountain became too steep to walk, making him crawl on all fours. Halfway up the steep slippery slope he felt like turning back, the climb was proving more than his casual estimation. He persevered walking until he reached his hut in the early hours of the morning. Shivering cold and drenched in mud, he showered, dried himself and went to bed.

Continuous knocking awoke him. Gretchen was hammering at the door. Her voice called, "Gus! Hello...are you here? Are you okay?"

He staggered out of bed and opened his door.

She was amazed to hear how, after a full day's work, he had walked 20 km in a lightning storm at night. Afterwards, she told him to get dressed. She knew someone who owned a truck that could help get his car out the ditch.

By 10:30 am, thanks to Gretchen's contacts, Gus got his car back and returned driving it home. The onions had become hot in the car causing Gus to tear up. Afterwards, the hot issue of Joe Varella onions was shared around and received by all with tearful thanks.

***

A few days later Gus received a call from a dairy farm down the road.

"Doc, I have a sick cow."

Gus listened to the farmer explain the cow's symptoms. To Gus it sounded as if the cow might have ingested wire, but he kept quiet. It was no use jumping to conclusions without first seeing the animal.

"How do I get to your place?" Gus asked.

As the farmer explained, Gus realised it was the farm he had passed on the way to Modjadjiskloof where he spotted a cow eating an umbrella. As he hung-up, Gus knew he had an advantage.

"Where are you going?" Gretchen asked. "To visit Len Cheeseman's dairy. He's got a sick cow that might need surgery."

Gretchen's brows furrowed. "Ah. He's a tricky customer. Rumour has it he doesn't like you. He thinks young vets lack experience and can't be trusted. I know his regular vet is on holiday now, so maybe he's desperate."

"Huh," Gus said. "I'll fix his bad attitude."

Gretchen's jaw dropped. "But what can you do?"

Gus smiled. "I might tell you after I'm done.

<u>CHAPTER SEVENTEEN</u>

Umbrella Sickness

WGus arrived at Len Cheeseman's dairy, the old farmer came out to greet him with a dour look on his face. "So, you're the new vet."

"Some still call me that."

"Huh! I'm not sure what such a young fellow like you knows. Young vets don't have much life experience."

"I've studied hard and know my job."

"Your accent's odd. Where are you from?"

"Sydney, Australia."

Len shook his large grey head and clicked his tongue. "I don't suppose you know much about African diseases."

"I'm learning fast," Gus replied.

"Well, I doubt whether you'll be able to figure out what's wrong with my cow. She's my best milk producer, and so far, she has given me heifer calves every year, so I really don't want to lose her."

"Where is she?"

"Follow me."

Len Cheeseman led the way to the cattle yards behind his dairy. A lone Friesian cow stood with her head down but was not eating. Her back was hunched into an arch shape.

Gus shook his head as he observed her. "She's in a bad way."

A herdsman moved the cow towards the crush for examination. She ambled forward with dragging hooves. Her back arched higher with every step. She let out one low, groaning bellow and stopped. The herdsman nudged her on until she went into the holding.

In an instant, Gus recognised the Friesian cow as the *umbrella chomper*, for it had a unique marking in the formation of a paw print on its left side. Gus took out his stethoscope, plugged it into his ears and listened to the cow's stomach and respiration. He took his time, allowing tension to build. Finally, he unplugged his ears and stood to face Len Cheeseman's frowning expression.

"So, what do you think?" Cheeseman asked.

Gus shook his head slowly. "Mr Cheeseman--it's very serious. I'm glad you called me because this cow must be operated on immediately."

Cheeseman looked doubtful. "Are you sure?"

Gus nodded.

Cheeseman rubbed his chin thoughtfully. "Why can't you just give her a few injections and then we can see how she goes?"

"Because," Gus said with authority, "injections won't work. This cow must have surgery--today."

Cheeseman looked doubtful. "Tell me," he said, "what do you think is wrong with her?"

Gus folded his arms across his chest, looked Cheeseman in the eyes and said, "This cow has the worst case of *Umbrella Sickness* I've ever seen in my life."

If Cheeseman had doubts beforehand, now they manifested with a dose of rage. "*What*?" he bellowed. "I've never heard of such nonsense. What rubbish is this you're prattling on about?"

Unflinching, Gus stood firm. "Umbrella Sickness--I swear to you it could kill your cow. And I've got a hunch it's a colourful problem too."

"What if we don't operate?" Cheeseman asked.

"Then your cow will die a slow and painful death."

Cheeseman grunted. "And if I let you operate, what then?"

Gus cocked his head thoughtfully. "I reckon she'll have a good chance of survival, but we must act fast before she gets too weak. We don't want her rumen to stop working."

Cheeseman let out an agonised sigh of discontent. His back was against the wall. He shook his head and said, "Okay. Operate if you insist."

Gus smiled. "Thank you. You won't be disappointed with my diagnosis. Please stay here and watch--I might need your help."

Cheeseman scowled. "I don't believe you, so don't take me for a fool. I know there is nothing called *Umbrella Sickness*, but anyway, get on with it."

A herdsman brought two buckets of clean water. Gus injected some local anaesthetic into the cow's side and administered a paralumbar injection to help block pain. Then he began shaving and preparing her flank for surgery. He scrubbed the area with iodine and then took a new scalpel blade and made a long incision down through the skin. Then he cut through the next layer with surgical scissors and put his hand inside the cow and delved around her four stomachs until he got hold of her rumen. He grabbed it with a pair of forceps and asked Cheeseman to hold onto it while he cut it open. Cheeseman stared in horror as he watched Gus cut into his cow's stomach and pull out half-digested grass.

Gus bent his head in quiet concentration as he groped his way around.

"Ah! Just as I thought," Gus said. "Now you will believe me. It is *Umbrella Sickness*." Slowly, like a magician pulling scarves from a hat, he pulled out long, brightly coloured pieces of nylon, all joined together.

"What the hell is that?" Cheeseman asked.

"An umbrella."

"No! You're kidding."

"Afraid not," Gus replied as he pulled out more crumpled remnants of masticated, indigestible brolly with multiple sharp wire attachments.

"Well, I never!" Cheeseman appeared incredulous. "*Umbrella Sickness* indeed! How did you know?"

Gus shrugged. "Just put it down to life experience."

Cheeseman went quiet.

As Gus sewed up the cow, he told Cheeseman about the benefits of putting magnets into all his cows' stomachs. "It's an ideal way to collect all those small pieces of wire that cows pick up over a lifetime. But I must say, Len, whether this cow had a magnet or not, she would have still needed this operation. The umbrella was too big to pass or stay inside her gut."

"Well, I never," Cheeseman marvelled. "Honestly, you must come around again soon as you can and put magnets into my cows. And when you return--you might as well do a few pregnancy tests too."

Gus smiled. "Sure. I'll do that." He finished sewing up the cow and stood back to admire his handiwork. "Stitches come out in two weeks' time. How about I return then and do your other work?"

"Sure!" Cheeseman said. "See you then."

***

A few days later Gretchen said to Gus, "Ever since you went to Cheeseman's farm, rumour has it that you can do no wrong. He's been telling everyone what a wonderful vet you are. He even told old Mrs Batty that you are unusually gifted and bright."

Gus preened.

Gretchen stared at him over the top of her glasses. "I get the feeling you haven't told me everything about this."

"Knowledge is power. Put it down to my excellent veterinary training back in Sydney."

CHAPTER EIGHTEEN

Wingnut

On Monday morning, Miranda brought in a tiny brown puppy.

"What have we here?" Gus asked as he held the warm, wriggly pup in one hand.

"She's mine!" Miranda beamed with pride. "And I've named her Mini."

Gus chuckled. "Mini and Miranda? No! That won't do. It sounds ridiculous."

"Don't mock," she warned, "not unless you can think of a better name."

Gus cocked his head to one side as he considered the shivering scrap now parked on his cold table. "First, are you sure it's a dog?"

Miranda rolled her eyes, landing a playful punch on his shoulder. "Stop it! You're mean. If you can't think of anything better, then *Mini* will do."

"No way! Look at its ears--they stick out sideways. And it has a flattish snout. To me, its face looks like a fruit bat and those ears make it look like a wingnut."

"A *wingnut*? What do you mean?"

"Surely you must know? It's one of those screw-thread nuts with two flanges on the sides."

Miranda screwed up her nose. "Oh, I know what you mean. But *Wingnut*?"

"Yeah."

She smiled. "Okay. *Wingnut* she is. Miranda and Wingnut--it sounds better. I like the idea because you came up with it." As an afterthought, she added, "My Dad calls it a *stoepkakker*."

Gus raised his brows. "What the heck is a *stoepkakker*?"

Miranda giggled. "It's an Afrikaans word used for little dogs that poo around the house. Directly translated, it means *veranda-pooper*, because they never walk too far from the house."

"Well," Gus replied, "it's a fitting description. It's easy to see how the phrase came about."

"Hopefully, Wingnut will be better than that. I fully expect her to behave like a decent dog."

Gus gave a wry smile. "That remains to be seen. Where did you find it?"

"Dumped on the roadside at the edge of town. Can you believe it?"

"Sadly, yes."

"How old do you reckon Wingnut is?"

"Maybe about six weeks. She looks like a cross between a miniature pincher, a pug and maybe an alien."

Miranda laughed. "I know she looks weird, but she's irresistibly cute."

"Wingnut needs to be vaccinated and dewormed," Gus said. "She looks like a worm bus."

Miranda's eyes widened. "Don't be horrible! Wingnut's far too cute to have worms; besides, she's too young."

Gus chuckled. "Don't fool yourself. Worms are no respecter of cuteness. Trust me; Wingnut has worms."

"How can you tell simply by looking at her?"

"She has a pot-belly, a dry coat and I can see her ribs under her coat. Allow me to de-worm her right now. If you don't she could get sick and die. Hookworms are a real problem in puppies."

Miranda wavered as she hugged the pup close to her chest.

"Trust me. I'll deworm and vaccinate her for free. Give here."

"Okay, if you insist."

Wingnut stood still while Gus treated her and then gave her back to Miranda. "There. All done. Give that dewormer about a day to work. From now on when you feed her, Wingnut, and not the worms, will be utilising the food. And here, use this shampoo to kill fleas. It's safe for puppies. Make sure you rinse it off well."

"Thanks. I'll wash her right now outside in a bucket."

The phone rang so Gus answered it. Afterwards, he hung up and went to find Miranda.

"Hey," Gus said, "that was Steve Prinsloo, my boss from Phalaborwa, on the phone."

She looked up. "Yes?"

"He's working in Lydenburg on a dairy for a few days. He says he received a couple of veterinary calls in Hoedspruit that he can't attend. He wants me to go and do the work. If we leave now, I'll probably be gone all day. Do you want to come along?"

Miranda's eyes shone. "Yeah, sure! I'm keen to see what you do but where can I leave Wingnut?"

"Leave her here with Gretchen."

"Okay. Let me help you pack. What do you need?"

"The first call is to a farm with dying cattle, so I'd better take my microscope, slides, medication...." He rattled off a long list. "Then I have to see a horse with a sore leg at the Air Force Base Stables."

After Gus had packed his car, he did a mental check to ensure everything was with him that might be needed. "Right. It's about a two-hour-drive. Let's get going."

As they chugged along, Gus thought it was time to pop a few questions. "So, Miranda, I've heard you have another boyfriend."

Alert, she looked up.

"I hope you're not two-timing me because I won't stand for any nonsense."

"I was dating a guy named Piet who stands to inherit some farm land. My father is keen for me to marry him so that our family estate can grow, but I don't like him."

"What changed your mind about the guy?"

Miranda sighed. "He's already cheated on me twice, and he drinks too much. To be honest, I find him scary."

"Who is this guy? Piet, who?"

"Piet van der Skiet."

Gus swallowed. "Is he any relation to Bruno van der Skiet?"

"Yes, Bruno is his father."

<u>CHAPTER NINETEEN</u>

Hoedspruit Cattle Call

Gus drove along in silence as he digested Miranda's news of her connections with the van der Skiets. No wonder she wanted to break off her old relationship. The possibility of a van der Skiet vengeance crossed his mind.

Hendrik Groenewald waited in his truck at the entrance to his farm when Gus arrived. "Good day," he called. "Thanks for coming. Since I phoned, another three cattle have died. Follow my truck and I'll show you."

Gus and Miranda followed Hendrik until he pulled up under the shade of a thorn tree. Then they followed Hendrik into a dry bushy paddock.

"So far," Hendrik said as he stood pointing to bloated cattle corpses dotted around his field, "I've lost 17 highly bred Brahman cows. They were due for sale at the Pretoria Agricultural show next month. This is a major loss. I don't know what's killing them--they seem to be dropping like flies."

Gus stood with his hands on his hips as he turned slowly, surveying the animals. They were all fat and shiny with glossy coats--the picture of fine breeding and excellent health, except that many were dead. A herdsman came running. He pointed back over his shoulder while talking excitedly in his lingo.

"Darn!" Hendrik said. "He reckons another one just went down."

Gus sprinted over to see the ailing cow but it was too late; the beast had already taken its last breath and fallen over stone dead. A sigh of air rushed from its lungs, forced out by its own sheer weight as it lay on its side--the final exhale. The cow's eyes remained open in death, causing a frenzy of greedy flies to settle in their moisture, already feeding, copulating and laying eggs.

Hendrik whipped his hat off and slapped his thigh with frustration. "Doctor, help me. *Please!* Do something. How many more are going to die? I can't afford to lose them all. Please, I beg you--work fast. We must stop this carnage now."

Miranda remained silent as she watched Gus's jaw clench. She knew he was perplexed and deep in thought. Hendrik demanded answers that Gus could not give.

Hendrik's body went taut while his eyes shone with unshed tears. He was a man on the verge of losing his sanity and there was no consolation to offer. His eyes turned to Gus, filled with questions, his mouth opening and closing but without words as he struggled to express his devastation.

"How many cattle are on this farm?" Gus asked.

"Two hundred and fifty before these deaths."

"Are they all in this paddock?"

"No. Only 30 cows here. I've been keeping them aside for sale."

Gus scratched his head. "Have there been any other deaths on your farm beside the ones in this paddock?"

"No," Hendrik answered. "So far, they've only died here."

"When did you last dip?" Gus asked.

"A week ago."

"Are you sure the concentrate was correct?"

"Yes. My other cattle went through first and they're all right."

"Okay," Gus said. "I'll do a few post-mortems. It's no use guessing until we find concrete evidence to work with."

Miranda followed Gus back to his car. "Do you have any idea?" she whispered.

He shook his head. "Clueless."

His anxiety rubbed off onto her. She couldn't but help feel sorry for him. 18 cows were dead and within five minutes of arriving the farmer demanded impossible answers. She sighed. Now she wished she hadn't come. It wasn't much fun sharing in Gus's worries and misery; but seeing she was here, she might as well help where possible. She carried things, hoping to ease his mind with helpfulness and a compliant demeanour.

Gus set up his microscope and then took a few blood smears from the cows' ears. He checked them all for signs of disease.

After that he opened a few cows and took brain smears that he analysed under his microscope. He stood back with a sigh.

"Found anything?" Hendrik asked.

"No," Gus said. "They are free of tickborne diseases--no sign of Redwater Fever or Heartwater, so your dipping is good. No sign of anthrax either--so that's good for all of us."

Hendrik frowned. "What could it be?"

"I suspect it's poisoning. Have you checked this camp for toxic plants?"

"Yes," Hendrik replied. I check my paddocks regularly for toxic plants--I swear to you there are none here. I checked this paddock thoroughly before I put the cows in."

Gus pulled out a book of indigenous toxic plants and flipped through the pictures with Hendrik. The farmer recognised most of them but claimed to have none.

"What about this--gousiekte?" Gus asked.

Hendrik shook his head.

"Right," Gus said. "I'll cut open their stomachs and look for anything strange."

Miranda watched with interest as Gus cut open the first cow's stomach. Warm, heavy air escaped, delivering a wave of putrid stench. Miranda flew backwards, almost gagging. Her eyes watered. She stood at a safe distance observing Gus, marvelling at the strength of his tolerance to offensive odours.

Hendrik paced up and down, muttering to himself as he watched Gus move from dead cow to dead cow.

"Can you see anything noteworthy?" Miranda whispered.

"There's fluid in the lungs. See that froth in the tubes? And there's fluid around the heart. It kind of looks like congestive cardiac failure."

"Have you found anything significant in the stomach?"

Gus shook his head. "The food is too well chewed in this cow, but I'll look in the others--maybe I'll get lucky."

When Gus got to the fourth cow's stomach, he held up a long, dark green undigested leaf. "Does anyone recognise this? It's odd. It's not the normal shape of an indigenous leaf."

Hendrik and Miranda shook their heads. Gus bit his lower lip. The leaf looked familiar, but for now, he couldn't place it. "Ask the herdsmen if they have seen this leaf anywhere," Gus asked.

Hendrik took the leaf and showed the herdsmen. They all mumbled and shook their heads. Suddenly, one lad came forward, nodding. He ran pointing to a pile of sawn-off branches near the fence. Gus followed him and looked. Most of the branches had been eaten, but some leaves remained.

"Where did this foliage come from?" Gus asked.

Hendrik spoke to the herdsman in his lingo before turning to Gus. "They say the gardener throws my wife's garden clippings over the fence here."

Gus's eyes lit up. "Please take me to your garden. I wish to try to identify this leaf."

"Sure, follow me."

Gus said, "Tell the herdsmen to keep the cattle away from these leaves. They mustn't eat any more."

Hendrik gave orders. Heads nodded. He and Gus went to the garden and walked around. "Ta-da!" Gus exclaimed. "Look- -the leaf matches this bush."

"What is it?" Hendrik asked.

"Nerium Oleander," Gus replied. "More commonly known as *oleander*--it is highly toxic and fast acting. Your cows must have gorged themselves on it."

Hendrik paled. His expression was a mixture of sorrow and relief. He didn't know whether to laugh because the cause of his needless cattle deaths had been found, or to cry because of the stupidity of it all. He took a deep breath and buried his face in his hands. "Oh, my. Oh, my," was all he seemed to say until he looked up and said, "Thank you, Doctor. You have saved me from losing more."

Gus said, "I'm glad I could be of service. Now, move the cows out of that paddock and burn the remains of those garden clippings. In future, all garden clippings should be burnt inside a special area inside the garden and not be put over the fence where livestock roam."

Hendrik hung his head. "This lesson has cost me thousands, but you have saved me from losing more. I just can't thank you enough."

***

Gus called Miranda. "Come on. Let's pack-up. I must still see that horse with a sore leg at the Air Force Base."

Miranda grabbed what she could and headed towards the car. "I hope we can stop for a cool drink somewhere. I'm parched."

Gus smiled. "Yeah, a couple of celebration coolies sounds good."

<u>CHAPTER TWENTY</u>

Hoedspruit Horse Call

They drove down the road and stopped in the tiny town of Hoedspruit where they purchased refreshments and downed them. Gus emitted a burp of satisfaction.

"Excuse me, but that's better."

Miranda giggled. "For a rough diamond, you're surprisingly sharp."

Gus cocked an eyebrow. "Explain?"

"The way you figured out the cause of those cattle deaths was impressive."

He shrugged. "A day's work. Right, let's head off to see that horse."

As they drove along the desolate tar road, heat waves danced and shimmered on the horizon. They wound their windows right down; hot air blasted over their flushed faces. On arrival, their hair stood awry, and perspiration trickled down in rivulets under their clothing.

"Man, I stink," Gus said.

Miranda smiled. "Not too badly, and I'm sure the horse won't mind."

A young woman came out to greet them. "Hi, I'm Grace."

"Pleased to meet you." Gus smiled.

"Come this way. I'll take you to Nutmeg."

Gus carried his black bag while Miranda followed.

Grace led them to a pole and rail enclosure where a bay horse stood on three legs munching teff from a hay net. It was tethered to a pole by its headcollar. Gus patted the horse's neck. "Hello, Nutmeg." It turned to wipe its wet, dusty nose across his chest, leaving a muddied snot streak across his shirt. Gus looked down. "He's resting his near fore."

"Yes. He's very lame today."

Gus untethered the horse and gave the lead to Miranda to hold. He stooped and picked up the problem hoof and scratched around with a hoof knife. "He's got a seedy toe," Gus said. "I reckon Nutmeg has an abscess. In future, you should get him shod."

"I hoped to save on shoeing costs," Grace replied.

"In the long run, shoeing him will work out cheaper than getting a vet out to lance hoof abscesses. It's all part of owning a horse."

"Yes, okay."

Gus nodded. "Yeah, the ground's too hard for a heavy horse like this--especially when you add a rider's weight and saddle on top of his withers; it puts extra weight on the front hooves. After I've dug down, he'll be out of action for at least a week, unless you find a good farrier really quick."

Grace sighed. "Getting a farrier out here is difficult. He only passes by every five weeks. He's due in another three weeks' time--that's why I called you."

"Good. You did the right thing. We don't want the infection to spread up the hoof and come out the top by the coronet--if that happens you'll end up with a damaged horse. No hoof, no horse."

"You're right," Grace replied.

Gus said, "Miranda, hold him. I'm digging down."

Miranda braced herself as the horse began to rear slightly. Gus hung onto the front hoof and dug. The horse hopped around. Miranda hung on to its head and Gus almost lost his balance. He stopped and let the horse rest, and then he dug again. This time, a foul-smelling dark fluid was released. Immediately, the horse seemed calmer. Gus cleaned out the area, making the hole deeper and wider. After that, he applied a bran and Epsom Salts poultice. He showed Grace what to do.

"Right, do this treatment three times a day for two days. Once the cotton wool pad shows oozing has stopped, then you can plug the hole with a piece of cotton wool dipped in iodine. Then place another piece dipped in formalin over that to help harden the area." Gus demonstrated how to apply the poultice and how to plug the hole afterwards so that no more dirt could enter. "Check the cotton wool doesn't fall out until the hoof hole has healed. It's a long recovery that requires constant attention to avoid any recurrence."

Grace beamed. "Thank you for coming and helping me out."

Gus rubbed Nutmeg's neck. The horse tilted its head and stretched its neck out for a bit more while lifting its top lip, displaying his long teeth.

"Oh, he's smiling again," Grace said. "I think he likes you."

Just then another young woman walked past them carrying a saddle. "Hi, everyone," she called as she plonked her saddle down on the pole and rail fence.

"Hey, Jill, did you have a good ride?" Grace asked.

"Yeah. I'm glad to be back--it's way too hot."

"Meet the vet, Gus, and his assistant, Miranda."

Jill smiled. "Hi, ya' all?"

"In which paddock did you put, Misty?" Grace asked.

Jill pointed over her shoulder. "Back there under that tree. He was enjoying a good roll in the sand when I left."

Grace stood up on tiptoes. "I can't see him. Are you sure the gate's closed?"

"Yes, it is. Don't worry; Misty won't go anywhere. He's waiting for treats."

Grace squinted her eyes, frowning. "I can't see him. He should be up by now. I hope he's not cast himself against that tree."

"Okay, I'll go and check." Jill ambled back.

Gus said, "Well, it looks like Nutmeg is on the road to recovery. I'll just give him a shot of long acting antibiotics. Is his anti-tetanus shot up to date? This is typically the sort of wound that is prone to tetanus."

"Yes, thank you. It's okay."

A shriek rang out. They all looked up and saw Jill hurtling towards them at breakneck speed with flaying arms.

"OH, MY GOD! Get inside quick. Get Nutmeg inside. MOVE!" Tears streamed down her face. She screamed almost incoherently.

Grace put one hand on her hip. "For goodness sake, Jill. Calm down. Nobody can understand what you're on about..."

Jill trembled violently.

Gus looked up, alarm written all over his face. "What's wrong?"

Jill lifted a shaking finger and pointed backwards. Tears streamed down her face as she sniffed and sobbed. "Misty's dead!"

"You're not making any sense," Grace said. "What are you talking about?"

Jill almost collapsed into Gus's arms. "HELP! You gotta do something!"

Gus gripped her firmly by the shoulders. "Jill, calm down. What's the matter?"

She sank to her knees, sobbing and hitting the ground. "Stop those lions eating my horse!"

"Stay here," Gus ordered as he turned to go see.

"Don't!" Miranda cried.

He shook her hand off and jogged towards Misty.

He went far enough for a glimpse but ended up with an adrenaline rush that almost stopped his heart. A trio of lion huddled around the horse carcase, eating its stomach. Gus froze; suppressing an urge for spontaneous urination. One lion turned towards him with blood smeared on its chin, gave a deep-throated growl and then turned back to feed.

Gus moved backwards slowly and carefully. He shot into the tack room with the women as fast as he could and jerked the door shut. He stood rigid, breathing hard. Miranda grabbed his hand. "Thank God, you made it back. You, foolish man!"

"I phoned for help," Grace said. "My husband's coming with a rifle. He'll fire into the ground and scare them away."

Gus swallowed. "Jill, you're right; it's too late for Misty. I'm truly sorry."

CHAPTER TWENTY-ONE

Two-Timing

On their way home, Gus and Miranda stopped at the Hoedspruit convenience store and bought two more cool drinks. They drank these as they journeyed along the flat tar road, flanked to the left side by the Mariepskop Mountains to their right the Olifants River.

Miranda said, "Today was the most terrifying day of my life. I thought lions would kill you."

Gus winced. "Yeah, so did I. How do you reckon those lions got there?"

"The Kruger National Park is close by, and although it's surrounded by high electric fences, occasionally they break. And, there are several smaller private safari lodges nearby that keep lions."

"How do the fences get broken?" Gus asked.

Miranda pursed her lips in thought. "I've heard that illegal immigrants from Mozambique cut fences when passing through."

"Don't they get eaten by lions?" Gus asked.

"Yeah, some do. And I've heard stories of elephants throwing their calves against the fence to flatten it and then the herd tramples through."

"Amazing," Gus said. "I reckon Rangers have a full-time job maintaining the place."

"And now they have three lions to track and dart."

"I hope they find them before anyone dies."

"I'm sure they will."

As they drove along, Gus said, "It feels strange to travel in the flat Lowveld where right alongside us loom the Marieskop cliffs, a section of the Drakensberg Mountains."

Miranda smiled. "To me, it's normal because I've lived here all my life. Hey, do you see all those white streaks that run perpendicular to the horizontal rock strata on the cliffs?"

"Yeah?"

"That's dry vulture poo. Everyone knows vultures live in lion country."

"If I'd known, that would have warned me."

Miranda smiled and continued, "Just over these mountains the road passes through a tunnel, the J.G. Strydom Tunnel, and then twists along a perilous pass until it comes out near Ohrigstad. After that, the road continues towards Lydenburg, a scenic, productive farming area."

Gus turned the car right towards the Olifants River and later stopped on the verge before the bridge. "I want to view the river."

He and Miranda walked along the bridge and peered down. Hippo floated peacefully in the river below while the sound of barking baboons in the bush drifted up.

"Look!" Miranda said, pointing. "There's a crocodile lying on the river bank with its mouth open. See those little birds pecking its teeth?"

Gus's eyes followed her finger.

"They're called Egyptian Plovers. They clean crocs' teeth and warn them of danger by squawking and flying away. It's your lucky day, Gus. One does not always see crocs this close to the bridge."

After they had enjoyed the view, Gus said, "I guess we'd better head back."

***

On their return, Miranda took Wingnut from Gretchen. "Thank you for caring for my pup."

"It was my pleasure. Wingnut's so cute!" Gretchen laughed. "I wish you saw the worms she passed, urgh!"

Miranda's eyes widened. "Wingnut had worms?"

Gus chuckled. "When will you learn to trust my diagnostic powers?"

Miranda blushed. "Thanks for deworming her. You were right."

"So how was your day?" Gretchen asked.

Gus raised one eyebrow. "Eventful."

***

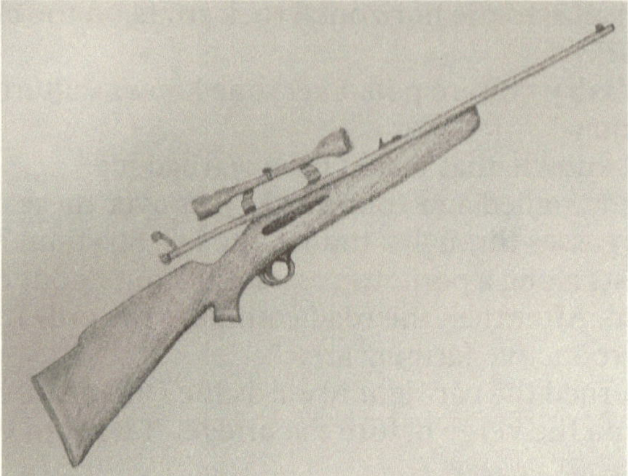

The following Friday night, Miranda dropped by Gus's place after hours for a tête-à-tête. Energetic Gus was delighted with her company and was willing to oblige. As things were about to get underway, their romantic moment was broken by the strains of a large car engine pulling up into his driveway. Miranda groaned, yanked her top back on and hid in the corner of Gus's bedroom while he answered his front door.

Amour van der Skiet's voice was instantly recognisable, so Miranda kept quiet, staying out of sight. Amour had a dog with her. It sounded as if she was more concerned about flirting with Gus than with her dog's wellbeing. Jealousy and annoyance needled Miranda as she hid away eavesdropping. Gus laughed nervously, as he attempted to duck and dive Amour's suggestive advances.

Within minutes, another large vehicle accelerated down the drive and screeched to a halt. Miranda heard the car door slam followed by the *stomp, stomp* sounds of a man's heavy footsteps. She peeped through the curtains and saw Bruno van der Skiet, armed with a rifle, head towards Gus's consultation room and kick the door wide.

Terrified and wide-eyed, Miranda's hands flung to her mouth as she pressed herself hard against the wall as far back into the shadows as she could go.

"Ah, woman!" Bruno raged. "I caught you out."

Gus put his hands up. "Amour has a dog with a sore back."

Unconvinced, Bruno's eyes assessed his wife's skimpy attire. "Nonsense! Something's going on here--and I want answers--now!"

"There's nothing more to say," Gus replied.

Miranda heard Bruno cock his rifle. She screamed and ran out into the consulting room. "Don't shoot! Please don't shoot. I swear to you--there is nothing between your wife and Gus."

Bruno hesitated, lowering his rifle. "How would you know?"

"Because Gus is my lover!" Her heart pounded with fear and desperation as she challenged Bruno who was once supposed to be her future father-in-law.

Bruno shook his head. "No! Don't tell me that this pathetic Englishman has stolen your childish heart too."

"Excuse me, Sir," Gus interjected. "I am not an Englishman. I am Australian."

Bruno's eyes blazed as he lifted his rifle and took aim at Gus's chest. "I hate the Australians more than the English. It was you guys who put the Boers' children and wives into concentration camps during the Boer War. Your Aussie friend, Breaker Morant, was notorious for killing civilians and Boers who had surrendered."

"That was almost one hundred years ago, 1899 to 1902," Gus replied. "I can assure you; Breaker Morant was no friend of mine. Anyway, he was sentenced to death for his war crimes."

"I don't care," Bruno shouted. "I hate Englishmen and Australians--you included. You're nothing but a *soutpiel*."

Miranda gasped. "Stop it! Take your wife away and go home. You have no right to threaten Gus like this. He's just a vet who is doing his job."

Bruno turned and spat. "Miranda, you're nothing but a traitor. Wait until I tell your fiancé, Piet, about your affair with this *soutpiel*."

"Tell him! I don't care," Miranda yelled. "Piet is no longer my fiancé. I broke it off--but he won't listen."

Bruno grabbed Amour by the top of her arm and dragged her around. "Come, we're going."

She picked up her dog and went with him.

After they had left, Gus turned to Miranda and said, "That was a bit hair-raising. Do you really think he might have shot me?"

Miranda shrugged. "I don't know. But I couldn't stand by and take the risk."

"Thanks for saving my life." Gus hugged her. She was still trembling. "It's okay. Don't worry; he's gone. I'm sure he won't be back."

Miranda rolled her eyes. "Yeah, but it's his son, Piet, I'm worried about."

Gus said, "Have you really broken up with Piet?"

"Yes, ages ago. But he can't stand being jilted by a girl."

"It's time he learned," Gus said.

Miranda's hands fidgeted. "I never told Piet that I was going out with you because I didn't want him to be jealous and do anything daft. Now his dad will tell him."

Gus bit his lower lip. "You can't keep these sorts of things private. It was always going to be a matter of time before he found out about us. And in my opinion, the sooner, the better."

Miranda gave a sickly smile. "I hope you're right."

Gus changed the subject. "By the way, what is a *soutpiel*?"

Miranda blushed. "*Sout* means salt, and *piel* means penis. It's an insulting word given to people who are not committed to staying in Africa for their whole lives. If a man stands with one foot in Africa and has his other foot in an overseas country, then it is said his penis hangs in the sea. Therefore his progeny has no roots and are mere drifters."

"Oh," Gus said. "Thank you for enlightenment. Tell me, how do you feel about going out with a *soutpiel*?"

She smiled. "Happy."

<u>CHAPTER TWENTY-TWO</u>

Missing

That night, Gus lay in bed procrastinating whether he should file a police report against Bruno van der Skiet for threatening behaviour. As a foreigner, he didn't want to cause a stink against his own name. The complications of a lawsuit had the potential to gobble up money faster than a Christmas turkey might be eaten. Money was better saved. There was also a chance that Miranda might endure negative consequences if he pressurised van der Skiet. Odds were that Bruno and his wife wouldn't return. His son, Piet, was yet an unknown entity, who made Gus feel uneasy. It was no use worrying about possibilities because things might blow over.

***

The next day unfolded with business as usual. Later that evening Miranda phoned.

"Gus, please help!" she cried. "Bruno van der Skiet told my father we were having an affair, and now I'm no longer fit for his son, Piet."

"But I thought you guys broke up?"

"Yes, I broke up with Piet, but he thinks I still belong to him." Miranda stifled a sob. "My father's furious with me for upsetting the van der Skiets. He says I've ruined my chances of a prosperous marriage and now he wants me out of his house."

Gus's head reeled. "He's your father! Why would he evict you?"

"He's very strict and doesn't believe in sex before marriage. Now I've brought shame on him by our affair. He says, seeing I won't carry out his wishes; it's time for me to get out and lead the life I've carved."

Gus screwed up his eyes. His dalliance with Miranda had turned serious, but he didn't feel ready for a long-term commitment--she was too young. "Where will you go?" Gus asked.

"I was hoping to move in with you."

"Mmm. I'm not sure that's a good idea. You're too young and I don't feel ready...."

"Fine!" she yelled. "I've just trashed my life for you--but you think I'm too young because you can't commit!" She sobbed and sniffed. "Excuses, excuses. Screw you, Gus. You're no better than Piet. You're nothing but a loose ball!"

"Wait," Gus said.

CLICK.

Too late, Miranda hung up.

"Darn," he moaned and punched his pillow. He had to admit she was sexy, fun, gutsy and smart. Her simple loyalty and devotion appealed, but now he had broken her heart. Finding a girl that devoted and willing to please sure took him by surprise. He had let her down because of misgivings about age. An insidious guilty feeling trickled into his heart. He knew he loved her, but his commitment was hindered because at some time he must return to Australia. The South African law prohibited him from marrying unless he applied for immigration, and that was out of the question; Australia was his home.

***

The following morning Gus phoned Miranda's house and her father, Karl Kaalvoet Mostert, answered.

"No, she's not here," Karl replied. "She's gone to live with her aunt."

"Please, may I have a contact number?" Gus asked.

"If she wanted you to have it she would have given it to you. Goodbye."

After that, Gus phoned the Tzaneen Hospital where she worked and asked to speak to her. Instead, Matron came on the line. "I must inform you Nurse Miranda Mostert resigned, so please don't phone again."

"Thank you." Gus sighed and hung up.

The joy had gone from his life. A day of 250 cattle pregnancy tests loomed ahead. It would be a long, shitty day, only made tougher by the weight inside his heart.

"What's wrong?" Gretchen asked, watching him chuck stuff on the table as he gathered supplies.

"Nothing."

She frowned. "How's Miranda?"

"I have no idea."

Understanding dawned. "Try to have a nice day."

"Thanks. You too." He marched out the door.

***

Three weeks later, Gus's mood still hadn't improved. He went about his work like a robot. His thoughts frequently turned to Miranda. He wished to see her again and talk, but she had vanished into thin air. He felt empty inside. Maybe it was time to return to Australia.

The phone rang, and Gretchen answered it. After she had hung up, she said, "That was Mrs Batty at Howl at The Moon farm."

Gus looked up with weary eyes. His haunted soul felt darker than the inside of a cow. "Oh, no. That's the old woman with the fancy teacup I broke. What does she want?"

"She wants you to make a house call as soon as possible. When will you see her?"

"Never--I wish."

Gretchen laughed. "I have to phone her back with an appointment."

"What does she want me to see?"

Gretchen giggled. "You know that old woman is mad as a hatter. She kept saying she has a sick pussy."

"Crikey," Gus said. "Last time her cat attacked me. Now she expects me to treat it at her home?"

"What Mrs Batty wants, Mrs Batty gets. When?"

"Tell her; I'll be there 10:30 am tomorrow."

"Thanks. I'll call her back."

CHAPTER TWENTY-THREE

Solutions

A sinking feeling settled in the pit of Gus's stomach as his VW trundled up Mrs Batty's driveway. Armed with his medical bag, he climbed out and headed towards her front door, watching as he walked along the garden path, hoping to spot the killer-cat, Bouncer, first. The feral feline was nowhere to be seen; maybe he was today's patient.

A servant came to the door and showed Gus into the hallway. Soon after that, Mrs Batty appeared.

"Good day, Dr Gus."

Gus smiled politely. "Good morning, Mrs Batty. How are you keeping?"

"Bah!" she said. "Enough of your crap. Go and sit over there." She pointed to a low pouffe stool.

He obeyed while the awful feeling inside his stomach tightened.

She sat opposite him in an elegantly wing-backed Parker chair with mahogany ball and claw feet. Seated higher than he, she knew how to make a man feel small as her stern countenance bore down.

Gus opened his mouth to speak, but she raised her hand indicating a halt.

"Stop right there," she said. "I have a bone or two to pick with you."

He knew what was coming. *Curse her old teacup!*

"The last time you came here..."

He nodded.

"I believe you broke my teacup."

He stopped nodding.

"You can't deny it," she said. "My gardener saw you climb out the window to retrieve it."

Gus felt the blood drain from his face.

"What have you to say for yourself?"

He looked up, observing her tight lips and beady eyes. There were hateful aspects of his work, for veterinary wasn't all about working with animals, it also concerned working with difficult people.

"Mrs Batty, I deeply regret breaking your cup...."

"I bet you do! Did you not have the balls to own up?"

Gus swallowed. He wasn't sure what alarmed him more-- her confrontation or her language. Was she about to lose it? He raised his hand to his chin, half covering his mouth. "It was an accident..."

"Yes, a most regrettable one indeed. Not everything that is broken can be mended."

"True. But I hope your cup can be fixed. Would you like me to glue it together?"

"Somebody already has--but the scar will always be there."

Gus checked his watch. "Mrs Batty, I believe you have a sick cat."

Her eyes narrowed. "Would you care to treat it?"

"Naturally. That is my job."

She leant closer. "See that you do it well."

Gus cleared his throat. "Where?"

"Follow me." She rose to lead the way further along the passage, around a corner and then turned right. "In there."

"After you," Gus said.

"No. You're on your own. I'm not getting involved." She held the door open as he entered and then closed it behind him.

His eyes turned to an unmade king-size bed, topped with sumptuous pillows with Bouncer perched at the end. As he moved closer, Bouncer's ears flattened, his eyes narrowed, and he emitted a deep-throated growl. Gus hesitated, watching his swishing tail. Bouncer yowled and lunged forward with claws spread-out, landing squarely on his thigh. A lump in the bed moved. The bedcovers jerked back and Miranda, dressed in cat pyjamas, sprang out and prised Bouncer's claws off his body, one by one. Then she hopped back into bed, placing Bouncer under the sheets.

Gus reeled with pain and surprise as he rubbed his thigh. "What are you doing here?"

She scowled. "I'm the one who should be asking! So, what are *you* doing here?"

"Mrs Batty said she had a sick..."

"What?"

"Pussy."

Miranda laughed. "My aunt, said *that*?" She appeared incredulous.

Gus shrugged. "Yeah. I presumed Bouncer was sick."

"Sick of you," Miranda supplied.

"Is he ill?" Gus asked.

"No, of course not."

Relieved, Gus said, "I didn't know you were related."

Miranda shrugged. "It's a small community. Most families are related in one way or another. Mrs Batty is my great aunt. If you care to work it out, she's my grandmother's sister."

"Okay." Gus shook his head slowly. "Look, I'm sorry. I really didn't mean to turn you away. It's just that I'll be returning to Australia soon."

The excitement faded from her eyes. "But, why?"

"Because that's my home; it's where I belong."

She picked at the bedcover. "Can't you apply to live here?"

He sighed. "I suppose I could, but I don't want to."

"Why not?"

He shook his head. "When I look at the turbulent history of Africa, sporadic violence appears to be ongoing. I love Australia--it's my home. I only came for a break and to get life experience."

Miranda sat up in bed and crossed her arms. "Are you telling me that I was just part of your fun experience?"

"No, that's not what I meant. I came here for a break--I didn't expect to fall in love."

Her interest perked. "Have you fallen in love?"

"Yes." He hung his head. "Truth is, I've been sick as a dog ever since you disappeared."

"Where do we go from here?" she asked.

"I don't know. The last thing I wish to do is to take you away from your family and everything that is precious to you."

"My mother is dead, and my father wants me to marry Pieter van der Skiet. Do you honestly think I would mind leaving them behind?"

Gus looked up. "I'm not sure. Only you can make that decision. Are you old enough?"

"Of course, I'm old enough to know what I want. I don't want to marry Piet! He's a hunter--he loves killing animals. That's why I went nursing--it's a three-year course, and it gave me time to delay that marriage."

"Why did you resign?"

Miranda sighed. "In our culture, a woman is not supposed to have a career. Her mission in life is to create a comfortable home and to raise children. Career-orientated women are deemed sinful--that's why my father wouldn't pay for my tertiary education. The state trains nurses for free in return for a small wage. Naturally, I grabbed the opportunity to delay marriage to Piet."

"Mmm, I see," Gus said. "But why did you resign?"

"I don't enjoy nursing--it gets depressing. And, I can assure you, I've seen enough car accident victims in this small town to know it's just not my thing. The worst was when I saw a child that...."

"Okay," Gus soothed. "You don't have to talk about it."

"Are you starting to understand?" she asked. "I've always wanted to work with animals, and when I met you--I liked you. Straight away, I envisioned our life together."

"Whoa! That was quick."

"Quick thinkers know what they want--and I want you-- even if it means moving to Australia. I love you because you're an honest sort. You're also kind and clever. Both those qualities are admirable in a man. Trust me; it's a hard combination to find."

Gus tilted his head. "Thank you. Now it's my turn. I admire you because you know what you want. You don't let others push you around. The thing I like best is that you have a genuine interest and respect for my work which is rare." He grinned. "The bonus is that you are sexy."

She smiled. "Do you think we'll make a great team?"

"Yes, I do." He hugged her. "Now tell me, what happens when your father ages, and you live in Australia?"

She shrugged. "Hopefully, there'll be enough money to visit him; but he'll be okay. I'll keep in touch and send him birthday and Christmas cards. Might even phone him now and then. But to be honest, he's proved he doesn't care for me by almost forcing me to marry Piet. There are enough extended family members to look after him, should he need it."

Gus smiled. "Well, Miranda, you thought things through better than me. You know your mind." He knelt next to her bed and took her hand. "Will you, Miranda, move in with me?"

She threw her arms around his neck. "Of course, I will! When?"

"Today."

"Right-o. Let me pack my bags."

Mrs Batty knocked on the door. "Are you two lovebirds ready for tea?"

"Yes, thanks!" Miranda yelled. "Hang on! I'll pour it."

Gus rolled back on the bed, clutching his stomach with silent laughter, then he turned to her and whispered. "You'd better go quick before that dratted flyswatter comes out!"

CHAPTER TWENTY-FOUR

Emergency!

Miranda and Gus moved in together and got along well. She enjoyed accompanying him on veterinary trips and made herself useful whenever possible by carrying equipment and passing instruments needed for surgery. Every morning, Gus enjoyed benefitting from her cooked breakfasts. Her companionship was great in bed, and out of it too, especially when undertaking long road trips.

One morning Gretchen poked her head into Gus's consulting room. "That was Mr Steenkamp on the phone. He thinks his dog was bitten by a snake."

"What kind of snake?"

"A black mamba."

Gus groaned. "Poor thing. If his dog's not dead on arrival, then I reckon we'll have a busy day."

Minutes later, Mr Steenkamp's car pulled up. He dashed straight through to Gus's consulting table with his little black and white patched fox terrier tucked under his arm.

"Twiggy's her name," he said with a concerned look while his hand stroked her back.

Twiggy appeared well; she wagged her tail as she licked Gus's hand. Gus listened to her respiration and heart. All her vital signs appeared normal and well--nothing unusual. Gus folded his arms across his chest and frowned as he considered options.

"Mr Steenkamp, are you sure the dog was bitten?"

He shook his head. "I can't be absolutely certain because things happened so fast. I saw the snake strike towards Twiggy just before she killed it."

Gus pursed his lips. "Did you bring the snake's body along, so I can identify it?"

"Yes. It's in a box in the car. I'll fetch it." Mr Steenkamp disappeared briefly and returned with a smallish, slender grey snake with a pale underbelly and coffin-shaped head.

Gus consulted his snake book, checking the pattern of scales on the top of the snake's head. "Yes, it is a black mamba--the deadliest and most feared African snake."

Keeping a safe distance, Miranda peered into the box, and she too, confirmed it was a black mamba.

Gus listened to Twiggy's chest again but picked up no sign of abnormality. He stepped back from the table and said, "I shouldn't give Twiggy antivenom if she wasn't bitten and she looks okay because there is a chance of a severe allergic reaction; also, the antivenom is expensive. Most dogs that are bitten need several bottles to have a chance of survival. It's possible that the snake bite did not release venom, and without symptoms, it's hard to tell."

Twiggy sat quietly, bright-eyed, listening to their conversation.

Gus frowned. "A black mamba's venom is extremely fast-acting. I'm certain that if Twiggy was bitten, she would be showing symptoms by now. The best thing is to take her home and if there is any change bring her back and we'll go from there."

"Okay, thank you. I'll do that." Mr Steenkamp lifted Twiggy off the table and carried her back to his car and drove home.

"I'll make us all a cup of tea," Miranda suggested after Mr Steenkamp left.

"Good idea, thank you," Gretchen said.

Fifteen minutes later, just as Miranda gathered the teacups to put in the sink, the phone rang. Gretchen answered and spoke. Afterwards, she turned to Gus. "That was Mr Steenkamp."

"Yes?" Gus looked up sharply.

"Twiggy died."

Miranda gasped. Her eyes clouded over.

"*What*?" Round eyed, Gus's face epitomised shock.

Gretchen said, "He put her in the back seat, but when he got home to let her out, Twiggy didn't respond--she was dead."

Gus slumped back into his chair where he sat clutching his head. "If only I had kept Twiggy here for observation--this wouldn't have happened."

Tears filled Miranda's eyes. Words failed her. The thought of poor little dead Twiggy and of her beloved Gus taking the rap was almost more than she could bear. She sat rubbing Gus's back. His eyes stayed shut as his jaw muscles tensed. "You mustn't blame yourself," she crooned. "You can't save everything all the time."

"I should have observed her for longer." He rose and went outside by himself, taking a little walk down the drive and out of sight.

Miranda wanted to follow, but Gretchen held her arm. "Just let him go. I think he needs time to himself. He'll return when he feels ready."

"Okay."

***

That night together was the first they never made love. Miranda felt sorry for him; she understood he always tried his best and hated failure. Over the next few days, Gus began to recover, and Miranda was wise enough not to raise the matter again. There were some nights when he struggled to fall asleep, and all she could do was be loving and supportive.

He nuzzled her neck. "I'm lucky to have you," he whispered hoarsely.

"And I'm even luckier to have you, my darling," she murmured, snuggling closer. She knew they had more hard times ahead to get through--his profession would always have wonderful highs and terrible lows.

CHAPTER TWENTY-FIVE

Cobra Bite

The following morning was quiet. Miranda spied Gus poring over a book at his desk and asked, "What are you reading?"

His knitted brows indicated concentration. "How to treat snakebites."

"Interesting. Have you learned anything new?"

"It says Black Mambas get their name from the black colour inside their mouths that is seen just before the snake strikes. They are the fastest moving snakes in the world, and the second longest venomous snake, only beaten by the Asian King Cobra."

"And?"

"When venom is released, Black Mamba bites have a virtual 100% mortality rate if not treated. It's known as *The Kiss of Death*. It can kill an adult within 20 to 60 minutes."

Miranda shivered. "So, what's the treatment?"

"Antivenom--the same type we keep in the fridge--it covers adder, Black Mamba and cobra. The amount given depends on the amount of venom injected into the victim."

"So, the bigger the snake, the more anti-venom required."

"Yes."

Deep in thought, Miranda pursed her lips. "Is there any snakebite *not* covered by our antivenom?"

"Boomslang. That antivenom would be a specific and exceptionally expensive order."

"Do you think we should get some?"

"No, it's too costly, and if not used, expires fairly fast. Let's face it--Boomslang tend to stay in trees so they shouldn't bite dogs."

"Can you explain how a Black Mamba's venom works?"

Gus consulted his book. "Death results in paralysis of the lungs followed by sudden cardiac arrest."

"But," Miranda said, "are there any warning symptoms first?"

"Humans say they feel dizzy. Sometimes they experience coughing and might have an erratic heartbeat--but that would be just before their heart stops."

"Ah, well, a dog can't tell you that," Miranda said. "So, I suppose they remain symptomless to the viewer--unless they have an increased heartbeat--which Twiggy didn't. It's impossible to see needle-sharp fang marks in dog hair if the venom does not produce swelling."

"I still feel bad about losing Twiggy--I missed the opportunity to try."

Miranda sighed. "Stop blaming yourself. No one else does."

"That's not true."

She looked up quickly. "What do you mean?"

"Mrs Steenkamp phoned and tore strips off me for letting the dog die."

A cold feeling trickled down Miranda's spine.

"I told her I was sorry for their loss--and do you know what she said?"

Dumbstruck, Miranda shook her head.

"She said, *I bet you're not as sorry as we are.*"

Miranda's gaze connected with his and witnessed his pain. Immediately, she sprung to his defence. "I'm pleased she never told *me* that. I might have torn strips off her."

"You can't do that to clients; it's best to let them vent."

She sighed. "I suppose you're right, but hers was an ungracious comment. What does she expect? You to commit suicide because of a mistake? Chances are Twiggy might not have survived anyway. I know from human nursing, not all snakebite patients make it."

Gus arose with a heavy sigh and placed his hands in his pockets as he faced gathering storm clouds through the window. "It's no wonder so many vets commit suicide."

Her pulse quickened. "Please, explain yourself."

He shrugged. "It's a well-known fact. Vets see euthanasia as a way of relieving suffering; sometimes they are tempted to extrapolate it to themselves too. It's hard when you try to do good but fail. People are unforgiving; they always want somebody to be accountable and pay for their loss even if it is impossible to salvage anything."

Miranda's fingers fidgeted with the ends of her hair. His words aroused discomfort. "Gus, please don't talk that way."

"It's true. They commit suicide because of human resentment. They start out in the profession because of a passion for animals; instead, they end up dealing with bitter people. In comparison to other professionals, they earn less and yet have huge study loans to repay. At times, it all gets too depressing."

"I love you," Miranda murmured. "I know you're a good person with a kind heart." She held Wingnut up to his face. The little dog wiggled and licked the tip of his nose. "See--even Wingnut adores you."

He smiled. "You are worth living for. You make me want to win."

"You will." She touched his hand. "Come on; I'll make tea and biscuits. That'll help cheer you up. Don't let people get you down. We have a bright future together. Things will improve--you'll see." She stood on tippy toes to kiss him.

***

The following week as Gus bade the last customer of the day farewell, a truck pulled up in a cloud of orange dust. The noisy Marlow family trooped in.

The eldest son carried a crossbred bull terrier, placing it on the table. "Doctor," he said, sounding breathless. "Dodger was bitten by a massive cobra!"

Gus's pulse quickened. This was his chance to redeem himself. "Are you sure it was a cobra?"

"Yes, sir. Look inside the box my Dad's got. See for yourself."

Miranda and Gus peered into the box; bloodied snake coils filled it to overflowing, its half-severed head visible.

"That Snouted Cobra's huge!" Miranda cried.

"Two and a half metres long," Mr Marlow exclaimed. "Dodger saved my youngest boy's life by killing it first. We saw it happen, but the cobra struck Dodger twice. He went mad, shook it by the neck and snapped its head off."

The dog was already showing signs of distress with an elevated heart beat and copious salivation.

Gus spoke fast. "Mr Marlow. I hate to talk business now--but snakebite costs a fortune to treat. A snake that size could take up to seven ampoules of antivenom to counter, maybe more. Do you wish me to put Dodger down now and put him out of his misery? Or do you wish to pay for a very expensive treatment where I cannot guarantee any success."

Mr Marlow looked appalled. "Doctor, this dog saved my son's life! I don't care how much it costs--save his life too! Dodger deserves it--he's part of our family. Do whatever you must--spare no expense." His voice broke, and he turned away, mopping his eyes with a soiled hankie.

"Miranda, fetch me one bottle of anti-venom," Gus said. Anticipating Dodger going into shock, Gus was already in the throes of setting up an intravenous infusion before the dog's veins could collapse.

She returned with the glass vial.

"Open it and draw it up," Gus commanded.

Her hands shook as she tried to cut the glass with the small metal file provided.

Dodger began to shake and retch. Vomit spilt over the edge of the table. The youngest child squealed and moved away, clinging to his father's leg.

"Hurry!" Gus said.

Miranda couldn't open the vial with the rasp; it was only halfway through, so she snapped the glass top off with her fingers, cutting her finger in the process. She managed to draw up the antivenom and hand it over.

Gus began infusing it into the porthole in the intravenous line.

Dodger flopped on to his side, retching. Muscle spasms convulsed his body as his bowels and bladder emptied involuntarily.

"Fetch me another ampule of antivenom," Gus commanded.

Miranda did his bidding. This time she managed to open and draw it up faster. Her finger still bled; there was no time to find a plaster.

Gus administered the anti-venom, but the dog's condition continued to deteriorate.

The Marlow children began to snivel and cry.

Gretchen entered and drew the family outside. "Mr Marlow, why don't you take your children home. Gus will phone you when he's finished. By the looks of things, Dodger is too sick to go anywhere tonight--I just hope he makes it."

Mr Marlow thanked Gretchen, turned and left.

By now, the dog had received the third bottle of antivenom with little sign of improvement. Its eyes began to glaze over, and its breathing became erratic.

"Oh, Christ," Gus prayed. "Please don't let Dodger die. Miranda, put some eye gel into his eyes to stop them drying."

Miranda did as she was asked. She stood in silence biting her lip while waiting for Gus's next instruction. She watched him put the stethoscope to his ears and then dash them aside.

"God, he's stopped breathing! I'll intubate him while you fetch the Ambu Bag."

Miranda returned armed with the Ambu Bag. Gus connected it and began rhythmic air compressions, desperately trying to oxygenate Dodger's lungs with fresh air.

Gretchen poked her head into the doorway. "Do you need help?"

"No, thanks. We'll be a long time yet," Gus answered.

"Seeing there's nothing I can do; do you mind if I go home?"

"Sure. See you tomorrow."

"Thanks. I left Mr Marlow's telephone number in my diary."

"Okay. Cheers." Then Gus turned to Miranda. "Fetch more antivenom."

Two hours later, Dodger remained motionless. Visible muscle spasms had ceased, no more bowel action and no vomiting. Only a continual, dribbling urine leakage as the intravenous fluid was processed by Dodger's kidneys.

Gus and Miranda took half-hour turns to compress the Ambu Bag manually. For Dodger, every breath was vital. Five hours and seven ampoules of anti-venom later, Dodger remained unbreathing and unresponsive.

"Oh," Miranda moaned. "My back aches. I wish we had a ventilator. This manual Ambu Bagging is killing me. I don't know if I can last much longer."

Gus looked wrecked. "If we stop now--we'll lose Dodger and leave the Marlows with a hefty bill to pay with nothing to show for. If only the dog would live, we'd all feel so much better. I could live with myself, and they'd be happy to pay. But if Dodger dies, we'll all feel terrible, and no matter how sorry I feel for them, I simply can't afford to foot their bill."

"Nobody expects you to."

"Yes, but people feel angry when they spend big money, and their animal dies."

"You're doing your best," Miranda encouraged.

He snorted. "Sometimes, that isn't enough. I need this dog to live."

She shook her head. "I hope you get your wish. God decides."

At twenty minutes past midnight, Gus raised weary, bloodshot eyes to Miranda's. "I hate to admit it--but we've lost him. We can't go on forever."

She sighed. "Honestly, we did our best. My hands are cramping up. We've been Ambu-bagging for seven hours without food or drink. I'm exhausted. And you have a big day tomorrow."

Gus stopped Ambu-bagging and listened to Dodger's chest. No heartbeat, no breathing. He pushed his hand back through his dishevelled hair and pronounced him dead.

"Are you sure?" Miranda asked.

He swallowed and nodded.

She took the stethoscope and listened. She too confirmed, not a breath, not a beat. Her eyes met his. "I'm sorry. Let's bathe and get some sleep--forget food."

Gus lifted Dodger's body off the table and carried it outside to the shed for tomorrow's collection or burial. He staggered inside and opened Gretchen's diary and read her note under Marlow's number:

> *Mr Marlow wishes you to phone him, no matter how late you finish, to inform him whether Dodger makes it or not.*

These were the sort of calls Gus loathed. He dialled the number. An expectant Mr Marlow answered.

"Good evening, Mr Marlow. Gus speaking."

"Yes?"

"I am afraid it's bad news. Dodger didn't make it."

"Oh," Marlow's voice cracked. "Thank you for calling. My kids will be very sad."

After Gus had hung up, he bathed and went to bed. A long, restless night ensued as his tortured mind became plagued by troubled dreams.

<u>CHAPTER TWENTY-SIX</u>

Retraction

Gus arose first, bringing a cup of tea to Miranda in bed. "Thanks." She sat up, taking the steaming cup. "How was your sleep?"

"Not good. Today, I'm tired before I start."

"What's booked?" she asked.

"Four hundred cattle tuberculosis tests."

She groaned. "I suppose we should leave soon."

"I'd prefer to wait for Mr Marlow to collect Dodger's body before we go. I hope he doesn't arrive too late."

"Can't Gretchen show him where it is?"

"She could, but I would prefer to carry it to his car--it's the least I can do."

They dressed for the day, Miranda began cooking breakfast while Gus went outside to put Dodger's body into a thick plastic bag. Moments later Gus stuck his head in through the kitchen window and said, "I can't find Dodger's body. Something must have taken it during the night."

"Oh, no, that's all we need," Miranda muttered. "I just wish things would go well for a change."

"I can't imagine explaining to a client their beloved pet's body was dragged off into the bush and eaten by bush pigs."

"Well, next time, you must lock the cadavers up somewhere. Perhaps it's time to get a deep freeze."

Gus froze and stared off into the distance.

"What's wrong?" Miranda asked.

He rubbed his eyes. "Come out here. I think I'm hallucinating."

"What are you talking about?" She threw her kitchen towel down, turned off the stove and marched outside.

Gus stood eyes agog, as he pointed underneath a large tree in their driveway.

Her eyes followed his gaze. "Whose dog is that?"

He grinned. "It's Dodger!"

"What?" she peered closer. "Wow! It is. He's alive! How the hell did that happen?"

Gus sprinted over to the tree, picked Dodger up, and returned placing him on his consultation table. "It's Dodger all right--he's alive and looking jolly well."

Miranda clutched her face, beaming from ear to ear. "How on earth will you explain to Mr Marlow?"

Gus grinned. "With difficulty, but I'll be happy to try. First, l will give him a thorough examination because he doesn't totally look right."

After a while, Gus put his stethoscope aside and said, "He's weak and smelly--needs a bath later. I don't want to stress him out now. There's only one thing wrong...."

"What's that?"

"Dodger's blind."

"Oh, what a pity. Why?"

"Unfortunately, when we left him for dead, we stopped caring for his eyes, and they must have dried out while he was still paralysed before he could blink."

"Do you think his sight will ever recover?"

Gus pursed his lips. "Probably not."

"That's a pity. I wonder what Mr Marlow will have to say about all of this."

"We'll soon find out. I'll phone him now and try to explain this inexplicable resurrection."

Miranda giggled. "Rather you than me. Good luck!"

After Gus had phoned and hung up, Miranda said, "What did he say?"

Gus grinned. "His happiness was infectious. He told the kids while on the phone, and all I heard were whoops of joy!"

"Does he know Dodger's blind?"

"Yes. He says it makes no difference--they love the dog and they're coming right away to collect him."

When the Marlow's arrived, although still shaky, Dodger stood to greet them. His tail wagged frantically as soon as he recognised their voices and smell. The kids rushed to pet him, and he rolled over on his back begging for his tummy to be tickled. Mr Marlow picked him up and put him on the floor in the front of his car. With tears in his eyes, he turned to shake Gus's hand. "Dr, thank you so much. You'll never know what this means to my family--we love this dog so much. He saved my son's life."

Miranda sidled up to Gus, entwining her arm around his waist as they waved goodbye to the happy family. After they had left, she turned and kissed him. "You see, miracles do happen. That dog wasn't named Dodger for nothing."

CHAPTER TWENTY-SEVEN

Lightning

Fierce storm clouds drifted and gathered low across the darkening sky. Thunder rumbled. A cool wind gust swirled fallen leaves high into the air causing tree tops to sway.

"Yikes," Gus said. "It looks like we're in for a massive thunderstorm. Gretchen, go home now. Once the deluge starts, you won't be able to see where you're driving. I don't want your car getting stuck in the mud."

She peered out the window anxiously. "Thanks, I will." She gathered her car keys, bag and canary cage and rushed out the door saying a hurried farewell.

Moments later, lightning flashed, followed by an ear-splitting thunder crack. Gus moved the curtain back and stared down the driveway. "Oh, bother!"

Miranda looked up from painting her toenails. "What's wrong?"

"I left my car parked under that big syringa tree. I'm worried it might fall."

"The wind is fierce," she agreed. "I'll fetch a jersey."

CRACK!

A shriek escaped Miranda's lips. "Lord, that was close!" She reeled as a blue lightning ball darted and flicked erratically inside the room before dispersing out through the open doorway.

"That was amazing," Gus said. "I've never seen one of those before."

Miranda put rubber slip-slops on her feet. "Close that door!"

"I'm going to move my car." About to head through the door, Gus picked up his car keys.

Miranda yanked him back. "Don't be a fool! Leave the wretched car alone. If the tree falls--so be it. Stay safe inside with me. It's too late now to do anything; just hope and pray."

"I'll be quick."

"No, you won't." She snatched the keys from him. "I'm confiscating them. You can't go--I won't let you."

A draft blew papers around inside their hut as she slammed the door shut.

Another almighty thunder crack split the air, jarring their nerves. Deep rumbling sounds followed. A power surge coursed through the electric lights, making them flicker and fade. Wind gusts rattled windows, shook trees and outdoor lines. They stared through the window in horror as they saw the heavy topped Syringa tree swaying precariously to and fro. It bowed for the last time, falling with a sighing crackle onto Gus's VW, squashing the roof.

Gus groaned. "I should have moved it."

"Too late now." Miranda clicked her tongue. "You would be dead if I hadn't stopped you. Look at that roof--it's crushed. There's no way you would have survived."

"Yeah, true. I hope insurance pays."

***

The following morning blossomed into a beautiful, sunny clear-sky day. Birds sang as they set about repairing their nests. Butterflies flitted along the pathway above Spy's head, taunting the cat by keeping just out of his lazy, sun-drugged reach.

Refreshed and dust-free, the earth smelled wet and clean. When Gretchen arrived, she gave Gus her car keys allowing him and Miranda to drive into town, so they could visit the bank and buy another car.

By ten o'clock, Gus returned driving Gretchen's car with Miranda close behind driving his new second-hand Suzuki 4 x 4 van.

Gretchen smiled. "It looks like you got yourself a good deal there. It's a much more practical car too."

"I hope so," Gus replied.

"While you were out, Sarel Botha phoned to say his horse died. He wants you to do a post mortem to see what killed it."

"Okay. Phone him and let him know we're on our way."

***

Gus stared at the dead horse on the steep, exposed grassy slope.

"Do you think it died from colic or a snakebite?" Sarel asked.

Gus shook his head. "Looking around here," Gus pointed to some burnt grass near a large tree where the fallen horse lay. "I reckon there's a good chance it died from a lightning strike."

"Are you sure?"

"Yes, but I'll do a post-mortem."

Gus set about his grisly task as flies honed in. After a while, he stood up and said, "Yes, definitely a lightning strike." He showed Sarel the burn pathway under the horse's skin.

"Well, I never would have guessed," Sarel said. "I'm busy building a stable for my other horse, but in the meanwhile, they have had to sleep outdoors. Bad luck to lose this mare. I'll have to buy another one." He shuffled his feet. "Horses are expensive, but you know the old saying; lightning doesn't strike twice."

Gus packed his bags and then walked back to the house where he washed underneath Sarel's garden tap. A big black horse with a wavy mane and tail sauntered by.

"That's my favourite horse," Sarel said with pride.

"He's a beaut," Gus said. "What's his name?"

"Satan."

Miranda scowled, her expression indicating she didn't approve of his name choice.

Gus replied diplomatically, "He's a fine-looking animal. I'm sure you're proud of him."

"I am. He's a stallion, so I plan to breed from him."

***

On the way home Miranda said, "There's a three-phase horse trial coming up in Johannesburg next month that I want to attend with my horse. Will you drive us there? It's about a 500 km trip."

"Is it over a weekend?"

"Yes."

"Sure. You haven't spoken to your father since moving in with me. Do you think he'll allow you to fetch your horse?"

She rolled her eyes. "I hope so."

On their return, Miranda told Gretchen she feared her father's reaction if she went home to collect her horse.

"Leave him to me," Gretchen said. "I'll speak to him. Hopefully, he'll come around. After all, you are his only child. He must love you."

***

The following week, Gretchen said, "Miranda, I visited your father and took him a cake. He agreed for you to collect your horse."

"Thank you, Gretchen! How did you persuade him?"

Gretchen smiled. "Now, that would be telling. I think it best you phone him and start the communication ball rolling again. He's longing to hear from you. I told him you were happy with Gus and that you two get along well--he has no need for concern. I begged him not to alienate his only child over her partner choice."

"Oh, thanks, Gretchen!" Miranda hugged her.

"And I reminded him of the van der Skiets' bad reputation. Surely, he doesn't want you married off to a wife-beater. He was surprised I thought Pieter would go that way. I reminded him children tend to follow their parent's examples. So, he's had a rethink. Parents can't live their aspirations through their children's lives."

Gus interrupted, "Miranda, you must arrange stabling in Johannesburg for next month, for your horse to stay overnight somewhere when we go."

"Okay, I will."

"And another thing," Gretchen said. "Mr Marlow came in and paid his account for that cobra bite in full. He's pleased with Dodger's recovery and says he's starting to get partial vision returning."

Gus grinned. "That success story keeps on improving every time I hear it."

Miranda closed the door against a sudden updraft. "Hey, it looks like we're in for another storm. Gus, get out there and move your Suzuki fast."

"Right-o. Hey, Gretchen, you'd better get home. Let's call it a day while we batten down the hatches."

Within an hour another angry storm pelted down. More thunder and lightning. Spy hid under the blankets while Wingnut shivered and nestled into the crook of Miranda's arm. The power surged, and the electricity went off again. They were safe inside their hut.

The following morning when Gretchen arrived in the office the phone rang. After hanging up, she turned to Gus and said, "That was Sarel Botha again."

"What's up this time?"

"He says to tell you, lightning strikes twice. His other horse, Satan, is dead. Same spot, same story."

Miranda shivered. "I think his horse was cursed."

<u>CHAPTER TWENTY-EIGHT</u>

Silent Visitor

As Gretchen continued working for Gus, she found it hard not to sigh with resigned envy whenever she saw Gus and Miranda together. There was no denying it-- they got along well. If only she too could find that kind of love again.

"Oh, no!" Miranda yelled.

"What's the matter?" Gus asked.

"Wingnut has pooped in the kitchen again! Honestly, I'm sick and tired of it. I'm at a loss to know how to stop her."

Gus said, "To make things easier, I'll cut a hole in the door, so Wingnut can go in and out whenever she wants. It's up to you, Miranda, to train her to use it."

"All right. I'll coax her with cold chicken."

True to his word, Gus created the doggy door by simply cutting a hole in the door that was six inches up from the base. Miranda soon had Wingnut jumping in and out with bouncing confidence during the day, but nights were different. Wingnut refused to go out at night.

Miranda sighed. "Gus, you seem to have wasted time making that doggy door. Wingnut refuses to use it at night."

"Mmm. I see so."

"I hope no snakes or unwanted creatures get in through there."

"I doubt it. Spy and Wingnut should keep them out."

A few weeks later, after dinner one evening, Miranda challenged Gus to a game of rummy. As they sat at the table, Gus's attention turned to his cat, Spy. The kitten had grown into a sleek-haired teenage feline. Despite having only one eye--it was sharp as radar.

"Go on," Miranda said, marvelling at how easily Gus appeared to get distracted. "Stop staring at your dumb cat--it's your turn."

Gus hesitated. "I wonder what Spy's staring at." He turned his head, following the cat's curious gaze until it came to rest on the curtain rail behind him. "Crikey!" Gus stiffened.

"What's up?"

"Spy's spotted a snake," Gus said pointing to a long, patterned thick body draped along the top of the curtain rod. Its lowered head, directed his way, with its flicking tongue was busily transmitting messages to its beady-eyed brain.

Miranda's eyes widened, on the verge of hysteria.

"Shush! Stay calm," Gus advised. "It's impossible to handle an angry snake safely. I'll get him."

"Are you insane?" Miranda hissed, shivering. "Will you kill him?"

"No," Gus said. "They're royal game, so I can't do that. Just look at him--he's beautiful! But we can't leave him here. He's not poisonous--he's only a rock python."

Her eyes bulged. "Yes, but a big one."

"Don't worry. I've handled pythons before. We get plenty of these fellows in Australia."

"I hope you realise their vicious bites tend to go septic."

He nodded as he rose, creeping towards the corner of the room to fetch his broom, returning armed. "Miranda, please fetch me a sack from outside to put him in."

"Sure." She went out, moments later returning with his request.

"Hold it open while I put him in." Gus moved cautiously, so as not to alarm the snake. With the broom handle, he lifted its middle. He lowered it off the curtain rod and onto the floor where it began to slither away. Miranda jumped up onto a chair. He used the broom handle to pin its head down to the ground before grabbing it by the back of its neck. Its coils tried to wind around his forearm, but he held it firmly in the middle with his other hand.

With pounding heart and shaking hands, Miranda got off the chair and opened the sack as he held the python with two hands, lowering it in. As he did so, he uncoiled the python's tail from his left forearm. It took a while to extricate himself and secure the top of the bag. "I reckon it's about three and a half metres long. Big enough to eat Spy for an hors d'oeuvre."

"Ugh! I'm glad it didn't get that far. Lucky, we saw it before we went to sleep."

Gus grinned. "Now what should we do with him?"

Miranda wagged her finger. "It's no use letting him go near our house--he'll come back and maybe eat Spy and Wingnut."

"Should I let it go down the road?"

"No, that's too near the neighbours--they keep chickens."

"What if I take him down to the T-junction?"

Miranda shook her head. "No good either. He'll get run over by traffic."

Gus rolled his eyes. "Where?"

"Ah! I know," Miranda said. "There's a small nature reserve down by the Tzaneen Dam. We can release him there."

"Good idea," Gus replied. "Let's go now before they lock the gates for the night."

Gus put the sack in the back of the car.

Miranda shuddered. "I hope you secured that knot tight."

"Yeah. You can check it if you want."

"No, thanks. I'll trust you."

By the time they reached the Tzaneen Dam Nature Reserve the boom across the road was locked down. Gus checked his watch. "Gosh, they close earlier than I thought."

Miranda craned her neck out the window. "Hey, look! There's a night watchman sitting in a chair inside the little gate house."

"Good, I'll go ask him if we can go through."

Miranda sat in the car while Gus went and spoke. Moments later, he returned. "It's no use. He won't open the gate. He says it's too late. I think he hinted for a bribe, but I have no cash."

"Huh! Well, I'm not going home with this snake in the car. He must open the gate--I'll make him."

"You can't make him do anything."

Miranda put her hands on her hips and turned towards him. "You want to bet? Watch *him* fly! I know these Sotho people--they're superstitious about snakes--because they fear and hate them."

She knocked on his glass door. "Please open. I want to speak with you."

"No. Go away," he said. "It's too late. Eight o'clock--gates closed."

She watched him reclining in his chair with his hands behind his head. His feet were parked up on the small desk in front of him. Such indifference made her anger rise. She wrapped again, more urgently. "We have a big python to release."

"Go away."

"We have a *nyoka*." This word he would understand.

His head turned towards her. "No."

"Yes! A big *nyoka*!"

His feet came off the desk as he stood to face her through the glass. "I don't believe you--go home."

Miranda smiled. "Okay. If you don't believe me--I'll show you. I'll let it go here next to your office--then you'll see it. You can sleep near each other. When you walk to the toilet--nyoka will see you."

He stood in silence behind his locked door. Now she had his attention.

Miranda yelled to Gus, "Bring out the snake. The watchman wants us to release big *nyoka* here next to his office."

The whites of the watchman's eyes glinted fearfully. He seemed to freeze, only his lips trembled.

Gus climbed out the car, laden with his heavy burden and placed it in front of the car's headlights so he could see where to untie the bag.

The nervous watchman sprang to attention. "*Stop!*" he shouted. "Wait--don't release *nyoka* here. You must drive through. I open gate."

Miranda smiled. "Thank you!"

The watchman unlocked his door, saluted and raised the boom as if he were a parading military man holding an erect rifle. He pointed towards the horizon. "Drive straight! Go twenty kilometres that way. Don't stop. Just keep moving."

"Thank you." Gus nodded as he and Miranda entered the reserve on their blessed special mission.

Miranda chuckled wickedly. "It helps to know how things work."

When they reached a remote bushy area near the water's edge, Gus climbed out with his heavy sack while Miranda, no better than the watchman, sat inside the safety of his car; protected by glass and steel. Gus placed the sack on the dirt track in front of the car's headlights while he untied the knot. Carefully, he gently tipped the bag as he stepped back out of the way.

They watched in breathless silence and awe as the long, elegant python's head rose half its length off the ground. It stood erect, tall and regal as its tongue flicked, sensing its new bushy surroundings, and then, ever so gracefully, it came down to ground level and slithered away into the night where it's rich dark markings blended into camouflaged obscurity within a twinkle of an eye.

Afterwards, Gus climbed slowly back into his car. "Isn't that one of the most beautiful moments ever witnessed?"

Miranda tilted her head. "Mmm. Impressive, but I've seen something better."

He was incredulous. "What was that?"

She smiled, moving her hand towards his crotch. "Your one-eyed snake can do some tricks...."

A slow grin crossed his face.

CHAPTER THIRTY

Rocky Road

Barefoot, as usual, Karl Kaalvoet stood at his doorway as he welcomed Gus and Miranda into his luxurious newly built home.

"Hello, Daddy!" Miranda hugged her father. The old man's face wrinkled with reserved pleasure.

Gus extended his hand. Karl shook it and said, "Please, take a seat."

Fat Chops, Miranda's large Boerboel dog came bounding towards her. Its giant body and stumpy tail wiggling madly, giving way to smelly flatulence. Everyone coughed, choked and laughed. Fat Chops woofed and howled, singing a special welcome for Miranda as she petted the dog's head but pushed her giant, slobbery face away from her clothing.

Gus and Miranda's footsteps clip-clopped over the beautifully laid Italian floor tiles as they walked to the sunken lounge with its sumptuous L-shaped leather settee and highly polished hardwood coffee table. The modern lounge expanse overlooked a crystal-clear blue swimming pool nestled in a semi-protected courtyard. Gus's eyes browsed the rich oil paintings of African wildlife that adorned the walls.

"It's good to see you two," Karl said. "So, tell me, Gus, what are your plans for my daughter's future?"

"Oh, Daddy, stop it!"

"Shush, please. I want to hear what he has to say."

Gus shifted uncomfortably. "It's not something we've discussed yet."

Karl leaned forward. "Why not? You are living together as man and wife. If you don't marry my daughter, her name will be dragged through the mud. This is not the way I raised her."

Miranda's face turned red.

Gus was uncertain if rage or humiliation was the cause; maybe a bit of both.

"Put it this way," Karl said. "Are you going back to Australia?"

"Yes. It's a wonderful place, and I'm thinking of moving to Queensland."

"And what will become of Miranda when you go?"

"She's welcome to travel with me."

Karl shook his head. "She's not an Australian citizen--they won't let her stay."

Gus smiled. "If we were to marry then that wouldn't be an issue."

"Have you proposed?"

"No, not yet."

"Why not?"

"I planned to propose next month on her birthday. But seeing you are putting pressure on now--let's resolve the issue." Gus turned to face Miranda, taking her hand in his. "Miranda, will you marry me?"

She sprang to her feet, glaring towards her father. "How dare you force Gus to do this? This isn't the way it should be. You're ruining everything!"

Gus reached up and gently pulled her back into his arms, holding her close as if he were trying to sooth a startled kitten. "Miranda, I'm not intimidated by your father, nor anyone else for that matter. This is between you and me. Will you marry me? I want your honest answer."

She pursed her lips hard, fighting to hide a spreading Cheshire Cat grin.

Sparkles in her eyes already showed the answer.

"Yes! I will." A squeal of excitement broke from her lips.

A proud moment was shared as the couple hugged, grinned and kissed.

Instantly, Karl's harsh demeanour changed. He shook Gus's hand. "Congratulations, son! Welcome to my family. I'm pleased you two chose to do the right thing." He fetched a bottle of champagne from his fridge. "Let's celebrate!"

After a few glasses of champagne, Karl said, "Miranda, I've worked hard to keep this farm going. I've given you horses and everything your heart desired. How can you turn your back on it all? I'm not angry with you; I'm just trying to understand."

"I'm not sure what the future holds for South African farmers," Miranda said. "If you look at the history of most countries up north like Kenya, Congo, Angola, Mozambique and Zimbabwe; realistically, I don't think there's a safe future. And, I'm doing no worse than our ancestors did almost three hundred years ago when they left Europe to settle in Africa."

"I disagree," her father replied. "South Africa will be different."

She smiled sadly. "Dad, I don't want to argue with you. You are entitled to believe whatever you wish, but I'd prefer to raise my children elsewhere."

Karl's eyes filled with tears. "You are my *only* child. I can't bear the thought of living without you."

"Maybe you could sell the farm and use the money to buy a place in Australia."

He shook his head. "This is my motherland. I'd struggle to leave it. All my friends are here."

"Just not your daughter--not for much longer," Miranda supplied.

"You've put me in a terrible situation."

"No, Dad. I haven't. Politics has. Take your time, and when you feel ready to move or to visit us, I'll make sure there's a room waiting for you."

"Thank you, Miranda. I will visit you there one day. Who knows what may happen? First, you two need time to settle."

Miranda smiled. "Thanks, Dad. I knew you'd come around." She kissed his cheek. "I'll always love you. You've been the best father--ever."

After lunch, Miranda and Gus stood to leave. Karl handed Gus the keys to his truck. "Use it to tow Miranda's horse box; it's a much safer vehicle than your little Suzuki."

"Thank you," Gus replied.

"And on your return, Miranda, I'd like you to take Fat Chops away. The dog misses you terribly."

She turned to Gus, "Is that okay?"

"Yeah, sure," he said with a sly wink. "She'll make a handy blood-donor."

<u>CHAPTER THIRTY-ONE</u>

Horse People

Early on the morning of Gus and Miranda's departure to the Johannesburg equestrian trials, Ruby strolled into his horse box as if he were entering a stable.

"What a beaut!" Gus said, patting Ruby's neck. "There's nothing better than an easy loader."

"Yes, he has the ideal temperament. He's fearless and fast under saddle and completely bombproof."

Ruby stood pulling greedy mouthfuls of high-quality Teff grass from his hay net. He turned his head with tufts sticking out from his lips and whinnied.

"He knows we're going somewhere exciting. Ruby enjoys outings."

"Right, let's get going." Gus reached for the truck keys and waved a cheerful goodbye to his future father-in-law.

"Good luck and go well!" Karl shouted from behind their departing vehicle.

Miranda turned to Gus. "Thanks for driving. A five-hour journey with a horse box in tow is too tiring for me--especially after competing. It's nice to have help."

"Thanks," Gus replied. "Did you confirm your booking for the stables Ruby is staying at tonight?"

She shrugged. "I made the booking three weeks ago. I've stabled with Smith's Riding School before. Don't worry; there'll be no issues."

"Good. Where do you want to go first? To the show or to the stables?"

She glanced at her watch. "Show first, please. I ride at approximately 2:00 pm."

"Okay."

Gus drove up Magoebaskloof Mountain Pass, then through the winding Haenertsburg area. After that, the road became straight as they headed towards Pietersburg and along the Highveld plateau.

"These are beautiful, wide roads. It makes for easy driving," Gus said.

Miranda chuckled. "Just wait till we reach Johannesburg! It's a maze of highways and bridges."

"I don't mind. I'm used to Sydney traffic. If you direct me well there'll be no problem. I'd hate to get lost."

"No chance of that. I know the area."

***

Gus pulled into the show grounds and reversed the horsebox up alongside rows of others.

"Hey, you know how to reverse a trailer!" Miranda exclaimed. "Not everyone can do that well."

He helped her back Ruby out of the box. Ruby snorted and whinnied to the other horses.

"I'll go and walk him around for a while," Miranda said. "I want him to stretch and relax before I saddle up."

"Good idea." Gus surveyed the busy showgrounds with its array of fine horseflesh and expensive vehicles. People walked to and fro, leading sweating horses under sweat rugs. Others were saddling up and trotting around in the warm-up arena. Overhead, the loudspeakers played pop music that was occasionally interrupted by announcements.

By 1:30 pm, Miranda was mounted on Ruby. Gus stepped back giving her the thumbs up. "Ride well--good luck. I'm rooting for you."

At 2:05 pm Ruby and Miranda's number was called. Gus felt a tremor of nervousness; he feared for Miranda because after the dressage test the jumps would be high.

Miranda passed the dressage test with an excellent score. An hour after that she participated in the show jumping circuit. Her results were spectacular, yielding her with a clear round and a fast time. Afterwards, she jumped off Ruby and patted his neck. His sides heaved as he wiped the foamy, white sweat from his neck onto her arm. She pushed him aside, leading him to a tap where she hosed him down and then put a sweat rug over him to prevent his muscles from chilling.

Gus looked up into the clear blue sky with sunglasses. "It's a lovely, hot day. You couldn't have wished for better weather."

An hour later, the show jumping results were announced. They waited with bated breath as they heard the third-place winner and then the second-place winner.

The loudspeaker blared out, "First Place goes to Miranda Mostert on Ruby!"

A round of applause went up as Miranda jogged to the podium and collected her silver trophy and certificate. It was a proud moment for her and Gus. Victory and joy shone from her pretty face.

"Congratulations!" Gus hugged her. "That was an amazing round."

"Thanks, but tomorrow's our biggest challenge," she said. "When we jump fixed jumps across the countryside."

"Yeah, I saw some of them. Are you sure you're up to it? I think you're crazy."

"To be honest, I'm feeling a bit nervous."

"Oh, well, I reckon we should be heading over to that riding school where Ruby's booked in to stay the night."

"Okay, let's go before it gets dark."

Miranda directed Gus to the stables she booked at. On arrival, the gates were locked.

She frowned. "That's odd. They never lock their gates." She climbed out the car and pushed the gates, but they were chained closed and secured with a heavy-duty padlock.

"I don't know what to do," she said. "This is weird. We need to phone them. I saw a phone booth back that way."

Gus manoeuvred the horse box with difficulty back out the driveway and onto the road. He drove to the phone booth and parked at the side of the road. Miranda rummaged in her handbag looking for the number. An exclamation of relief escaped her lips when she retrieved the telephone number written on paper. She went into the booth and made her call.

Moments later she jumped into the truck and slammed the door with an anxious look. "You won't believe this."

"What?" Gus asked.

"They've put an answering machine on for callers and can't be contacted."

"What does it say?"

She rolled her eyes. "This is a recorded message. Please note our stables are closed due to the recent viral outbreak of Horse Flu. The stables are under quarantine until further notice."

Gus slumped his forehead onto the steering wheel. "That's not good. Now what?"

"I don't know!" Miranda began to cry. "It's too late to drive home now--and the horse is tired. I don't think it would be wise. He needs to lie down and rest somewhere."

"Can you try phoning some other stables?"

She sniffed and wiped her eyes. "Okay, I'll try. But it's getting dark now and I don't think anyone else will take us in."

She went back to the phone booth and pored through the yellow pages making calls. After twenty minutes, she climbed back into the truck and flopped into the seat looking harassed and wilted.

"Any luck?"

She shook her head.

"So, where are we staying tonight?" Gus asked.

"At my old uncle Richard Quick-Flippe's place. He's a real estate agent and a bit of a snooty bachelor. He lives in Hurlingham near Sandton City."

"Hurlingham?"

"Yes."

Gus tried to alleviate tension by emitting a pig-like snort. "Surely he can't afford to be snobbish if he lives in a suburb named *Hurlingham*. That name could easily be misinterpreted for *Puking-Pig*."

"Gus! Don't let my uncle Richard hear you say that! He's half Jewish and hates pork. It's a very smart area. His place is a modern townhouse. You know--one of those small, residential places that interconnect with a common driveway, electric gate and shared swimming pool. Each place has its own garden behind a security wall."

"I'm feeling tired. We need to get there."

"What about Ruby?"

"He'll have to sleep in the box."

"He can't! He might cast himself inside and get injured."

"Okay. Leave it to me," Gus said.

"What will you do?"

"I'll think of something. Now, concentrate and direct me. I'm not sure where to go."

"Sure."

<u>CHAPTER THIRTY-TWO</u>

Nosy Neighbour

As they drove along, Miranda asked, "Do you think Ruby's in danger of getting Equine Flu?"

"No, when I vaccinated him I made sure he got everything available. He'll be okay. Stop worrying your pretty head."

Half an hour later Gus pulled up into Richard Quick-Flippe's driveway, leaned out the window to press the intercom's buzzer. Rosina, Richard's maid, answered. Miranda greeted Rosina like a long-lost friend over the speaker. Immediately, the tall iron security gates rolled aside. Gus drove through and they closed automatically behind. Next, he backed up the horsebox into Richard's carport.

"Phew! That's a tight squeeze," Miranda exclaimed looking at the two-inch space on her side of the truck. "You're an excellent driver. Excuse me, but I'll have to get out on your side."

Gus smiled and switched off the engine. Climbing out with Miranda close behind, he peered into Richard's garage window. A blood-red 1982 Ferrari 512 BBi sports car was inside. An approving low whistle escaped his lips.

Miranda said, "Apparently that Ferrari Boxer is worth more than some houses."

"Yeah! I bet. Old Rich must be loaded with cash."

"Being a successful real estate agent did it for the old guy."

Rosina, the portly maid, came out to hug Miranda and greet Gus. "Richard's coming. He's on the phone with a client. Let me help you carry your things."

"Thanks, Rosina. Meet my boyfriend, Gus."

She nodded a smiley greeting. Gus stepped closer. "Pleased to meet you."

A tall dark-haired man in his mid-thirties bounced out with arms stretched wide in greeting. His muscle-man shirt revealed tanned skin and large gym-style biceps. "Hello, everyone! And welcome to my humble abode."

"Meet my uncle Richard," Miranda said.

"Pleased to meet you. I'm Gus." They shook hands. Gus couldn't take his eyes off Richard's slicked-back pony tail hair style.

"Call me Rich. Come in. Rosina will show you where to put your stuff." He paused, cocked his head and listened. "Is that a horse I hear and *smell* in the box?"

Miranda shuffled her feet. "Yeah. I'd like to borrow your phone and do some quick calling around. The place where I booked stabling let us down."

His eyebrows jerked. "Oh, that's not good. Go on--you know where everything is. Help yourself."

Gus followed Rich into the hallway. A massive painting depicting zebra drinking at a waterhole stretched from ceiling to floor. It was the sort of painting that demanded instant in-your-face attention and got it.

Gus gasped. "Wow, that's incredible."

Rich smiled. "It's by Keith Joubert. I collect originals. There's more in the dining room by Izidro Duarte. Do you enjoy art?"

Gus hesitated. "Y-yeah, it's wonderful. Excuse me for a moment; I must check on Miranda and see how the phoning's going."

"Sure. I'll fix you a drink. What can I get?"

"Beer, thanks."

Rich hesitated. "Uh, I don't have any. May I offer you wine, scotch-on the rocks or a fruit juice?"

"Orange juice, thanks."

"A good, healthy choice."

Gus made his way through to the bedroom they were to share, closing the door behind him. His eyes scanned the crystal chandelier and marble floor tiles before roaming to the exquisite hardwood furniture. For a small place, it oozed extravagant, luxurious charm in every priceless detail. Heavy, cream-coloured drapes, detailed with gold brocade adorned the sparkling windows. Flamboyant, silken tie-backs held the sumptuous drapes aside. He felt too intimidated to touch anything in case a smudge got left behind.

After a while, Miranda hung up and faced him. "Nothing. Absolutely no stabling available anywhere. The last three people were positively rude--didn't want to know my story. The one guy told me I was mad and had a cheek to phone at night. That's it--we're stuck." She began to cry. "What can we do?"

Gus drew her against his chest and patted her back. "There, there. It's no use crying. It's not the end of the world. Ruby will have to sleep here."

She pulled back. "*Where*? We can't leave him in the box--it's too dangerous."

"Ask Rich if we can put him in his garage."

"No, that won't do. Rich won't agree to leave his car out at night. And there's no bedding to put on the garage floor; Ruby could end up with a capped hock or knee--it's too hard."

"True."

She thumped his chest. "Come on; you said you had an idea."

"Yeah. I saw the garden, and I reckon Ruby could sleep out there. It's a nice little patch of grass for him to lie on. He'll be okay."

Her eyes widened. "This is a smart, residential suburb! Chickens can't be kept here--never mind a horse! What if the neighbours see? They might report us to the police, the SPCA or the animal pound. Lord knows what trouble they could cause. It might damage your reputation as a vet. And Rich would have his name brandished negatively all over the newspapers."

Gus shook his head. "It's no use worrying about *what ifs*. Right now, that horse needs to get out, get water, be fed and lie down."

"I don't know if Rich will agree to that--it's illegal."

"You won't know until you ask."

She shook her head. "No, you ask."

"No way! He's *your* uncle--*you* ask. And by the way, you told me he was *old*. The guy only looks about seven years older than I."

"Yes, but he can't help that. I'll go and ask."

Much to her surprise and relief, Rich agreed to put Ruby in his garden on the provision they hid him properly. As a well-respected member of the local community, he couldn't afford to have his reputation tarnished.

Miranda repeated the conversation to Gus.

He grinned. "All good! Nice to know there's no pressure."

Miranda rolled her eyes. "This is the worst day of my life."

"Well then, you're lucky. Things aren't too bad--we've been offered a solution," Gus said. "I reckon it's dark enough. Let's get Ruby out and walk him through the garden gate at the side."

"Do you think it's wide enough?" Miranda asked.

"I hope so. We'll soon find out."

"He might go nuts if he gets stuck."

"Stop stressing--I'm sure he'll fit through."

"Yes, but what if he just gets in and tomorrow he goes goofy, as horses can, and decides not to squeeze back out. Then he'll be stuck in the garden, and we'll be caught. Everyone will know when builders arrive and break down the wall!"

Gus shook her gently. "Stop doing this to yourself. He's a calm horse. I reckon he'll be okay."

They sneaked out into the car port and checked the vicinity was clear. Night lights illuminated the massive, shared driveway. Hopefully, they wouldn't be seen. Gus was about to give Miranda the thumbs up when he spotted a woman out walking her little pooch.

"Good evening!" she called in a cheery voice as the dog trotted ahead.

Miranda clenched her fists and shrunk back into the shadows.

"Evening!" Gus smiled and waved.

The woman stopped while pooch strained on the lead and began barking. She faced Gus. "I'm Felicity Oppenheimer. Pleased to meet you." She and Gus shook hands. "You must be ... a friend of Richard's?"

Gus guffawed. "Yeah, yeah. Just visiting...."

Just then, Ruby stomped his hoof inside the box and emitted a loud, snorting exhale.

Felicity's dog strained forward on the lead, yapping madly.

"Gosh!" she exclaimed. "Is there a *horse* in there?"

Miranda burst out from the shadows. "Gus! You promised to water the garden. What are you doing? Hurry--we want you back inside. For goodness sake, come and be sociable!"

Gus grinned. "This is Miranda. We recently got engaged."

"Oh, congratulations!" Felicity exclaimed.

"Thanks," Miranda replied snappishly, not looking too pleased. She quickly turned on the garden tap and then attempted to attach the hose. Water sprayed everywhere--soaking Felicity and Gus.

Felicity shot back with a squeal.

"Sorry!" Miranda yelled as she got the hose connected and began spraying the flower bed. Ruby sighed and stretched before a flood of urine began trickling out the back of the horse box. Miranda quickly turned the hosepipe onto the puddle and diluted it.

Felicity wrinkled her nose. "There's a bad smell around here."

Miranda grinned. "Yeah, I know. There's a bit of horse pee leaking out from the box. Excuse me please, I'm trying to hose it away and into the drain." Miranda stepped forward spraying water onto the paving so that it splashed up onto Felicity's legs.

The woman shot back. "Oh, I'm all wet!"

Miranda smiled. "Sorry! I'm just trying to get things done so we can all go to bed and relax. We've got an early start tomorrow."

Felicity gushed, "Okay, I won't keep you. Good night, and if I don't see you in the morning--have a safe trip."

"Thank you!" Gus and Miranda called as she turned and walked back to her apartment.

"Phew, that was a close shave."

"It serves you right for being too friendly," Miranda replied.

"I had to be friendly! You get more out of people if you're nice. It's no good being rude--that gets people riled."

"Okay, Mr Nice Guy. Is the road clear?"

Gus craned his neck. "Yes."

"Keep watering the garden while whistling--that should cover any noise."

Miranda backed Ruby down the ramp, turned him and led him straight through the gate. It was a tight squeeze, but he made it. Once inside, he pooped and then put his head down to graze.

Gus poked his head over the wall. "How's he doing?"

Ruby answered with a whinny and a snort.

Miranda cringed and clutched her ears. "I swear, I can't take any more of this--I'm so stressed out."

"Relax," Gus said. "There's enough traffic noise to mask sound. It's time to unwind. Come inside."

Miranda hesitated. "Ruby's fiddling with the barbeque and dustbin. I'm afraid he may hurt himself."

"I've got some white string here. Let's string it up across the garden so that it acts as a boundary between him and the other stuff."

"Do you think it'll work?"

"He knows what an electric fence is, so hopefully he'll think the string is one of them and simply keep away."

"Great idea!"

That night they went to bed, craning their ears for any troublesome noises. But all was quiet. Exhausted, they fell into a deep sleep. In the early hours of the morning, a loud bang rang out from the garden followed by silence.

Miranda sat bolt upright. "Dear, Lord! What was that?"

They listened for more noise--nothing. "I'll check on him," Gus offered. He returned minutes later. "It's so dark out there; I can't see much. But Ruby's lying down. He seems relaxed. There's nothing we can do until daylight. Go back to sleep."

Sleep was elusive. At first light, they were up.

"Right," Gus said. "Let's get Ruby into the box before anyone wakes up and decides to go jogging or go to work."

Miranda was up in a flash, stuffing their overnight bag full and getting dressed. Rich met them in the hallway. "Do you want breakfast?"

"No thank you, Rich. Thanks for everything--we'll just get going before people rise."

"Okay, I understand. Drive carefully."

"Thank you so much," Miranda said. "You've been such a sport--I can't thank you enough."

He smiled. "Hopefully, this won't happen again."

"*Never!*"

Gus packed the car while Miranda fetched Ruby. During the night, Ruby must have leaned over the white string and tipped the dustbin that had made noise during the night. She shone a small torch onto his legs and was pleased to see no harm. After they loaded Ruby into the box with a fresh hay net, they went back to tidy the garden.

"Oh, no! Look at that!" Miranda exclaimed as she pointed to the mud patch where Ruby had rolled and slept.

"It's just grass," Gus said. "It'll grow again. Help me pick up the rubbish and manure. Hopefully, dustbin day is soon. Otherwise, this bin will stink."

"Poor Rich!" Miranda said. "Now, let's get the hell out of here."

Ruby stomped and kicked inside his box while emitting three great whinnies in anticipation of the next stage of his journey.

Felicity Oppenheimer's lights came on. Miranda heard Felicity's back door open and close.

Miranda jumped into the truck slamming the door. "Gus--quick! Let's go before that nosy Felicity *Poochandwhiner* checks out the crime scene and sets off the alarm."

Gus started the truck and headed out through the gates. "Where to now?"

"Stuff the show!" Miranda exclaimed. "No more jumping. And in any case, without stabling the cross-country course will be far too tiring for Ruby to travel home on the same day. Please, take us home. My stress levels are beyond belief. I want to rest and unwind."

"Yeah, me too."

CHAPTER THIRTY-THREE

Biliary Fever

Karl and Gretchen came out to greet the returned, weary travellers.

"I'm glad to see my truck back in one piece," Karl boomed cheerfully.

Gretchen slapped his arm playfully. "Stop it! I told you Gus was a good driver."

Miranda whispered into Gus's ear, "That's a surprise--seeing them together. Do you think something romantic is going on?"

"Yeah, it looks like it."

"Come in and tell us all about it!" Karl called. "We've saved some lunch for you. And Gretchen's made a super chocolate cake."

Miranda smiled. "Thanks, Dad. We'll come as soon as I've put Ruby out to graze."

***

On Monday morning, Mrs Turnbull brought in a sick Alsatian. Gus took a blood slide and examined it under the microscope before announcing his diagnosis, "I'm afraid Spock has a severe case of Biliary."

Mrs Turnbull scowled. "Biliary? How would he get that?"

"It's a common tick-borne disease that causes animals' red blood cells to break down. There is no vaccination against it, so prevention is better than cure."

She stroked Spock's head. The prostrate animal appeared feeble and listless. "How could I have prevented this illness?"

"The best way is to dip your dog once a fortnight, or to use an anti-tick collar."

Her frown increased. "Do you mean to say I should regularly put poison on my dog?"

Gus drew in his breath as he delved deep into his soul in search of patience. "This is Africa, and the disease is endemic. Prevention is better than cure. If you don't use dips or anti-tick collars, then your dog will continually be at risk. If Spock survives this bout, he could get it again and again--unless you take measures to prevent another infection."

"Oh, I suppose I should buy an anti-tick collar now."

Gus shook his head. "No. It's too late for prevention. Spock is too ill to be exposed to any poison now."

"Okay then, give him medication today and then I'll buy a tick collar for next time."

Gus removed the stethoscope from his ears. "I'm afraid it's not that simple. It's already too late for simple medication. Spock is critically ill. His chances of pulling through are marginal."

Her face paled. "I didn't realise..."

"How long has he been off his food?"

"A few days."

Gus sighed. "If only you had brought him in immediately, his chances may have been better."

Her hands trembled as she wiped her eyes and nose with a tissue. "I didn't realise he was that sick. I thought he was fussy."

"Is he normally a fussy eater?"

She shook her head.

"Spock's illness has progressed to the point where his red blood cell count is so low that his body is struggling to stay oxygenated."

Her anxiety manifested by the way she twisted the tissue in her shaking fingers. "Please, don't let him die! Surely, there must be something you could try?"

Gus pursed his lips. "Has Spock ever had a blood transfusion?"

"No. Why?"

"As a last resort, I can try a blood transfusion, but only if the dog has not ever received one before. If a dog has had a previous transfusion, the chances are high of having an allergic reaction the second-time round."

"Why is that?"

"Because most bush vets do not have access to the sophisticated blood grouping tests that humans receive. It's not normally an issue with the first transfusion. Problems arrive the second time around."

Her eyes lit up. "So, he's got a chance this time?"

"Mrs Turnbull, his chances of recovery are slim. A blood transfusion is costly, and I cannot guarantee it will work. The transfusion must be used in conjunction with medication."

"Oh, please try your best to save him! I'd like to take the chance. I feel bad for not bringing him in sooner."

"Okay, thank you. You best go home and get some rest. I won't know for a day or two if he's going to make it or not, but I'll phone when there's a change in his condition."

"Thank you." It was a whisper. She collected her handbag and left.

Gus called to Miranda who was busy grooming Ruby outside.

"Yes?"

"Do you mind if I use Fat Chops as a blood donor?"

"*What?* Are you joking?"

"No. This patient here, old Spock, needs blood urgently."

She looked at Fat Chops who stood wagging her stumpy tail. "Yeah, sure. If it's a matter of life and death, let's do it."

"Okay," Gus said. "Make her lie down and remove her collar. She must lie flat on her side."

"All right."

Gus fetched a vacuum bottle, an intravenous line and a wide gauge needle. Miranda stroked Fat Chops's head and held it firmly while Gus shaved and disinfected an area on her neck before jabbing the needle into her jugular vein. Fat Chops flinched slightly. Miranda's reassuring voice soothed, "Stay, Chops, stay. Good girl. Stay."

Gus held the bottle as Chops's blood flowed into it. After a few minutes, he said, "Great! This is enough." Then he pulled the needle out and gave Miranda a cotton wool swab to apply pressure with over the wound. "Apply pressure there for about three minutes, then you can put her collar on, and she's free to go."

Gus prepared Spock for a blood transfusion.

Miranda said, "Do you think he'll survive?"

"Honestly, I don't know. Let's hope this blood pulls him through."

The next day, Spock drank a little water and then ate a small amount of food. Miranda took him outside for a short, wobbly walk, but Spock's urine still looked dark.

"Don't worry," Gus said. "If he continues to eat and drink, then he'll get stronger. If he stops eating and his gums turn jaundice, then we'll know it's not working."

On the third day, Gus felt satisfied with Spock's progress, so he phoned Mrs Turnbull to collect. When she arrived, Spock barked and wagged his tail.

"I reckon he's well on the road to recovery," Gus said. "Keep his diet simple, just water and meat protein. Stay away from fat and milk for a while. In a week or two, you can go back to feeding him normally and make sure you start practising tick-bite prevention. Once a dog has had Biliary this bad, the second time is far worse. With each bout, their liver gets weaker."

"Thank you, Doctor. In future, I'll see to it that Spock gets regular anti-tick collars."

Fat Chops sat outside the doorway sunning herself as Spock climbed onto the back seat in Mrs Turnbull's car.

Gus turned to Miranda. "Thank you. We were lucky to have Fat Chops with us. I've got a feeling this will be the first of many Biliary patients her blood will help save. Tonight, we must give her a meaty meal and some extra doggy nutrients."

Fat Chops heard her name, stood up and wagged her stumpy tail. Then she nuzzled Miranda's hand with her healthy wet nose.

<u>CHAPTER THIRTY-FOUR</u>

Baobab and Cycads

On Wednesday afternoon, after a visit to a game farm, Gus returned armed with a huge venison leg.

"Whoa!" Miranda exclaimed. "That's a massive leg roast."

Gus beamed with pride. "Yeah, it was generous of the guy to give it to me, but it's in lieu of payment."

"What did you do there?"

"Not much really. I vaccinated all his dogs and one cat. Then we sat down to lunch while I offered him some herd management advice."

"So, this roast is instead of payment?"

"Yeah. He said he had no money, but he had heaps of meat from a hunting trip."

"Well, I suppose it's all right this time but please don't make a habit of it. We need cash to pay our bills."

"I know but look at this meat! When did you last see such a hunk of venison?"

"It's too much for two people."

"Then we'll organise a dinner party."

"Who should we invite?"

Gus's eyes lit up. "How about your Dad and Gretchen?"

"Okay. But you must help me prepare it--I don't have a clue."

"Sure," Gus said. "I'll make a quick marinade."

Miranda watched with interest as Gus mixed a bottle of wine, a bottle of cooking oil, some crushed garlic, salt, pepper and a dash of brown vinegar into a clean plastic bucket together with some fresh garden herbs. Next, he placed the meat into the bucket and put it in the fridge.

"How long must it stay there?" Miranda asked.

"Three days. Arrange the dinner party for Saturday night."

"Okay, leave it to me."

***

After breakfast on Saturday morning, Miranda spoke to Gus, "It looks quiet today. How about we go for a picnic lunch somewhere interesting?"

"Yeah, sounds great. Where?"

She rolled her eyes thoughtfully. "I don't think you've visited The Modjadji Cycad Forest yet."

"No, I haven't."

"Nor the largest Baobab tree in the world?"

"Nope. Haven't seen that either."

"Right!" Miranda slapped her hands together. "Let's get packing. We need to be back by 3:00 pm to start cooking the roast."

"Sure thing."

***

"This is an amazing collection of cycads," Gus said. "It's the biggest forest I've ever seen of these prehistoric plants. They look like palm trees, only their leaves are much harder and stick straight up."

"They're fascinating," Miranda agreed. "It's strange how so many of them grow here in such abundance, and yet, nowhere else that I can think of. Some seem to think it has something to do with the mist in this particular valley."

Gus touched the stiff, shiny, dark green leaf. "Imagine dinosaurs appearing out of the mist and eating this foliage."

Miranda giggled. "They had big teeth, so I'm sure it wasn't difficult."

Gus pulled out his camera. "Sit over there on those twisted trunks and pose for me."

"Like a cave woman?"

"You're too pretty to be one."

"Thank you!" She sat down smiling and crossed her legs, letting her hair fall over her left shoulder.

"Oh, nice shot!" Gus exclaimed. "I reckon I'll frame it."

"Here, take a picture of this cycad flower," Miranda said, pointing to a large, yellow cone that looked like a primitive pineapple growing out of the middle of the stiff, jagged foliage.

They walked around, arm in arm as Miranda explained about the Modjadji Rain Queen. "It's believed that the Balobedu people settled in this vicinity about four hundred years ago after fleeing from the ancient kingdom of Monomotapa in the eastern highlands of Zimbabwe."

"This area must have been rife with malaria and other diseases back then."

"It was," Miranda continued. "The tribe's history is filled with rumours of trouble, incest, weird rituals and superstition. It's the only South African tribe to have a woman leader--the Rain Queen."

"How did she get that title?"

"She is believed to hold power to bring rain to this dry land. The power used to belong to the King, but his sons lusted after his wives, so he took the title away from them about 200 years ago. I'm not sure of all the details, but the honour was passed onto a woman. Problems arose when one Rain Queen was barren, so she took wives from four related royal families."

"It sounds complicated."

"It is. I think the rules got altered every time things didn't go to plan. Anyway, for the last six generations, the Rain Queen has always been a woman. And I think it's likely to stay that way."

"Interesting," Gus said. Then he glanced at his watch. "I think we'd better go and see the big Baobab before it gets too late."

"Yes. We'll see the bar and have our picnic lunch."

Gus's brows raised. "Is there a bar there?"

Miranda grinned. "The inside of the tree is hollow, and the people who own it have made a rustic bar inside it."

"It sounds fun! Let's go."

***

Half an hour later, after trundling along several dusty roads, they turned into the farm where the big Baobab tree grew.

Gus said, "I can't believe how many times I've driven nearby here and not stopped to see this before." He stood gazing up at the monstrous, gnarled old tree with its grey bark and dense emerald green foliage. The sheer size, grey colour and rough texture reminded him of elephant skin.

"I knew you'd appreciate seeing it," Miranda said. "Experts reckon it's over 1700 years old and is the widest Baobab tree in the world. It's also the only sizable one nearby. Most others grow further north towards the Limpopo River where it's flat and dry."

"Amazing!" Gus's eyes filled with wonderment.

"I read that Baobabs start going hollow in the middle once they're over 1000 years old."

"Let's go inside." Gus made his way to the hollow that served as a doorway. He stooped down as he entered through. Once inside the cavern, there was plenty of room to stand up in. A roughly hewn wooden bench bar stood inside with several makeshift bar stools in front of it. "Where are the drinks?"

Miranda laughed. "They only serve drinks here for weddings and special functions, so the property owners are kind to allow us in for a look around. They said we could eat our picnic lunch here too as long as we clean up afterwards."

They went outside and sat at a wooden picnic table under the Baobab tree's luxurious shade. Miranda unpacked cool drinks and sandwiches.

Gus took a long swig of cool juice and smiled. His held Miranda's hand, giving it an affectionate, gentle squeeze. "Thanks for bringing me here. This is a memory I'll always treasure. It's really special."

She leant forward and kissed him.

Afterwards, they packed up their things and headed towards the carpark. As they were climbing into Gus's Suzuki, a large black truck pulled up alongside. Miranda's eyes widened as she gasped. "Quick, Gus. Get in the car--let's get out of here fast."

"What's the hurry?"

The black truck's driver jumped out with a handgun holstered to his hip. "Well, look who's here," he drawled. "Slutty Miranda and her Soutpiel!"

"Shut-up, Piet. We're over," Miranda yelled.

Gus surveyed his well-built, thick-necked rival as he considered the thick-headed remark. "That's no way to talk to a lady."

"She's no lady. She's a cheating bitch!" Piet spat into the dirt.

"Come on, Gus. Let's go."

Gus heard a fearful tremor in her voice and was about to say something when Miranda pushed him back. "Gus, this idiot's not worth it. Leave him to fry in his own hatred. We've got better things to do. Come on; I want to go."

Gus and Miranda climbed in the car. As Gus prepared to drive away, Piet called out, "I'll get you son of a bitch. Mark my words. You haven't seen the last of me so stay out of my way."

As Gus put the pedal to the metal, Miranda said, "Phew! That was a close shave. He has a reputation for fighting. Trust me, Gus, you don't want to be on the receiving side of his fists."

"I don't like the way he spoke to you."

"Forget it. Let's just get home and cook that roast."

CHAPTER THIRTY-FIVE

Dinner

Gretchen and Karl arrived at 6:30 pm and sat outside on the veranda sipping wine while Gus cracked a beer and held up his bottle. "Cheers, mates. It's good to have you around."

Karl sat with his bare feet planted firmly on the ground and laughed. "Urgh, I'll never get used to being called *mate*."

"Okay," Gus said. "I promise to change it to Dad after I've married your daughter."

"And when will that be?" Gretchen asked with a wink.

"Oh, for goodness sake!" Miranda interjected. "We'll let you know as soon as we've sorted through all the ins and outs and mountains of paperwork. Remember, ours is not a simple marriage because we have citizenships in different countries."

Gus sprang to his feet. "Hey, I think the roast is ready. Miranda, come and check the vegetables please."

"Sure."

When she got to the kitchen, Gus said, "Hey, be kind to Gretchen. She's only being curious."

"Sorry, I didn't mean to sound waspish. This microwave cooking is driving me nuts."

Gus took the roast out of the oven, leaving it to rest for five minutes while he helped Miranda set the table. Soon everyone came inside and got seated.

"Welcome to my humble abode," Gus said. "Make yourselves comfortable."

Karl pulled out Gretchen's chair before seating himself. "Mmm!" he exclaimed. "That smells delicious."

Gus rubbed his hands together with anticipation as he sat.

"Wait," Karl said. "Let's first say grace. Dear, Heavenly Father, thank you for this meal set before us. We ask you to bless it to our bodies. Amen."

A unanimous 'amen' broke out.

Gus stood and carved the meat. He sawed and sawed and then stopped. "Miranda, this knife is blunt. Please fetch another."

"Sure." She handed him a sharper knife.

Gus tried cutting again and struggled on. "Look, I'm sorry, but I'm having trouble cutting this meat. Sorry, but I'm going to give you thicker slices, okay?"

Karl laughed. "The more, the better. No complaints."

Miranda dished up vegetables, and then everyone began to tuck in.

Gretchen struggled to cut her meat. Miranda battled hers too. Gus watched Karl trying to cut his as he battled his own. Silence ensued as they sat around the table chewing their meat. They chewed and chewed and chewed.

Gus was the first to push his plate away. "The stuff's inedible."

Gretchen's eyes bulged as she swallowed a mouthful that almost stuck in her throat. She reached for her glass of wine to wash it down. Afterwards, she patted her chest and wheezed, "That's better."

Old Karl appeared to be having trouble with his dentures. Finally, he too put his knife and fork together. "Sorry, but I can't eat this antelope. I reckon it ran all the way from the Cape Province to Cairo, and back down to Kenya and then onto the Kalahari before it was shot."

Miranda tried not to choke as she spat it out. "It's as tough as old boots!"

"We could play tennis with it," Gus chipped in.

Everyone put their knives and forks together and pushed their plates away.

Karl mopped his mouth. "Never mind. We'll just eat pudding. What's on offer, Miranda?"

She smiled. "I made a microwaved steam pudding."

"Ah," Karl said. "So, Gus has one of those new modern micro-oven-thingy-ma-bobbins."

Miranda grinned. "Yes. It's the first time I've used it. I'll fetch the pudding." She went to the kitchen and opened the microwave door." A wail escaped her lips.

"What's up?" Gus asked watching smoke billow out the kitchen.

"It's all burnt!"

Karl smiled. "I love burnt pudding. Bring it here--I'll eat it."

"I'm afraid not, Dad." Miranda ventured near the table bearing her charcoal-briquette gift with oven mitts.

Gretchen coughed as smoke fumes assailed her nostrils.

Karl's enthusiasm waned. "Good Lord! It looks like a heathen shrunken head from hell."

"How long did you cook it in the microwave?" Gretchen asked.

"Three hours."

"Oh, dear! I think that was too long."

Gus scratched his head. "Understatement of the year."

Gretchen replied, "I've heard microwaves cook much faster than conventional ovens."

"Oh, well," Karl said. "Let's go to the Magoebaskloof Hotel for dinner. I'll pay."

"But you've got no shoes--they won't let you in."

"I'll lend him some gumboots and long pants," Gus said. "If he hides the tops under the legs of his trousers, nobody will notice."

"Okay, thanks," Karl said. "It's good when family work together and help each other. That's how good things happen."

Gus smiled. "Agreed. Fat Chops will be the only one to benefit from our home-cooked dinner."

Fat Chops, hearing her name, came trotting to receive her after-dinner snack and was pleasantly surprised.

CHAPTER THIRTY-SIX

Nightmare

Later, during the week, Gus received a phone call from Mr de Kock, a nearby chicken farmer, asking whether the chicken vaccines he ordered could be delivered.

"Sure, mate" Gus replied. "No worries. I'll send Miranda over while I stay and attend to clients."

"Thanks. She'll find me working in my egg incubation shed."

"Right-o. Cheers."

Miranda took the mini cool box with the chicken vaccines out the fridge and headed towards Gus's Suzuki with Wingnut underarm. Jealous, Fat Chops followed, begging to go along. Her wiggly stumpy tail and pleading eyes were too irresistible to ignore. Miranda opened the back of Gus's Suzuki with a reluctant sigh. "Okay, you two. Get in." Both dogs leapt into the back, eager and panting with excitement, in anticipation of a simple journey down the dusty road.

After Miranda arrived at the de Kock's farm, she pulled the car up under the sprawling shade of a Flamboyant tree. She wound the windows down to help keep the car cool. Then she grabbed the vaccines and closed her door. Wingnut yapped and sprang through the open window. Miranda stooped to lift her with one hand and carried her along.

"Hello!" Flip de Kock called. "Thanks for the delivery. Today is a bad day for me."

"Oh? What's wrong?"

"Yesterday, one of my old egg incubators broke down, but I only found out this morning. So, I've had to remove the eggs-- throw them away. Now I'm busy sterilising fresh trays and equipment."

"Gosh, that's unfortunate. How many eggs did you lose?"

"Two thousand." He grimaced. "It's all part of living and learning."

"Here are your vaccines." She held up the box.

"Thanks. It's such a hot day; I'll put them in the fridge. Would you like a cool drink?"

"No, thank you. I've a dog in the car, so I can't stay."

"Where did you park?"

"Under the Flamboyant tree."

"It's nice and shady there, no need to fret. Come along," Flip insisted. "My wife baked this morning--she'll be disappointed if you don't sample her baking."

"All right, but I can't stay long."

Tea was served on the de Kock's patio overlooking their beautiful garden with sweeping valley views. Overhead, branches swayed as Samango monkeys clicked their tongues and screeched.

"It's beautiful out here," Miranda said. "You have a lovely view."

"Yes, it's pleasant on a clear day. On misty mornings it's also lovely, the only thing is, one can't see as far."

Ester, Flip's wife, offered Miranda a piece of her decadent chocolate cake.

"Ooh! It looks fantastic! Thank you."

Miranda tucked in. "Wow, you sure are a great baker! This is truly superb."

"I can give you the recipe," Ester offered.

"I'm not such a great cook."

Ester laughed. "Don't be modest."

"No, trust me; I'm honest."

After tea, Miranda thanked the de Kocks for their hospitality and carried Wingnut back to the car, only to discover that Fat Chops was missing. Miranda whistled and called, but Fat Chops didn't come. She hurried back and found Flip in his shed.

"Sorry, but my big dog's jumped out the car and gone missing. I don't want her chasing your chickens or getting into trouble. I must find her."

Flip checked his watch; he had plenty to do. "She can't get into the chicken runs. They're well fenced to keep vermin out."

"Where could she be?"

Flip put his finger on his nose. "To find a dog, you must think like one."

Miranda scowled. "What do you mean?"

"Follow your nose, as dogs do. They love bad smells." He walked outside behind the shed and pointed.

"Oh, no!" Miranda gasped. Her eyes fell on Fat Chops guzzling down piles of rotten eggs laying out in the hot sun.

"Oh, dear," Flip said. "Looks like she found the old eggs. I was planning to move them--just haven't had a chance yet."

Fat Chops's stomach had a round, bloated appearance as she looked up, wagging her stumpy tail. A wolfish grin spread across her yellowed, slobbery lips as she stood licking with victorious satisfaction.

Miranda groaned.

Flip chuckled. "You found her. No harm's done."

"Yeah, thanks. We best get home." Miranda tugged Fat Chops's collar while the prodigal hound trotted alongside emitting a deep-throated burp.

***

As soon as Miranda returned home, she left Fat Chops outside for the day, hoping the dog would expel her extra baggage out in the garden. She decided not to tell Gus their beloved blood donor had gone walkabout on a client's farm. What he didn't know, couldn't worry him.

Later that night as they prepared for bed, Gus said, "Call Fat Chops. Don't leave her outside. The last thing we need is her going hunting bush pig and coming off second best."

Miranda opened the door and yelled, "Come, Fatty Choppy! Fat Chops!" Followed by a short whistle.

The dog came bounding with a madly wagging tail. As her tail wiggled, a sulphurous odour wormed its way out, permeating the room.

Gus cursed and choked. His eyes watered. "What the hell?"

"Fat Chops just farted."

He coughed. "What the hell did you feed her?"

"Dog food."

"I reckon she devoured something dead. Put her in the kitchen. She's not sleeping near us tonight."

"Okay." Miranda put Fat Chop's mat on the kitchen floor and told her to lie down and stay. Then she went to back to bed. It didn't take long for them both to fall into a deep sleep.

Sometime during the early hours of the morning, Gus stirred. Miranda grumbled and turned onto her side, pulling the blankets over her head. Gus got up and walked through to the kitchen while Miranda dozed.

An almighty roar filled the air. She dreamt she was falling, falling, falling....

"*Miranda!*" The shout was a distant call. "*Miranda!*"

She awoke to urgent shaking. "Miranda! Wake-up!"

"What?" she moaned.

Gus spoke. "Seriously, you need to get up."

"Uh?" she sat up, rubbing her eyes.

He switched on the bedside lamp and stared down.

She squinted up. "Urgh? What's going on?"

He grimaced. "Come and see for yourself."

She yawned. Stopped midway and choked. "Crikey--what the hell is that?"

"Come." Gus led her with a firm hand to the kitchen and switched on the light.

Miranda gagged. "Oh, my..." Cough. Choke. Splutter. "What the...?"

"Your dog." Gus pointed to copious puddles of shit splattered everywhere.

Fat Chops sat on her mat with drooping ears, looking utterly ashamed of herself while surrounded by vast volumes of diarrhoetic shit. It was on the walls, floors and kitchen doors. Acrid sulphurous waves radiated from the crime scene. The sheer magnitude of the devastating horror was inconceivable. Worse than any science-fiction aftermath of alien chemical warfare; and way beyond the realms of human experience.

"Oh, no!" Miranda clamped both hands over her nose and mouth. Shocked, her wide eyes stared.

"Oh, yes. *Your* dog," Gus said. "You're going to help me clean it."

She backed off, shaking her head. "I can't..." she mumbled from behind clenched teeth. "I just can't."

"Yes, you will help. We'll do this together. Now, tell me, what did you feed that dog?"

She wagged her head.

"You're hiding something..."

"Okay. She feasted on rotten eggs at Flip de Kock's farm. Sorry, I had no idea this could happen..."

Gus clenched his jaw. "Fetch me a bucket of hot water while I find something to sterilise this place."

Eager to escape, she did his bidding, returning minutes later with a bucket of steaming water.

Gus handed her a pair of gloves. She pulled them on. Next, he handed her a rag. She bent down to start alongside; instead, she retched. She ran outside and vomited under a tree. Gus sauntered up to her, holding her hair back while she finished puking.

"Never mind, honey," he said. "You stay out here while I scrub. You keep me supplied with buckets of fresh water when needed."

Gratefully, she nodded and turned to face the starlit sky, sucking in a lungful of pure mountain air. Relief.

After an hour and a half of hard scrubbing, rinsing and washing, their kitchen smelled like a chemical plant had exploded inside their hut. Once Gus had finished sterilising every surface, he opened the windows to let out fumes. Then he sat down and said, "Miranda, please make us some hot chocolate."

<u>CHAPTER THIRTY-SEVEN</u>

Tasks at Hand

The morning got off to a quick start with a hit and run. Mrs Jones, surrounded by five young children, hurried into the clinic, crying. She placed, Taxi, a fox terrier crossbreed on the table and stood back saying, "He ran out onto the road and chased a car. It happened so fast. One moment he was with me and the next...." She dabbed her eyes with a tissue and then blew into it. "He was gone."

Her grubby, wide-eyed children clutched onto her cotton skirt in silent fear as they waited to hear the animal doctor's opinion.

Taxi shivered as Gus rolled him over to check his stomach. A horrified gasp escaped Miranda's lips at the sight of Taxi's shredded abdominal skin. The wound had the appearance of a pantyhose ladder. She could see right through into the little dog's gut. The gaping wound revealed the secret place where no daylight had shone before. His purple-grey intestines bulged and strained behind the bleeding cobwebbed skin.

A frown of concentration marked Gus's forehead as he bent low over the frightened animal and gently palpated and examined the extent of its injury.

Mrs Jones, her children and Miranda waited in silent hope to hear his verdict. "Doctor, can you save him?" the woman blurted, while her anxious children whimpered. "Please try. My children love that dog. I'll pay anything to see him well again; money is no issue."

Gus stroked the dog's head slowly. "It looks far worse than it is. Although there's some bruising, Taxi has no broken bones, and his gut doesn't appear ruptured. But he needs immediate surgery."

Mrs Jones sniffed and smiled. Her kids stopped whining and squirming as they stood listening with bright-eyed wonder.

"I'll open him up to check his gut properly. Then I'll irrigate it and suture him back together. Afterwards, he'll need antibiotics. Are you able to administer tablets?"

She beamed. "Yes. I had no problem giving de-worming, so antibiotics will be simple."

"I must start. Taxi's intestines mustn't dry. They must be cleaned and closed as soon as possible."

"Please start right away. You'll phone me when you're finished?"

"Yes. Leave your contact details with Gretchen, thanks."

"Thank you, Doctor. See you later. Goodbye."

***

From behind his surgical mask, Gus hummed along to the radio as he put the last suture in place on Taxi's stomach. "Miranda, please ask Gretchen to phone Mrs Jones. Taxi will be ready for collection later this afternoon. Everything went well."

"Okay."

***

After Miranda had passed on the message, Gretchen asked, "Is Gus ready to see another patient yet?"

"Almost. Give him five minutes."

"Good. Because Mrs Hilton-Fynes is here with an injured kitten."

Gus carried Taxi to a cage where he laid the small dog down on a thick warm blanket to sleep off the anaesthetic. Then he returned to his room and wiped his table clean. "Okay, Miranda, bring in Mrs Hilton-Fynes and her cat."

Mrs Hilton-Fynes carried a growling kitten wrapped in a thick blanket.

"Good day," Gus said, "What have we here?"

"Frisky, my kitten, tried to swallow a fish hook."

Gus clicked his tongue as he stretched out his arms. "Here, let me see." He unwrapped the blanket to find a tiny kitten with a huge fishing hook protruding from its mouth. He winced. "Ah, I bet that's painful." He felt Frisky's racing heart beat against his hand as he held him.

Frisky swished his tail and growled. The hook hung like a huge anchor from his bottom jaw, swinging to and fro like a pendulum with every movement. Gus peered closer and saw the hook had pierced its way straight through the kitten's jaw under its tongue. The top part of the hook protruded from its mouth while the nasty barbed arrow projected through its fur in the middle of its jaw.

Mrs Hilton-Fynes bit her nails anxiously. "Can you help him?"

Gus smiled. "Sure can. You go out there and take a seat. Gretchen will make you a cup of tea or coffee while you wait."

"What will you do?"

"Give him a quick anaesthetic, cut the hook with a pair of pliers and remove it."

Fifteen minutes later, Gus cradled the repentant purring kitten in his strong arms, returning it to its owner.

"Thank you, Doctor," Mrs Hilton-Fynes cried. "Frisky looks much happier!"

The kitten mewed as it kneaded her bosom.

Gus smiled. "No worries. Just make sure your husband keeps his fishing tackle locked away."

She laughed. "I will! Thank you."

***

No sooner had Gus and Miranda sat down to lunch when the phone rang. Gretchen answered, spoke and hung up.

"That was Len Cheeseman."

"Who's he?" Gus asked, frowning, as he tried to recall the name.

Gretchen rolled her eyes. "You know--the farmer who had the cow with *Umbrella Sickness*."

A spark of remembrance twinkled in Gus's eyes. "Oh, yeah. What's he want?"

"He has a cow with a prolapsed uterus and wants you to see it. No other vet will do. According to him, you're the best."

"Crikey," Gus said glancing at his watch. "Looks like I've got a reputation to maintain within a limited time frame. Tell him I'm on my way. I'll be there within half an hour; soon as I've packed my car."

***

As Gus and Miranda carried the veterinary equipment further into the field, a low, moaning bellow rose from a ditch.

"There she is," Len Cheeseman said, pointing to a small gulley. "Earlier, she was walking around, kicking her uterus with her hind legs. We tried to steer her towards the crush for your visit, but she stumbled and fell there."

Gus stared down into the ditch; the cow lay with her head and chest slightly elevated while her rear end sloped downhill. Still attached, her bloodied uterus lay behind her in the dirt with the lumpy cotyledons peppered with sandy grit. The situation was far from ideal. Her new-born calf stood nearby crying for milk.

Gus rubbed his temple; he could feel a headache coming on. "Look, I think we need to get her up and into the crush. It's too hard to work here. I'll be fighting an uphill battle against gravity when I try to push her uterus back."

"Okay," Cheeseman said, "we can only try."

Five people pushed and shoved, but the dead weight of a reluctant 700 kg cow proved too much for them.

Cheeseman smirked. "Okay, Doc, I'll leave you and the herdsman to do it. You know your job. Come and see me when you're done." He turned and walked away.

Miranda was appalled. "What now?"

Gus shrugged. "I'll just have to do my best. The guy thinks I'm a miracle worker. It's no good standing around. Let's start."

Miranda asked the herdsman to fetch two buckets of water. Five minutes later he returned with four child helpers. Each pair carried one brimming bucket between them.

Gus soaped his arms and lay the uterus, which was the size of an oblong weighty beach ball, onto a plastic sheet. Then he began washing off the sand with warm water. Next, he rinsed the uterus with an antiseptic solution in cold water to reduce swelling. Then he wrapped a large cotton towel around it and slowly twisted the towel tighter and tighter.

"Why are you doing that?" Miranda asked.

"It reduces swelling. Otherwise, it'll never fit back. It compresses the blood back into the cow's body."

"Oh. It looks tough."

"It is." He continued twisting the towel. Eventually, he said, "Right. Time to push the uterus back."

He lay down in the ditch behind the fallen cow and inch by inch; he pushed the uterus back into the suffering animal's body.

The beast mustered up enough energy to resist his efforts. As Gus pushed in, she pushed out. Gus cursed, gasped for breath and tried again.

Miranda watched with mounting anxiety as Gus fought to save the reluctant cow. He pushed up and in while she pushed down and out. Her efforts were assisted by gravity and the sloping ground that was in her favour. The sheer size and weight of her 700 kg body fighting against him was more than Miranda could bear to watch.

Miranda said, "Can't you give her an epidural? Then she might stop pushing."

"No. Can't do that. It will keep her down too long. She needs to stand up as soon as possible. Once she's up, it will take pressure off the prolapse. Hopefully, she'll feed her calf."

Time marched on and soon two hours passed as Gus fought on.

Miranda watched in horror as Gus heaved, gasped and strained. His face had turned an awful shade of deep red as the veins on his neck and arms bulged blue.

She sat down on a nearby log and held her head in despair, praying that Gus would not have a heart attack out in the bush. He looked exhausted as rivers of sweat trickled down his face, soaking through the overalls on his back.

"Oh, my God," Miranda cried as she stood looking down on him. "Please don't die on me!"

He stared up into her pleading face with bloodshot eyes that were red from dust and sweat. He gasped one word, "Water."

"Uh?"

"I must drink."

"Sure." She held a plastic bottle to his mouth while his arm stayed inside the cow. He drank until satisfied.

"Are you winning?" Miranda asked.

A deep moan escaped his lips. "I'm not sure if I can get it back far enough to make it stay. She keeps pushing it out."

Recharged, he fought back. "This is my last attempt."

He took a deep breath and with one last straining push, he thrust his lubricated arm with all his might into the cow, forcing the uterus back in. Veins on his forehead stood out like angry blue cords as his arm shook with exertion. Finally, the uterus returned, and the cow stopped pushing.

Quickly, he placed an antibiotic vaginal pessary into the cow's uterus and then placed a large, thick glass bottle into her vagina. He sewed her vulva closed with broad cotton tape to keep the bottle in place. Job completed, he rolled back panting. Perspiration dripped from every pore in his body. He gulped down more water.

"What's that glass bottle inside the cow do?" Miranda asked.

"It will keep the uterus out of the vagina so that the cow strains less. It maintains sufficient pressure to keep the uterus in place until swelling subsides."

"How long must it stay there?"

"Two weeks, and then she'll be good."

Weak and weary, Gus stood and packed his stuff. Miranda helped. As they were about to leave, the cow bellowed, staggered to her feet and walked over to her calf. The calf butted her udder and began feeding.

Smiling, the herdsman came forward bearing an enamel bowl filled with fresh water, a cake of Lifebuoy carbolic soap and a rough towel.

"Thanks, mate." Gus washed and dried his hands.

Just then, Len Cheeseman appeared and said, "Marvellous! I knew you could do it. See--it wasn't that difficult."

<u>CHAPTER THIRTY-EIGHT</u>

Jumbo Problem

Miranda knew something was up on the Saturday afternoon her father invited her and Gus to a special occasion at his home. When they turned into his driveway, they saw numerous cars parked and happy kids tearing around the garden. She got out and slammed the door. "Things look festive. I wonder what Dad's got up his sleeve."

Her father met them and greeted her with a warm hug before quickly pulling her aside. "Come with me. I have good news to share."

Curious, she followed him down the passage and into his office. He closed the door behind him. Smiling, he said, "I want you to be the first to know..."

"Yes?"

"Today, Gretchen and I are engaged. I'll make our announcement before lunch."

Miranda's eyes and mouth became astonished orbs. "Oh."

His smile waned. "Is that all you have to say?"

"No, of course not.... It's a bit soon since Mum died."

He took her hand. "I loved your mother, but she's not coming back. You, my only child, will be heading off to Australia. Surely, you don't want me to be sad and lonely?"

She hung her head, biting her lip. "It's a bit of a shock, that's all. I thought you'd ask me first."

He shook his head sadly. "My child, I love you. Just like you, I don't need anyone's permission to choose whom I marry."

"Ah, Dad, you have such a way with words. What can I say?" she smiled. "Congratulations!" Then she kissed his cheek and hugged him. "Gretchen's a good woman. She'll make you happy. Promise to look after her, okay?"

His eyes shone with joy and relief. "Of course! Thanks for understanding."

"To be honest, I'll feel better leaving you behind if I know you are cared for and loved."

***

Mrs Jones, accompanied by her brood of lively kids, arrived twelve days after Taxi's accident to have his sutures removed.

"I'm pleased with his excellent recovery," Gus said.

"So am I!" she exclaimed. "He finished all his antibiotic tablets, and my children are grateful he lived. Thank you so much, Doctor."

As Mrs Jones was about to leave, Gretchen asked her to settle her bill because Gus had given her a special low price.

The woman rummaged around in her handbag. "I'm sorry, but I seem to have left my purse at home. I'll drop by and pay you tomorrow. Is that okay?"

"I understand," Gretchen said. "I can see you have a busy life. Give me your address, and I'll post your account--that'll save you making another special trip back here."

"I'd appreciate that. Thank you," Mrs Jones replied.

Gretchen wrote her contact details down before she left.

***

"Miranda, are you coming?" Gus asked.

"Where are you going?"

"To Cheeseman's farm to see the cow that had the prolapsed uterus. After that, I've got a call to visit an elephant."

"Yeah! Count me in. Who keeps an elephant in their backyard?"

"The circus," Gus said, bowing and clowning around trying to balance a cup on his head. "It surprised me to hear of a circus travelling in South Africa. But, the truth is, just like the USA where bison were shot to clear farmland, the same thing applies here with elephants. These days, the only places they are seen are in circuses, zoos and in game reserves."

"And only the wealthy can afford to visit game reserves," Miranda said. "So, it stands to reason that hundreds and thousands of poor people would queue to see an elephant up close."

"Well," Gus said, "They're in town today and tomorrow. The last thing they need is a dead elephant on hand--the press would have a field day."

She frowned. "I bet you haven't treated one before."

"No."

"How'll you know what's wrong?"

"I'll examine it."

She shivered. "I hope you know African elephants are treacherous; they're not the same as Indian elephants."

"If needed, I'm sure the trainer will intervene."

***

When they arrived at Cheeseman's farm, his cow was already in the yard waiting with her calf at foot. Gus's eyes lit up. "She's looking good. I'm pleased those sutures held everything in."

The herdsman rounded her up into the crush, placing wooden poles in front and behind her, to keep her still while Gus worked.

It didn't take long to snip the thick cotton sutures and remove them. Next, he placed his hand into her vagina and retrieved the bottle. After that, he placed another bovine pessary into her vagina. Gus stepped back as a herdsman steered the cow out through the crush and back to her calf. With a satisfied grin, he washed his arm under a nearby tap and said, "Right. Off to Tzaneen to see that elephant."

Miranda helped carry his stuff as they hurried to his car and prepared for the next destination.

***

Locating the circus in the small town was easy; they only had to follow crowds of people until they spotted the blue and white striped tent that was surrounded by colourful trailers, parked in a circle, end to end, for security. The makeshift campsite was set up at the rear-end of town behind the industrial area. A large, open field with lush grass stretched out behind an old industrial warehouse; making for an ideal site. Nearby were other open fields with short, rough grass that made ideal car parking.

Gus locked his car. Miranda helped carry things as they headed towards the entrance that was currently closed. After knocking on several trailer doors, eventually, somebody helped put them in touch with the circus manager. A handsome middle-aged man appeared. His eyes lit up as soon as he heard Gus was the vet. "Thank goodness you're here. My name's Dan, and I own the circus."

Gus inclined his head. "Call me Gus. Pleased to meet you, Dan. Tell me, what's the problem?"

Dan's forehead furrowed. "We've never had a sick elephant before. Can't think what happened. Let me take you to her trainer, Siphiwe; he knows more."

Siphiwe, a lithe, muscular, black man shook Gus's hand. "Thank you for coming, Sir. Ellie is sick. She stopped eating and is listless. She seems upset and is not heeding commands."

On Dan's instruction, Miranda watched the elephant from a safe distance while she overheard Gus's barraging questions.

"When did she stop eating? When did she start looking agitated? Do you know of any other sick animals? What do you feed her? How old is she? Do you know her weight?" But it was the last question that spiked her attention. "Can I go into the trailer to examine her?"

Alert and worried, Miranda saw anxiety flicker across Siphiwe's face.

"No, don't get inside the trailer. Please stand back. I'll try to entice her out."

Gus stood aside.

Siphiwe made several attempts to steer the elephant out and onto the grass before he permitted Gus to move forward.

Miranda noted the heavy chain around Ellie's leg and presumed it was there for safety in case she attempted to break free.

"Move slowly," Siphiwe cautioned. "She doesn't know you."

Miranda watched the elephant's trunk flicker and sway. Its giant ears flapped back and forth as it pawed the ground.

Miranda knew agitated elephants did that as warning signs. She observed Siphiwe's fearful face as he attempted to steer its trunk away from reaching Gus.

"Stop!" Siphiwe called. "Don't come closer. She's angry."

Miranda saw beads of perspiration trickling down the sides of Siphiwe's face and knew he was anxious. Ellie was unpredictable. Miranda had heard that most wild animals could never become completely trustworthy.

Gus moved backwards and spoke softly. "Okay, I'm stepping back. I'll observe her from here for a while."

Relief came for all as Ellie visibly relaxed and stood still.

As Gus observed Ellie over the next few minutes, he noticed she pawed the ground while turning her great head towards her loudly rumbling stomach to look at her heaving flanks.

Miranda sidled up to him and whispered, "What are you thinking?"

"She has the appearance of a colicky horse."

"Oh?"

"She's not eating, and look at her pawing the ground. She keeps turning to face her stomach. From where I'm standing, I hear over-active gut sounds; typical of colic."

Miranda smiled. "Your intelligent deduction amazes me. I reckon you might be right."

He peered closer and pointed. "Look there, see those slight muscle tremors?"

"I hadn't noticed, but now that you mention them, yes."

He shook his head. "Those don't fit in with colic."

Miranda shrugged. "I don't know what to think."

"And look at her saliva," Gus said. "It's not normal. There's too much, and it looks foamy. And, her eyes are watering."

Ellie pawed the ground listlessly and then stopped.

"Siphiwe," Gus said. "Can you walk Ellie into the shade over there?"

"Okay." Siphiwe clicked his tongue and prodded Ellie towards the shady patch cast by an umbrella thorn tree. As she shuffled along, Gus noticed her feet knuckling over. She was weak.

"I need to check her eyes. May I come forward?" Gus asked.

"Okay, come slowly," Siphiwe cautioned.

Gus examined the pupils of Ellie's eyes and noticed they were unresponsive pin-pricks.

Miranda faced him. "What do you think?"

Deep in concentration, he pinched the top of his nose between thumb and forefinger while closing his eyes. After a while, he opened them and said, "The pupils of her eyes don't dilate in shade. To me, it's starting to look like organophosphate poisoning."

Gus asked Siphiwe if he might listen to her respiration and heart. The trainer soothed the elephant with gentle caresses while making wooing noises, a language that only he and Ellie understood. Then he nodded and crooked his finger towards Gus who inched his way forward and listened to the side of her chest with his stethoscope. Considering her level of agitation, her heart rate was surprisingly slow; he thought it odd.

Afterwards, he stood back and surveyed the wider scene, taking the current environment into consideration.

Dan, the circus owner, mopped perspiration from his anxious brow. "To me, she's looking worse than when I phoned you. I don't like the look of things. She mustn't die-- it'll cause such trouble for all of us. Come on, Gus, what do you think?"

"I suspect poisoning."

Dan shook his head. "No, that's not possible. Only Siphiwe accesses her. Nobody here would poison her; we admire her. She's the jewel in our crown that draws in the crowds."

"Show me what and where you feed her."

Siphiwe pointed to a large plastic trough. "Her food goes in there."

Gus peered into the trough and rummaged around in the uneaten food. "There's plenty of sand in here. Is there normally sand in her feed bin?"

"No," Siphiwe answered. "She picked it up and put it there since she became ill. She doesn't usually do that--it's odd behaviour."

"Show me her dung."

Siphiwe pointed to a few small mounds. "There."

After Gus had examined them, he said, "It looks a bit loose. I see she's been eating sand. It's in her dung. That might cause colic."

"But why is she shaking and salivating?" Dan asked.

"Organophosphate poisoning causes those symptoms."

"She only eats what we feed her."

"Is your food stored in a safe, clean place?"

"Yes, we have a special trailer for it," Dan answered.

"She must have eaten something else," Gus insisted.

Dan sighed and asked Siphiwe before turning back to Gus. "He says the only other food she's had is that lush, green grass over there." He pointed to a spot directly behind the industrial warehouse.

"Ah," Gus said. "I know that warehouse. I've been there a few times. They store chemicals in that shed against the fence. It's quite possible a damaged drum has leaked. After our recent rain, the leakage could easily have trickled down that slope and into that grass."

Dan clutched his head. "Urgh! Poisoning? If she dies--, there'll be a media frenzy. The consequences would damage us all. We'd all be out of work." His eyes pleaded with Gus. "Can you save her?"

"There are no guarantees with medicine, but I'll try."

"Money is no issue--spare no expense--just get her right."

"Okay," Gus said. "I have some medication that I can administer, but I need her weight."

It turned out Dan had Ellie's weight written down. Gus took the figure and made some calculations on a piece of paper before drawing up a series of injections.

Miranda watched as he drew up numerous 20 ml syringes asking her to hold them.

"Usually, one syringe is enough for a cow, but Ellie's weight compares with several."

The tricky part came next as she watched him and Siphiwe try to soothe angry, sick Ellie as he administered several injections through her thick hide and into the vein in her ear. Miranda's fingers trembled as she watched Ellie's irritation escalate with each uncomfortable shot. Gus danced and dodged, avoiding her trunk, as he homed in to get the job done and then shot back out of reach. Her ears flapped while she shook her head. Gus jumped back and stopped. Siphiwe moved away and spoke soothing words from a safer distance. He lit up a strange smelling pipe, and she began to calm.

"She must get these other three shots," Gus said. "She's flapping her ears too much. I'll have to give them intramuscularly."

Siphiwe manipulated Ellie to stand sideways before allowing Gus to come forward and finish his task.

Afterwards, Gus turned to Dan. "For now, that's all I can do. If I'm right, she'll improve. It takes time for the injections to work."

"Thanks, I really appreciate your help."

"Make sure she doesn't eat any more of that green grass behind the warehouse. I'll return later at nine-thirty tonight to check on her."

"Okay," Dan said. "See you later."

***

Gus and Miranda went home. Later that night, they returned as promised.

"How's Ellie?" Gus asked Dan.

He smiled as they walked towards Ellie's trailer. "There's been a definite improvement."

Siphiwe grinned and saluted Gus. "Good medicine."

"Where is she now?" Gus asked.

"Inside her trailer," Dan said.

"Look, mate--Dan, she might need another shot."

The whites of Siphiwe's eyes glinted fearfully in the dim light. "No, she's gone to bed now. It's best not to disturb her."

"I must make sure she's okay. I don't want her to have a relapse during the night," Gus reasoned.

Siphiwe looked agitated. "Okay, come." He stood by the opening to Ellie's trailer and whistled. She came forward chewing a mouthful of dry grass. Her eyes glinted in the night light. Slowly, Gus moved forward. She shot her trunk out, throwing Gus backwards into the dirt.

Miranda gasped, flinging both hands to her mouth. Then she ran forward to help him. "Are you okay?"

He doubled over in pain as he struggled to straighten. "Yeah. She winded me."

Dan pushed his hand back through his hair. "Elephants get aggressive at night. After the evening show, we always lock them up until daylight. Wild behaviour at night seems to be a primal thing."

Gus clutched his stomach and inhaled. "Well, if you're worried, give me a call, and I'll come."

"Thanks. But she's looking good and is eating again."

***

The next morning Dan phoned to say, "Thanks to you, Gus, Ellie's fully recovered. You honestly saved our world."

"Glad to be of service."

"Would you and Miranda like free tickets for our final show in town tonight? I'll settle your bill when you arrive."

After Gus had hung up, he yelled to Miranda, "Put on your glad rags! Tonight, we see the circus."

CHAPTER THIRTY-NINE

Priorities

As Miranda entered and approached the Veterinary reception desk, she saw Gretchen sitting down with her giant, handwritten cash book spread open. Gus stood behind, peering down at the neatly-written entries. Light streaming in through the window touched Gretchen's diamond engagement ring causing it to sparkle.

Miranda commented, "It's a beautiful ring--look how it shines."

Gretchen peered over the top of her spectacles, smiling. "Yes, it's gorgeous. Your father spoilt me; he's generous." Gretchen glanced at Miranda's left hand and observed no ring. She clucked her tongue and said, "Gus, when will you buy Miranda an engagement ring? You mustn't keep the poor girl waiting."

"Yeah, I know. That's why I'm checking the books. I want to know if I can draw money."

Gretchen sighed. "We have a horde of slow payers; they're causing a cash flow problem. And what's more, I've noticed our bad debtor list is growing weekly."

"Tell me," Miranda asked. "Did Mrs Jones ever pay for Taxi's surgery?"

"No. I've tried phoning numerous times, but the number's wrong. All the accounts I sent her got returned with *address unknown* stamped across them."

Gus said, "I suppose we'll just have to write it off to charity."

Gretchen wagged her finger. "Watch out. If too many people hear about that sort of thing, you'll be inundated with more non-payers."

Gus shrugged. "It can't be helped. It seems the bad debt collectors cost more than their worth. It's cheaper to write the debt off."

"My biggest challenge every month," Gretchen said, "is to set aside enough money to pay our drug suppliers' accounts. They all give 20% discount providing their accounts are paid within 30 days."

"Yeah, I know."

"But," Gretchen said, "Your markup on drugs is only 30%. With so many slow payments and bad debts, sometimes I can't pay the drug companies on time--and that's dangerous. You can't afford to lose those discounts."

Gus ran his hands through his hair. "I'm a bloody vet, not an accountant. Gosh, I hate books."

Gretchen smiled. "That's why you got me. This month you don't need to worry. Mr Cheeseman paid early, and so did the circus, so I was able to pay the accounts on time."

"Thank goodness."

"Those early payments were a lifesaver. This month, you'll be paid on time, and there's some extra cash you can draw for Miranda's ring."

"Ah, so that's why I've waited so long." Miranda poked Gus's ribs.

"Yeah, sorry, mate. You deserve to be put first, but..."

"But what?" Miranda tried sounding casual as she wondered what held him back.

He shuffled his feet. "It's just that I hoped to buy a respirator machine for future snakebites. A guy who deals with old hospital equipment phoned to say he has one. He reckons the old ones are hard to source, so he wants to know if I'm willing to purchase it or not."

"Yes! Get it," Miranda exclaimed. "What are you waiting for?"

"Yeah, but," he scratched his head thoughtfully.

"What?"

"It costs the same as your engagement ring, and I can't afford both this month."

Miranda rolled her eyes. "My ring can wait. Get off your butt and phone him quick! Tell him we want that machine today."

"Are you sure?"

She smiled. "Yes. I couldn't bear to wear a ring instead of saving a few more dogs' lives. Good things materialise in good time."

"Okay, Gretchen. Phone him and tell him to deliver the respirator as soon as possible."

"Sure."

***

That afternoon, the respirator machine was delivered. Gretchen wrote out the cheque while Gus and Miranda tested it.

"Impressive," Gus said. "Now I can't wait to get our next snakebite victim to try it out."

***

A retired police dog arrived next, not a snakebite victim.

"What have we here?" Gus asked as the police officer lifted the huge, black and tan German Shepard onto the consulting table.

Officer Mitchell removed his cap and stepped aside. "He was in the process of being trained as a working dog, but he must be put down."

Gus's brows arched. "What a pity. He's a beaut of a dog. Can't they re-home him?"

"No, he's too vicious. Instructions are to put him to sleep."

"Okay." Gus turned to unlock his scheduled drugs cupboard. As he drew up sufficient euthanasia and prepared for an intravenous injection, he thought, *I hate this part of my job, but I suppose somebody must do it.* He turned to face the dog. "Officer Mitchell, please hold him while I administer the injection."

Mitchell held the dog's head.

Gus approached and took the dog's right forearm. The dog growled. Gus glanced up. "You got him?"

"Yes, sir."

Gus bent down, looking closer as he felt for the dog's vein. *Found it.* He took a deep breath and proceeded with calm, deft precision. As the needle pricked the dog's skin a vicious noise exploded, ripping the airwaves apart. A quick series of frenzied bites ensued, landing squarely on Gus's scalp. He jerked away as Mitchell checked the dog and brought it back under control. Warm, sticky fluid rushed down the sides of Gus's face.

Mitchell's look of horror said it all.

"Hold him tight," Gus said in a tense voice. "Here, use this to tie his mouth." Gus tossed Mitchell a crepe bandage. "Next time, please muzzle your dog."

Mitchell secured the dog's mouth. Gus homed in again, pushing the lethal shot in as fast as the fluid could go without rupturing out. The dog collapsed onto its side in a final slump as its body relaxed into eternal sleep with glazed eyes, oblivious to the damage it left behind.

Blood trickled into Gus's eyes, blurring his vision, as he listened to the dog's heart with his stethoscope. He stepped away. "Job done."

Mitchell apologised as he removed the dog's collar and lead.

Having heard the noise from outside, Miranda rushed in through the door and shrieked. "Oh my God! What happened?" she pushed a chair forward. "Quick, sit down."

"I was bitten."

With shaking hands, she pushed his dangling piece of scalp back over his skull and worked fast as she wound two crepe bandages over his head, applying pressure, to staunch the blood loss.

Speechless, Gretchen's hands clutched the sides of her face as she gawked in horror.

Miranda surveyed Gus's pale face and trembling body with mounting anxiety. "How're you feeling?"

"Shocked--a bit shaky."

"Take a few deep breaths and hold them. Oxygenate yourself."

He did as was told.

"Better?"

He nodded weakly.

"Are you feeling strong enough to walk to the car?"

"Sure."

"Come. I'm taking you to the hospital."

Gretchen held the door open as Miranda led Gus out towards the car.

CHAPTER FORTY

Medical Machines

A couple of hours later, Gus returned to his clinic sporting twenty-seven stitches to his scalp and a packet of oral antibiotics in his hand.

"How are you feeling?" Gretchen asked after he drank the tea she made.

"Much better, thank you."

"I took the liberty of postponing some routine farm calls until next week. Is that okay?"

"Yes, thanks."

"But there's still two cats that came in for castrations--are you feeling up to doing surgery?"

"Yeah. I'll manage. Thanks for the tea. I'll get started."

Gus finished his surgery and then sat down to chicken sandwiches that Miranda had made for his belated lunch. Halfway through, a car careened into the driveway and screeched to a halt outside the clinic door. A man rushed in carrying a brindled Staffordshire terrier crossbreed dog.

"Doctor, Jerry's been bitten by a cobra!"

"Put him up here." Gus indicated the consulting table. "Are you sure it was a cobra?"

"Yes! A massive thing. I saw the whole attack. Jerry killed it."

"Did you bring the snake with you?"

"No. I know a cobra when I see one--there was no time to fiddle around."

As they spoke, copious salivation drooled from Jerry's mouth and onto the table.

"Miranda!" Gus called. "Quick, draw up some antivenom."

"Okay." She drew it up into a syringe while Gus set up an intravenous line into Jerry's front leg. The dog shivered before retching onto the table. Gus grabbed a bundle of paper roller towel to stop it from trickling off the table and splashing onto the floor where he stood.

Miranda handed Gus the antivenom and cleared the mess away.

Gus injected the fluid into the line. Jerry collapsed on his side, releasing his bowels and bladder in several squirts as involuntary muscle contractions wracked his body.

"Miranda," Gus called while he began intubating the dog. "Get the respirator. Jerry's not breathing."

Shocked, the client stepped back, clutching his head. "I hope it's not too late. Can you save him?"

"We'll try our best."

Gretchen entered. "Sir, come with me. Let's leave Gus to work on your dog."

"Brett Jackson's the name."

"Thanks, Brett. I'll write your details down and then you can go home. It'll take a long time before we know if Jerry's going to make it or not. Gus will phone as soon as he knows whether Jerry's going to survive or not."

After Mr Jackson left, Gus administered several more doses of antivenom. Jerry remained paralysed while the respirator breathed for him.

"That's all I can do," Gus said as he stepped back. "I'll put him down on a soft blanket on the floor and leave him attached to the machine. From here on it's a waiting game. We'll just turn him every two hours to avoid pressure sores."

****

The following morning during the early hours, Gus awoke to hear Jerry stirring and coughing. Gus disconnected the machine and removed the endotracheal tube. Although weak, Jerry wagged his tail slightly, staggered to his feet and then flopped back down.

Gus rubbed his head. "There's a boy. How y' doin' old fella?"

Jerry nuzzled his hand and rolled onto his back.

Gus rubbed Jerry's belly gently, marvelling at his wonderful recovery.

By the time Brett Jackson came in to collect Jerry, the dog could stand and follow his master. Jerry wagged his tail fast and furiously as Brett fondled his head and praised him.

"He's still a bit weak," Gus said, "but I reckon he'll be feeling much better in a week or two."

"Thank you, Doctor!"

Gus smiled.

After Brett left, Gus turned to Miranda. "That machine has already saved one life. I'm glad we bought it."

"Yeah," she laughed. "And it saved us hours of manual respiration."

"It's a real boon--a worthwhile investment for this clinic's future snakebite victims."

"It's the difference between life and death."

CHAPTER FORTY-ONE

Lucky

Twelve days after Gus was bitten Miranda said, "Sit here under the light so I can see to remove your stitches."

Gus obeyed. "How do they look?"

"Pretty good. The doctor did a great job, but you'll have scars forever."

"My hair will grow back and hide them."

Miranda laughed. "Yeah, for a few years. They'll resurface when you go bald."

He shrugged. "It'll be a roadmap of a life well-travelled amidst occupational hazards."

She shivered. "Sorry to say this, but I'm glad it wasn't my head."

"Me too. Yours is too pretty."

"Sit still," Miranda said. "Only one more stitch, but it's in deep. The skin's grown over it."

"Ouch!" Gus yelped as she dug down and yanked it out.

She slapped his shoulder. "Shut-up! You're making more fuss now than when the dog bit you."

"I was hoping for a bit of sympathy, mate."

"You'll get plenty later tonight."

Gretchen's voice came from her desk. "I heard that! You lovebirds."

Miranda blushed.

"Here," Gretchen said with a smile as she handed an official looking letter to Gus.

Gus tore it open.

"Who's it from?" Miranda asked.

"The Australian embassy."

"What do they say?"

"Officially, your paper work is in order. We're all set to get married. You may now relocate to Australia."

She hugged him. "Fantastic!"

"Yeah." His eyes twinkled as he stood and reached for a tin inside his scheduled drugs cupboard. "Miranda, please sit down." His eyes indicated the wooden chair he had just vacated.

She did his bidding.

"Close your eyes," he said. "On the count of three, open them."

"Okay."

"One, two, three!"

She opened her eyes to see him kneeling in front of her chair, holding a small, brightly wrapped box with a miniature gold bow adornment. A delighted gasp escaped her lips for she already knew what it contained.

"How long have you been hiding this from me?"

He grinned. "I was waiting for the paperwork to be passed. It's good enough reason to celebrate, is it not?"

"For sure!" She opened the ring box carefully and smiled as her eyes fell on the simple, modest diamond solitaire setting. "It's beautiful, thank you."

"Try it on. Does it fit?"

"Yes--it's perfect. How did you know my size?"

"I borrowed one of your silver rings for the right sizing."

"Thank you! I love it."

Gretchen rushed in. "Let me see!"

Miranda displayed her left hand with pride.

"It's lovely. Congratulations, you two."

"Thanks."

"Don't cook tonight," Gus said. "I've booked a table at the Magoebaskloof Hotel for our celebratory dinner."

***

The following morning, Miranda wore her new engagement ring with a sense of pride and importance, as they set off to visit Jack Brown's horse that was reported to have sore ears.

Jack met them on arrival in his driveway.

"Hi! Pleased to meet you, Jack. My name's Gus, and this is my assistant and fiancée, Miranda."

Jack inclined his head. "Thanks for coming. I got this horse yesterday from an insolvency estate. They were going to shoot it, but I said I'd take it and see what I could do."

"Sore ears?" Gus said.

"Yeah. I don't know what's wrong with them--I can't see because he won't let me near his head."

"Okay. Well, lead the way, and we'll see what we can do."

Jack showed them to a cattle yard with a small fenced in enclosure. The horse stood resting under the shade of a tree, looking malnourished and dejected despite the hay on the ground and nearby water bucket.

A fetid stench assailed their nostrils as they approached the horse.

Miranda coughed and choked. "Phew! He smells terrible. I know that stench--people with septic wounds smell similar."

"Crikey!" Gus exclaimed, walked closer, surveying the horse's suppurating ears. A mixture of dark, thick blood and yellow pus oozed out its ears, trickling down the sides of its head. "I know that smell too--it's flystrike."

"What's flystrike?" Jack asked.

"Wounds usually start off with tick bites that cause bleeding. Blood attracts flies. Blowflies approach and lay eggs. Blowflies like to lay eggs in dark, damp places like under sheep tails or in open wounds. The eggs hatch in about 72 hours that turn into flesh eating maggots. Biting flies join in the orgy, and the cycle continues as more and more good flesh is eroded. Eventually, if untreated, the animal dies."

Miranda winced. "Oh, poor, old horse. That's why I dip mine once a week and put tick-grease in his ears. I've heard about this problem but have never seen it before."

"It's not pretty," Gus said. "Put a clothes peg on your nose and hold tight, girl."

"Jack, bring him here."

A head-collar was already in place, so Jack walked up to it and took hold of it under the horse's throat. He patted the horse's shoulder as he led it towards Gus.

Gus stood to the side, avoiding the horse from potentially hitting him in the face if it should rear up. He peered into the horse's ear with his otoscope, viewing a multitude of seething white maggots eating away at the petrified flesh. The horse rolled its eyes, reared up and backed away.

"Miranda put a twitch on his nose and hold tight. Stand to the side of his head, so he doesn't knock your teeth out if he decides to go up."

"Can't you give him a tranquillizer?"

"I will, but Acepromazine, ACP, doesn't work that well. He's still going to dance around. I'll work as fast as I can--that's the best I can do."

Gus administered ACP into the horse's jugular and waited for it to take effect before starting. As soon as the steel curette entered the horse's ear, scraping out the first scoop of maggots, the horse rolled its eyes until the whites showed, scuffled with its hooves and tried to rear.

"Hold tight!" Gus commanded. "Don't mess around. If he flicks his head, he'll knock me out."

"Okay, okay," Miranda answered. "I'm doing my best."

"Use both hands. Don't let go--no matter what. It's him or me."

"Okay. Ready when you are."

Gus dug in again as Miranda's forearms bulged and strained to keep the twitch tight. Exhausted and weak, the horse finally stood still, allowing Gus to finish his grisly task. Miranda made soothing noises as she hung on.

Scoopfuls of moist, bloodied maggots plopped to the hot, dry sand where they squirmed, fighting against sun exposure, as they writhed in the throes of death in a slimy mass. The scorching heat seared them to a slow sizzling death.

Gus worked efficiently. After clearing out the ear canals on both sides, he swabbed the ears out with iodine, followed by Flamazine. Then he sprayed an oil-based fly repellent onto and around the horse's head. The horse fidgeted and pranced around until finally, Miranda said, "I can't hold him anymore."

"Okay. Take the twitch off."

She released the leather loop from the horse's nose and rubbed it gently to help get blood recirculating. Her diamond glinted in the sun; suddenly, it wasn't new anymore. Oblivious to her thoughts, the horse stretched his top lip, displaying long, sloping, brown-stained teeth.

Jack offered him a handful of horse-nuts which he devoured as Gus administered a long acting antibiotic injection.

Afterwards, Jack asked, "Do you think he'll be okay?"

Gus smiled. "Yeah. I reckon you called me out in the nick of time. If you had left it any longer, the horse would have died of septicaemia or meningitis. It's hard to know how much of his hearing will recover, only time will tell."

Jack stroked the horse's neck. "They wanted to shoot him. I just had to bring him home and give him a chance. Apparently, he was a good riding horse."

Gus looked down at the horse's legs. "He's got tick bites there too. You best dip him today. You don't need flystrike starting behind his fetlocks too. With damage like that to his legs, he'll only be good for riding around on the farm."

Jack nodded. "That's all I'll use him for. Casual riding. I will dip him starting today, and I'll see that he gets dipped once a week from now on."

Gus patted the horse's neck. "It looks like the old fellow has finally found a good home. What will you name him?"

"Lucky."

<u>CHAPTER FORTY-TWO</u>

Playing Chicken

Miranda woke up to see the early morning sunshine streaming in through her bedroom window. She drew the curtains back and smiled. "Another hot day ahead. Last night I had nightmares about those maggots." She shivered and gritted her teeth. "Urgh!"

Gus laughed.

"I'll go and dip Ruby after breakfast before it gets too hot."

"Good idea," Gus replied.

Miranda ambled down to Ruby's stable and mixed the correct dip measurement in a ten-litre bucket of water. Next, she got a hosepipe and sprayed Ruby all over to get his coat wet so that the dip wouldn't run off. Then she used a scraper to scrape excess water off. Ruby nodded his head and swished his tail as she sponged the cold, wet dip along his back, down each leg, between his legs and then on top of his head. The horse held his neck up high, stretching his top lip out as she sponged near his ears. That was the part he hated most--getting his ears wet. Over the years he had learnt to tolerate his weekly treatment and looked forward to his reward--a big, fat, juicy carrot. Miranda untied his head collar and set him free. He snorted, gathered himself up and took off at great speed with a buck and a fart as he galloped far out into the field. She chuckled as she watched his predictable antics that he did every week. It gave her a sense of pride to watch her happy and healthy horse release his pent-up energy in such a comical, explosive way.

As she strolled back to Gus's consulting room, she knew something was up. Miranda heard guffaws of laughter and excited chatter coming from behind a closed door. Gretchen spoke on the phone to a customer while her anxious eyes darted to and from the closed door.

Miranda, keen to see what all the fracas was about, opened Gus's door for a peep.

Three men's voices, one of them Gus's broke out in a joint chorus, "AH, NO!"

She saw two large, hairy men dodging and dancing on their tiptoes as Gus jumped up onto a chair, almost causing it to topple.

"What's going on?"

"CLOSE THE DOOR!" They yelled. "Don't let the *crocodile* escape!"

She gasped as a young croc flashed straight in front of her, heading towards the dancing men's feet, who were trying to avoid its gaping jaws.

She snapped the door shut, grateful to be on the safe side of it but feared for Gus's safety.

Gretchen hung-up. "There's a crocodile in there!" She pointed over her shoulder with her thumb.

"Yeah, I just saw it."

Gretchen laughed. "I hope they'll be okay--they've been having trouble catching it to treat its injured tail that another croc bit. Gus reckons if left untreated it could be prone to infection."

"Oh, so that's what it's all about."

"Yes. Now, that was Mr Weber on the phone. He wants his Arabian horses vaccinated and dewormed this afternoon."

"Sure. I'll tell Gus when he's finished."

Fifteen minutes later, Gus opened his door allowing the two men to carry the crocodile back to their truck.

"I'm pleased to see you still have all your fingers intact," Miranda said.

"So am I!"

"Who on earth keeps crocodiles around here?" Miranda asked.

"Crocodile farmers. They're new to our area."

"Ah, that explains it."

"They were telling me," Gus said. "They had a large crocodile farm on the south coast they used to open to tourists."

"So, what made them move up north to Tzaneen?"

"They decided to move after all their crocs died."

Miranda scowled. "*Died*? From what?"

"Oh, something like chickenpox."

"You're joking? Surely, crocodiles have eaten the odd chickenpox-infected human in the past?"

"I'm sure too, but who is to say whether they lived or died afterwards?"

"But surely some would have survived?"

"He reckons they all got a pox disease. Some died while others stayed ill for months. Tourists only wish to see healthy animals, not sick ones. So, he had them put down. Now he's moved here to start over."

"I hope they don't get ill here too."

"Since then, researchers have found that they can produce a basic vaccine by grinding up the pox sores and injecting small amounts under the skin of young, healthy crocodiles."

"Good. It seems crazy--vaccinating crocodiles."

"When animals are kept in captivity in large numbers together, diseases can become an issue. Just think of children going to school, and one of them gets a cold. It doesn't take long to pass it on to the others sitting next to them."

"True. So, do you think your croc patient will live?"

"Yes, and hopefully I won't see him again."

Miranda chuckled. "Agreed. Now pack your bags. Mr Weber wants you to vaccinate and deworm his Arabian horses."

"Good. I'm tired of playing chicken."

CHAPTER FORTY-THREE

Linebreeding

Arabian horses, glowing with good health, grazed in knee-deep lush, irrigated paddocks to the left and right of Weber's driveway on the way to his sprawling mansion. Well-manicured lawns graced the entrance, offset with an array of exotic shrubs bursting forth in a profusion of colours from his remarkable garden. To the side was a massive, sparkling, blue swimming pool, and behind that, a new tennis court.

"Wow!" Miranda exclaimed, eyeing the pedigree horse flesh over her shoulder and noting the smart white pole and rail fences lining the paddocks. "This guy's stacked with money."

Gus beamed. "Either that, or he's enjoying a massive overdraft facility."

"I've heard some Arabian horses sell for thousands."

"Yeah, but I'm not sure how many riders can afford to pay. In my opinion, a hobby-farm like this, stuck out in the middle of nowhere, caters more towards a personal pleasure."

"Surely, he made his money elsewhere."

Gus nodded. "Possibly a retired businessman."

Later, after introductions were made, it turned out Mr Weber was retired since selling his business in Germany. His move to Africa worked favourably to his advantage due to the foreign exchange rate. His days were now spent pursuing his lifelong passion--breeding horses.

His horses were well-behaved and easy to treat, except the last one. A feisty young, dapple-grey Arabian colt trotted freely inside the circular lunge arena. Elevating his elegantly dished head high, he arched his neck into a beautiful curve and snorted at their approach. He stopped and turned the other way, trotting off with his beautiful, long tail streaming gracefully behind his fat, cheeky, dimpled rump.

Gus said, "He's a beautiful animal, but he's far too fat. He shouldn't have dimples in his rump. Watch out he doesn't get laminitis."

"He's a happy horse." Weber dug his hands into his pockets. "What's laminitis?"

"It's inflammation of the tissue inside a horse's hoof that affects the coffin bone. Basically, the sensitive laminae bonds to the pedal bone. There's no cure. Once a horse goes lame, it becomes an irreversible condition."

Not fully understanding, Weber shook his head, scowling. "What causes it?"

"Too much rich food; particularly green grass and grain. Fat Arabian horses are prone to laminitis. Remember, the original breed stems from hardy desert horses. They're smaller than Thoroughbreds and inclined to put on condition faster and maintain it longer."

"I've never heard of *laminitis* before."

"Trust me; you don't want to see or hear of it--not in your horses. It's time to reduce their feed. Start by feeding more hay than green grass and reduce their grain."

Weber pursed his lips.

Gus smiled. "I know. In the horsey world *fat* is a beautiful colour, but it causes other problems. Laminitis being the worst."

"Okay, if you say so. I've invested heaps of money in them. I don't want anything going wrong."

Gus beamed, thinking, *it's easier when people co-operate.*

Weber caught the young colt, leading it to Gus for its vaccination and deworming. It fidgeted with its neck as Gus injected it, ending up with two pricks instead of one. Then it reared up onto its hind legs several times as Gus administered the de-wormer.

Miranda stepped back, fearfully, holding her breath as she watched the colt's hooves flailing inches away from Gus's head. A wave of relief washed over when the treatment was done.

Weber opened the lunge arena gate to set the colt free. They all watched the youngster take off at great speed and gallop to the far end of the paddock where he stood leaning over the pole and rail fence, stretching his neck into a maize patch. He munched the tall, tasty maize stalks with wicked relish.

Gus clicked his tongue. "He mustn't eat that maize; he's fat enough. A good dose of lush corn is all it takes to trigger the onset of laminitis."

Weber yelled instructions to a stable-hand, telling him to catch the colt and put it in another paddock. As the worker ran towards the colt waving his arms, the colt leaned over the fence, taking a final mouthful of the forbidden fruit. A huge corn plant dislodged from the damp soil, coming up by the roots. The young colt, frightened by the giant, languorous foliage hanging from its mouth, clenched his jaw right down on it and galloped off.

Everyone laughed as they enjoyed the ridiculous spectacle of the frightened colt galloping around with the huge corn stalk hanging from its naughty mouth as he tried to get away from it.

Miranda clutched her sides in mirth. "The silly fool only has to open his mouth and let it drop. But he's too greedy!" She continued to chuckle. "He's poop scared--being chased by a corn stalk that he's hanging on to!"

"Fright and flight," Gus said. "All reaction and no thought. Typical young horse."

The horse continued to career around the paddock until its flanks dripped with sweat, but still, it continued to gallop, frightened by the bedraggled corn stalk protruding from its mouth that it refused to relinquish.

Gus bit his lip. "I've never seen anything like this before."

"Do you think he'll ever stop?" Weber asked.

"Hopefully, he'll soon tire."

Five minutes later, the sweating colt stepped on the end of the maize stalk, accidentally pulling it from its mouth. Surprised and relieved, he slowed down and came to a heaving halt.

"Thank goodness!" Weber exclaimed.

Miranda picked up the colt's vaccination card and read its breeding lineage. "Hey, there's something wrong here."

"What?" Weber asked.

"I'm sure this is a mistake," Miranda replied, holding up the card. "It states here this colt has the same father as his grandfather."

"It's called *line breeding*," Weber said.

Gus frowned and paused before delivering a thoughtful reply, "Well, you know what they say about such matters, don't you?"

Weber shook his head.

"There's a fine line between *line breeding* and *inbreeding*."

"What are you saying?" Weber asked.

Gus drew in a deep breath and continued, "*Line breeding* and *inbreeding* are the same thing. The difference being, if it works, it's called *line breeding*. If it doesn't work, it's called *inbreeding*."

"Are you saying my horse is inbred?"

"His parentage is too close. You're lucky he wasn't born deformed. It's not something I'd recommend."

Weber compressed his lips while folding his arms.

"And," Gus said, "his intelligence appears questionable. You know, that sort of thing doesn't make for safe riding."

<u>CHAPTER FOURTY-FOUR</u>

Phila

As Gus and Miranda headed back to their car Mr Weber followed, still discussing the pros and cons of so-called line breeding. A dog rushed past carrying a dry bone in its mouth on its way to lie in a shady spot.

"Oh, look at that!" Miranda said pointing towards the dog.

Gus's eyes followed her direction. "What?"

"There's something wrong with his penis."

Mr Weber shuffled his feet, looking uncomfortable as he tried to dismiss the matter with a casual wave from his hand. Miranda's curiosity was not to be fobbed off. "Gus, please look at it. It's all swollen and red."

Gus approached the thin, yellow-eyed dog and after a quick glance said, "That looks like a CTV tumour."

"What's that?" Weber asked.

"It stands for *canine transmissible venereal tumour*. It's a common venereal disease in dogs. Basically, it's a contagious tumour, a form of cancer, that's transmitted through coitus."

"*Coitus*?" Weber didn't understand.

Miranda piped up, "You know--bonking."

He shook his head, still at a loss.

She smiled. "Breeding. It's spread through breeding--sexual contact."

"Oh." Weber's mouth rounded as understanding dawned. "What can I do? It's the stable hand's dog and he can't afford any treatment."

"To be honest," Gus said, "the poor dog should be put down. There's no cure for the disease."

Weber called to the stable hand who came running at great speed, smiling. "Yes, sir?"

Weber said, "Your dog's sick. The doctor says its sickness can be spread to other dogs, so your dog must be put down."

The stable hand shook his head. "Put down? I don't understand."

"It must die," Weber supplied.

A sad look came over the eager young man's face as he shook his head. "No, sir. He's a good dog. I can't kill him because he is sick."

Weber put his hands in his pockets and turned to Gus. "He won't agree to euthanise the dog. What can we do?"

Gus scratched his head. "The main thing is to stop that dog from spreading it to other dogs. I'd recommend you bring him in for castration. While he's on the table and under anaesthetic, I'll surgically remove the tumour as best as I can. Over time it'll grow back. But at least it'll stop him spreading the disease, and he might get a year or two more to live."

Weber explained the situation to his stable hand who now appeared hopeful. Then he said to Gus, "He agrees to castration and surgery, but he can't afford it."

Gus smiled as he shook the labourer's hand. "What's your dog's name?"

"Phila--it means healthy."

Gus maintained a straight face as he turned to Weber. "Okay. I'll do the surgery at a special low price, so that you, Mr Weber, can afford to foot that bill."

"*Me*?"

Gus laughed. "You're selling expensive horses here. You can't have customers put off by the appearance of a sick dog running around."

Weber pursed his lips. "Okay. You win. I'll bring him in tomorrow morning."

"Okay. Make sure he has no food or water after ten o'clock tonight."

***

The following day, Mr Weber brought his farm hand's dog in for surgery and asked if he could stay and watch Gus operate.

"No. I'm sorry, I don't allow people to watch when I do surgery. Please wait outside or come back later."

Weber's mouth downturned with disappointed as he left.

Miranda felt awkward. Afterwards, she turned to Gus and asked, "Why won't you let him stay and watch?"

"When I operate, I have to be the surgeon and the anaesthetist. It's a big responsibility to do both. My patient is my priority; not making small talk with emotional or interfering clients."

"I don't think he'd be emotional," Miranda countered.

"Perhaps not. But I once made the mistake of allowing a woman to watch surgery on her cat. She fainted while I was operating and fell backwards. She smacked her head on the floor with a sickening thud."

"Ah! What did you do?"

"Nothing. I had already scrubbed up and was halfway through the operation. Fortunately, she didn't hit her head on the corner of the trolley when she went down."

"So, you just left her there on the floor?"

"Yes. My job was to look after her cat and keep it alive when its gut was open--not to pander to a stubborn client who refused to wait outside. I had no choice."

"Was she okay?" Miranda asked.

"Luckily, apart from a bump on her head and a battered ego, she was. But for me it was stressful. Being midway through surgery was no joke. I had to concentrate on my haemorrhaging patient while wondering if she had a serious injury. Worrying when there was nothing I could do. That's why I prefer people to wait outside."

"That's understandable."

Gus spent well over an hour operating on Phila's penis. First, he castrated the dog, working from a clean wound to the dirty. Miranda watched in fascinated silence as he painstakingly cut away at the ugly tumour, cauterising numerous small blood vessels as he went. Finally, victorious, he held up the mass of cancerous flesh with his forceps. It was the size of a medium tomato. Then he threw it into the bin for later incineration.

Miranda shuddered. "Poor dog. I bet he'll feel happy to be rid of that nasty lump."

"Yeah. Let's hope he still gets a few good years to enjoy." As an afterthought, he said, "I wish all casual dog owners would castrate their dogs. I hate seeing animals suffer unnecessarily with such a debilitating disease."

A couple of hours later, Weber arrived with his stable hand in tow. Phila wagged his tail when he heard his master's voice.

Gretchen handed Weber the account.

"I see you vaccinated and dewormed him too."

"Yes, we did. A healthy dog recovers faster. Now, how would you like to pay, Mr Weber?"

"Cash."

Gretchen counted out the notes and smiled. "Thank you. Have a good day." She watched him exit the door and climb into his huge, new truck. The stable hand and Phila sat at the back as he drove off in a dusty cloud.

CHAPTER FORTY-FIVE

Gretchen

An assortment of huge cardboard boxes had just been delivered to the veterinary clinic reception area as Gus walked in. His eyes widened. "Gretchen, what on earth have we got here?"

She smiled. "Birdcages, pet bowls and pet accessories."

He looked appalled. "I never ordered this stuff."

"Well, I did."

Speechless, his eyes questioned her.

She held up her hands. "Stop right there. I know you're thinking we can't afford all this, but a sales rep from *PoshPet* dropped in last week while you were out. Sorry, I forgot to tell you."

"PoshPet? Never heard of it."

"It's a new company that distributes pet products. The guy said that if my first order exceeded a certain amount, he'd give us three months to pay--plus we'd get a massive discount if we pay on time."

Gus pushed his hand back through his hair and blew out his cheeks. "Mate, this is a lot to move. What if we can't sell it?"

"Of course, we'll sell it." She chuckled. "There's no pet shop in town. People want these products. Not everyone wishes to drive all the way to the next town for a birdcage or a new kitten collar or pet bowl."

Gus's expression remained anxious. "Remember, I have a wedding to plan and pay for. This isn't the time to take risks."

"That's exactly why we're going to sell this stuff. We can put a 100% markup on it, and the salesman reckons anything we don't sell can be returned after three months on the provision that it's still in the original packaging."

A slow smile replaced his anxiety. "You certainly got a great deal!"

"Thank you. Leave it to me. I've been breeding lovebirds and budgies at home. People are welcome to come over and choose whatever they wish."

Just then, Miranda came in from outside with Wingnut bouncing along at her heels. "Wow! This looks great. Do you need help putting it out?"

"Yes, please."

"I'll arrange a nice place along the wall to hang the leads and collars."

"Hey," Gretchen said. "Who's going to make your wedding cake?"

Gus and Miranda looked at one another and shrugged. "Don't know yet."

"Well," Gretchen said, "I know this woman who's an excellent baker and cake-icing star. I know she'd love to make it for a reasonable fee."

"Isn't it too early?" Miranda asked.

"No, not for a fruit cake. It needs time to mature."

"Okay. Give me her number, and I'll get in touch. Thanks."

"And, what about your wedding dress?" Gretchen asked.

Miranda shrugged. "I thought of buying one, but they cost too much, so I've put the idea on ice for a while."

"Do you know Marion Jessup?"

Miranda shook her head.

Gretchen laughed. "Yes, you do. Her mother owns the little store next to the petrol station."

"Oh, yeah."

"Well, she's an excellent seamstress. I've seen some of her work. She could sew a dress for you."

Miranda's eyes lit up. "Okay! I'll contact her."

Gretchen beamed. "You won't be disappointed; her work's fantastic."

Gus put his hands in his pockets. "It seems to me that you two ladies have everything sorted, so I'll leave you to it. I've kittens to deworm and vaccinate."

***

A few weeks later, Gretchen proved herself right, by managing to sell 50% of the new pet stock. Her sales were so good that she put in another two orders for replacement stock.

Impressed with her business skills, Gus offered her a small commission on sales. All around, things were running smoothly until the morning old Mrs Courtney-Crouch entered and spouted off her self-righteous mouth.

Gus was talking on his phone extension when he overheard a shrill, angry voice. He cut his conversation short and went to the reception desk to find out what the din was about.

Mrs Courtney-Crouch stood stiff and erect as she pointed an accusing finger in Gretchen's face. Her stiff white, curly hairstyle had the appearance of an impenetrable pubic helmet. Gretchen kept trying to say something, but the old battle-axe's mouth kept working at an alarming rate. Her cold, beady eyes bored holes into Gretchen's face. She over enunciated each word she spat in Gretchen's direction as if she were an imbecile. At a glance, it seemed to Gus that the hardest work Mrs Courtney-Crouch's blue-veined hands had ever done, was to carry the weight of several extravagant gold and diamond rings while her long fingernails jabbed like sharp daggers with every accusation made.

One quick glance towards Gretchen told Gus everything he need know. His precious receptionist's cheeks were flushed, and she was close to tears. "Okay," Gus said in a booming voice. "Enough!"

Mrs Courtney-Crouch drew in a deep breath as her cold eyes summed up Gus's presence. "Good day to you--Doctor." She waited for an acknowledgement.

He smiled pleasantly. "Good day to you too, Mrs Courtney-Crouch. What's the problem?"

Her face suffused with blood as she shook with rage and pointed towards him. "*You* are responsible!"

Momentarily, Gus feared she might die from apoplexy, and felt bewildered. "For what?"

While bursting with indignation, words temporarily failed before she could splutter, "For cruelty to animals!"

Gus's face paled. Although the accusation was absurd, it was not to be taken lightly. "Please explain yourself, madam."

"My name is Mrs Courtney-Crouch to you, young man. My parents were founder members of this community. We come from good genetic stock--not like you Australian criminals..."

"Whoa! Please stop right there, Mrs Courtney-Crouch. Enough insults! What's the problem?"

"*You*, young man, are the problem!"

He shook his head. "Why? What's wrong?"

She seethed with rage as she spoke. "You should be caring for animals--not running a peasant-market! All you care about is *money*!"

Surprised, Gus raised his brows and thought, *not unlike you, who already has more than enough.*

"You're so busy selling all these things..." her hands fluttered, indicating her colourful surroundings. "That you haven't bothered to feed your parrot."

"My *parrot*?" Gus said feeling stunned. "I don't own a parrot."

"Liar! Don't deny it. It's right there behind me in a cage--without food or water! You have the cheek to call yourself a vet. You're so busy selling stuff that you haven't noticed your parrot has *no* food and *no* water. You're a disgrace, that's what you are--a disgrace to your profession."

Wide-eyed, Gretchen bit her lower lip, in silence.

Gus took a deep breath, appearing to stay calm. "Come, Mrs Courtney-Crouch, please show me the parrot that concerns you."

The old woman shook her head scornfully. "Your place is jam-packed to the point where not even you can see your parrot! 'Tis no wonder the poor creature is suffering miserably."

Gus cleared his throat. "Please *show* me this parrot."

"Very well." She walked back to the area where Gretchen had piled the bird cages in a large pyramid display. "There!" she jabbed her finger towards the topmost cage.

Gretchen stifled a guffaw while Gus reached up and lifted the cage down. He took out the *parrot* and held it up, smiling. "This my dear, Mrs Courtney-Crouch, is an *artificial* parrot. It's made from dyed chicken-feathers glued onto polystyrene. It's a cheaply manufactured product that serves as a model for our cages."

Her eyes narrowed, squinting at the colourful, imitation macaw held up for close inspection. Flabbergasted and without comment, the old gladiator sniffed and stuck her snobbish nose in the air. She swivelled on one heel and exited with military precision.

Gus and Gretchen watched as she negotiated her way back to her Mercedes-Benz.

Afterwards, Gretchen shook her head. "Mad as a hatter."

Gus smiled. "You do a great job, Gretchen. Why don't you take the rest of the day off and relax?"

She laughed. "Thank you. After that, I need to."

<u>CHAPTER FORTY-SIX</u>

When Knives Come Out

One stifling hot morning, Miranda overheard Gus speaking into the black Bakelite phone at his desk. "A sick calf, you say?"

Intrigued, she watched Gus's strong arms as he reached for a pen and paper.

"Okay," he said. "Fire away. Yes, I know that road. Yes, that one too. Wait. Whereabout? Hold on; I'm writing it down. Yes, yes, okay. No, I'm not sure of that turn-off. Okay, got it. I'll leave right away."

She tilted her head. "It seems you have a farm call."

"Yeah. A sick calf. Do you want to come along?"

"Sure!"

"Okay. Give me five minutes to pack stuff; then we'll leave. I mustn't be too long because I have someone else bringing in a sheep this afternoon."

True to his word, five minutes later, they were packed and heading off down the mountain into the Lowveld. After driving along for twenty minutes and taking several turns, Gus said, "Hey, Miranda, please read those directions I wrote."

She reached for the paper in the cubbyhole and read, "Turn left at the T-junction." She scowled as she deciphered his scrawl. "Drive three kilometres until you reach the rusty gate. Take the middle road and head past the big thorn tree on your right."

"Okay, that'll do for now. Let me get there."

Miranda grinned. "I don't know how you manage to find these outlandish places. I'd get lost."

"Having you around helps."

When they got to the tree, it was on their left, not their right.

"Do you think this is the right tree referred to in the instructions?"

Gus's brow furrowed. "I'm not sure. Sometimes people on phones get confused between their right and left. It all depends on which way they're facing when they speak."

Miranda chuckled. "It appears so."

Gus turned the way he thought he should go, but the track petered out into a series of cattle footpaths. "No, this isn't right. It must be the other side of that tree." He reversed, turned his car around and headed the other way. He swerved his car, narrowly missing a sluggish, plump, beautifully patterned puff adder as it slithered across the sand track and into a grass clump.

"Nasty!" Miranda exclaimed. "I'm glad we're not stopping here."

"Yeah, for sure," he said. "Where now?"

"Drive past the compound with ten huts and follow the stick and barbed wire fence until you reach a steel gate. Turn left and drive another kilometre."

Gus trundled along the arid track, his car spewing up orange dust clouds behind as they went.

"Whoa! Stop," Miranda yelled, pointing to an old rusty roofed building. "That must be the iron shed where the calf is housed."

Gus pulled up under the shade of a thorn tree. A herdsman appeared, displaying a toothless grin while shaking his head.

"I don't understand his lingo," Gus said. "What's he saying?"

Miranda listened to the herdsman's soft-lipped linguistic explanation. His Sepedi words blended together into a drawn out monologue, that was utterly incomprehensible to Gus. Afterwards, she nodded wisely. "He says, we're too late. The calf's dead."

"Dead?" Gus's hands fell to his sides. "Oh, no. That's not what I expected after travelling all this way."

The herdsman shrugged.

"What now?" Miranda asked. "Should we head home?"

Gus shook his head. "Now we're here; I might as well figure out the cause of its death. It's no good having disease spread."

"That's true." Miranda watched Gus rummage around at the back of his car and heard him curse under his breath.

"What's wrong?"

He sighed. "Well, because I expected to treat a sick calf, I didn't come prepared to find a dead one."

"So, what does that mean now?"

He smirked. "I haven't brought a knife to do a post-mortem examination."

"I'll ask the herdsman if we can borrow his. He's bound to have a knife."

The herdsman rubbed his nose and nodded. Then he delved deep into his trouser pocket and produced a small, rusty penknife.

Gus thanked him, took the knife and tested it on a piece of paper. "Blunt as a banana." Then he picked up a stone and tried sharpening it, but to no avail.

Miranda sighed. "That's no good."

"It'll have to do." Gus considered the pale puddles of reeking diarrhoea the four-month-old calf had left behind and hoped whatever had caused it, wouldn't be contagious to other cattle. Bending down, he hauled the carcass away from the foul mess and commenced his post-mortem with a slash to the hide. The knife bounced back. Gus gritted his teeth and plunged harder, but the knife didn't penetrate.

"Wow, that's really blunt," Miranda said.

He clicked his tongue. "If only it would puncture the skin, then it'll be easier to tear open." He took a deep breath and plunged the knife with all his might into the carcass, managing to make a hole in the pelt. Then he held the blade against the skin as he attempted to rip it open towards the stomach. After several attempts, he stood astride and ripped down with all his might. The force of his strength enabled the blunt penknife to slice through the hide at such an alarming rate that it stabbed, full hilt, into the calf of his leg.

"Shit!" was the only expletive to hail from his lips.

Miranda gasped, clutching her face. "Gus are you okay?" As she watched him jerk the rusty, short blade from his leg.

"Yeah. Let's get this post-mortem over first; then I'll look at it."

Miranda bit her lower lip in silence as she watched Gus's blood trickle in a thick, steady stream down his leg, over his sock and shoe and on into the dirt where he stood.

The herdsman shook his head. "Eesh! Sorry."

Now that the dead calf's stomach was open, Gus pulled out its liver and examined it.

"What do you see?" Miranda asked.

"It's unusually swollen and has these white spots." He pointed to them.

"What does that mean?" she asked.

"To me, it looks like it might have died from E. coli, salmonella or some sort of clostridial disease."

She shook her head. "That's not good. Now its blood is inside your body."

He pursed his lips. "Yeah, I know."

She watched as he took a few blood slides and put them away. He washed the herdsman's knife in disinfectant and handed it back. "Miranda, tell him that he can't eat this meat. It must be burnt."

Miranda conveyed his message. The herdsman nodded.

Gus walked back to his car with Miranda close on his heels.

He pulled out a bottle of hydrogen peroxide and mixed it with sterile saline. Then he handed her a clean 20cc syringe and said, "Squirt this into my wound."

"Are you sure? It'll hurt like hell."

"Yeah. Do it now. The sooner, the better. It'll help kill any tetanus and most other bacteria because it releases oxygen deep into the wound, destroying bacterial cells."

"Okay. Sit down on that rock over there."

Gus sat down and held up his leg.

She filled the syringe to maximum capacity, placed it deep into his wound and squirted the whole lot in hard and fast.

Overcome with shock and pain, Gus gasped. His body went rigid as he froze in a static stance to the rock.

Miranda trembled as she spoke. "Are you okay?"

He didn't answer. Her heart pounded with fear and panic as she watched his screwed-up eyes sink deep into his eye sockets. His face went crimson as large veins stood out on his forehead. Tense, the muscles bulged on his forearms as he held his leg.

"Gus? You're not breathing! Stop it--you're scaring me."

His mouth remained in a compressed, solid white line as she observed peroxide cascade in rivulets of foam in ever increasing hot bubbles as it frothed out of his hardened leg.

"Gus! For God's sake--answer me! What have I done? Please talk!"

His eyelids flicked open just long enough for her to see the whites of his eyes as his eyeballs rolled back. He took a deep, rasping breath and bawled from between gritted teeth, "Get it out!"

"*How*?"

"Use your hands. Squeeze it out--fast!"

Her hands shook as she expressed the peroxide bubbles out from under his skin. It crackled and popped like plastic and felt like surgical emphysema. His leg was in a rock-hard cramp as she worked.

"Get it out faster!"

Panicked, she dithered. "It's deep inside. I can't get it all out."

"Irrigate it with sterile saline."

"Okay." She did as he asked and watched him nearly pass out with each squirt. "Gus--please breathe! I don't need you fainting--not now."

He took a deep, rasping breath as if he'd been under the sea for two minutes and was only just emerging.

She rinsed and expressed the wound until the foam stopped. "Right, that's the best I can do."

Gus visibly relaxed, but only slightly. "Thanks. Excuse me. I must go piss."

She watched him hobble off behind a tree and heard him relieve himself.

He returned while zipping up his fly. "Let's get home. I must start some oral antibiotics and be on time to see that sheep."

Concern filled her eyes. "Would you like me to drive?"

"Nah, mate. I'll be okay. I've had enough stress for one day."

<u>CHAPTER FORTY-SEVEN</u>

Intruder

As soon as they returned home, Miranda placed a hot poultice and bandage on Gus's wound and ensured he began his oral antibiotics.

"Are your anti-tetanus shots up to date?" she asked.

"Yes, stop fussing! Remember when I cut my thumb and met you at the hospital? I had a booster back then."

"Oh, yeah. It's just as well."

After a quick bite to eat, they heard car tyres scrunch to a halt outside the clinic. Miranda glanced out the window and saw a bleating sheep on its back seat. They went out to greet their client.

"Good afternoon, Mr Unwin," Gus said. "How are you?"

"Things could've been better," he said, huffing and puffing. "But I managed to get here on time."

Gus raised his brows as he peered through Unwin's car window and spotted a ram lying trussed up like a Christmas turkey on a blanket on the back seat. "What's wrong?"

"First, the old dodger was a beggar to catch. Then when I put him in the car, he head-butted the window and dived straight through. I caught him again and tied up his legs. Now he's peed and pooped on the seat."

"Worse than shit on a shoe," Gus remarked.

Miranda suppressed a giggle. "Why didn't you bring him in a trailer or truck?"

"I don't have one. We've only just moved to the country and bought a small-holding for retirement."

Gus smiled. "If you can't afford a truck, invest in a tow-hitch and trailer with high sides."

Unwin mopped his brow with his limp handkerchief. "Yeah, all in good time. I tried to save money by bringing him in because we live far away. It seems costs were miscalculated when the window broke."

"Mistakes happen," Gus said. "But what'll you say when the glass repair people ask how your window broke?"

Unwin slapped Gus's shoulder and chortled. "I'll tell them my ram thought it was an emergency exit."

"Won't you feel a bit sheepish?"

Unwin bleated.

Gus cleared his throat. "Enough bleating around the bush. What's wrong with him?"

"He's got sore feet."

Gus climbed into the car and examined the hooves. "He has foot rot. Where are you keeping him?"

"In a small, shady pen with my pet goat, near a leaking water trough."

"I'll give his hooves a trim. Then I'll treat them with special spray--you might as well take the tin home and use it again."

"Okay, thanks."

"And get him out into a bigger, sunnier field where he can walk about and wear down his hooves. They're far too long."

"Yes, I'm planning to do that."

"I tell you what," Gus said. "I'll deworm him too. Sheep require regular deworming, especially if you keep them near goats. Goats are hardier than sheep."

"Okay."

After Gus treated the ram, Unwin thanked him and headed home.

***

Later that evening, the air felt hot, so Miranda opened their bedroom windows wide and drew the curtains closed. A slight, cool breeze lifted them gently as they rose and fell softly against the iron burglar bars.

She sighed with relief, thinking, *that feels better.*

Then she applied a Hibitane-soaked bandage to Gus's leg. "That'll help draw out any impurities during the night."

"Thank you, nurse Miranda. Now come here, it's my turn to examine you closer."

Knowing his desire, she smiled and dived, giggling, into the bed and drew closer.

He kissed her lips tenderly. "You're the sexiest nurse a man could want."

"And you're the hardest man I've ever known."

His firmness nudged her thigh. "Lying next to you makes it easy."

"No, Gussy! I wasn't referring to *that*." Snorting humorously, she threw a pillow at his face.

"Ouch!" He feigned pain. "What did you mean?"

"I meant, you're the *toughest* man I've ever known. After stabbing your leg, you carried on working all day as if you were on Cloud 9."

"I am! Being with you is wonderful." He rolled on top of her, nuzzling her neck.

She squealed with delight as their passion unfolded.

Later that evening after a bath and a warm chocolate drink, she jumped into bed, turned off the light and kissed him. "Goodnight." It wasn't long before they fell into a deep slumber.

Sometime during the middle of the night, Gus stirred. Miranda also awoke and said, "What's wrong?"

"Sssh. Listen."

She heard Fat Chops growl outside. "Oh, my goodness. I forgot to bring her in the house." Miranda was about to switch on the light, but Gus grabbed her hand and held it tight.

"Keep still," he whispered. "It might be an intruder."

The idea hadn't occurred to her. Now her heart raced with fear as she lay in frozen silence while her body perspired. *Could Piet van der Skiet be lurking outside?*

Through the open window, they heard Fat Chops growl, a low, threatening grumble.

Gus slipped out from beneath the sheets and tip-toed cautiously towards the window. Slowly, he lifted the edge of the curtain and peered out through the chink into the night. Moonlight streamed through the slit, silhouetting his stark-naked body.

"Do you see anything?" Miranda whispered.

He shook his head while Fat Chops continued to growl in an unusually menacing fashion. He stood in the middle of the window and parted the curtains with both hands, one to the left, the other to the right, standing, bold as brass with his full nude facing the moonlight streaming through the open window with only wide-spaced burglar bars separating him from the outside world.

Shivering, Miranda pulled the sheets up to her neck as she stared at the back of his muscular physique.

Fat Chops exploded into a full-blown attack mode. Barking mad, she scrambled after something rustling in nearby bushes.

"What is it?" Miranda hissed.

They heard Fat Chops gallop at full speed, clearly chasing something, past the window and back again.

Gus pressed his face and body close to the burglar guards, straining to see.

Right then, something flung against the window, smacking the burglar bars with full force. The impact made an incredible 'whack' as what-ever-it-was came to a squealing halt.

From Miranda's viewpoint, she saw Gus clutch his balls with both hands. Alarmed, she sat up and gawked in wide-eyed terror as her petrified eyes latched onto the hugest Cane Rat she'd ever seen. Its huge grey, stout body compared with that of a sizable domestic cat. The two opponents faced each other, eyeball to eyeball, nose to nose and whisker to whisker as they challenged one another to make the first move. The monstrous rat, desperate to save its rump from the dog's snapping jaws, clung onto the burglar bars with both hands while Gus, equally as desperate, continued to hang onto his nut sack.

"Oh, my God!" Not knowing what to do, Miranda's reactive prayer burst forth in a flash of hysteria and mirth in one go. She shot out of bed, yelling commands to Fat Chops to *sit* and *stay*. The dog obeyed.

As a spectator of the momentary standoff, she waited in suspense. Would Ratty bite Gus? Or would it spring off the burglar bars into the hut and attack her?

A shrill scream escaped her lips as Ratty scrambled down the bars and sprang onto the lawn. Its weird, erratic hopping strides had the appearance of a drunken wallaby as it darted off into the night.

Relieved, they fell into each other's arms and laughed uproariously.

Eventually, Miranda caught her breath. "What mad, wild creature tries to enter a house in the face of human beings?"

"One that's being chased by a dog."

"Do you think it has rabies?"

"Nope." Gus shook his head. "I reckon we were mutually surprised and terrified. Now, call Fat Chops and bring her inside. Let that poor thing go free."

<u>CHAPTER FORTY-EIGHT</u>

Paradise Flycatcher

After two weeks Miranda was surprised at Gus's remarkable recovery. Only a raised, red scar on the calf of his leg served as a reminder of his blunt knife encounter.

"Your leg healed remarkably well," she said while making breakfast.

"Thanks to your excellent nursing care." Gus winked.

She stood buttering toast while waiting for the kettle to boil as she peered out the kitchen window.

"Oh, look!" she stood pointing up into the tree at their back door. "Those Paradise Flycatchers have returned."

Gus came and stood next to her. While he observed the birds in the tree, he placed his arm around her waist. He pointed. "They've built a nest right up there."

"Oh, yes! I see it." Miranda grew excited. "Ever since you hung that organic fly trap in the tree, they've been coming around to feed."

As she spoke, the male Paradise Flycatcher swooped down, displaying a flash of his long, graceful, russet-coloured tail as he caught flies attracted to the trap. His dark metallic blue head twinkled in the sun as he flitted and swooped before returning to his nest. Once there, he swapped places with his short-tailed mate, taking his turn to care for their eggs.

"They're fascinating little birds," Gus said with admiration. "Their long-tailed plumage reminds me of the birds of paradise from Papua New Guinea."

She smiled into his eyes. "I'd love to see them one day."

"You bet. I'll take you there."

***

By midday, Gus had finished the day's surgery. He ambled over to Gretchen's desk. "Do I have any farm calls today?"

She shook her head. "No, but Mr Pemberton-Lloyd wants you to call in to visit his Koi fish."

Gus frowned. "Pemberton-Lloyd? Who's he?"

Gretchen laughed. "Come on, everyone knows him. Don't you remember?"

"Nope. Not for the life of me--can't place him."

Gretchen smiled. "He's the guy who owns that massive newly-built mansion down in Silverstream Valley."

Gus looked blank.

"You know, he's the man I told you about who made his fortune from selling cabbages. One year there was a nationwide cabbage shortage due to hail, but his hundreds of acres survived. That year prices hit the jackpot, and he made a fortune. So, he built a mansion and painted it green."

Finally, recognition dawned. "Oh! Of course, I know him. He's the guy who owns Cabbage Castle."

"*Cabbage Castle*. That's a good name! It's green enough and matches his stinky attitude." Gretchen chuckled. "I believe his house has twenty-three toilets."

"Twenty-three?" Gus was appalled.

Gretchen said, "It's a mystery why he wanted so many toilets."

"Maybe he had diarrhoea in mind?"

Gretchen chuckled. "For goodness sake, don't let him hear you say that."

"Sick Koi? Mmm. I'll see what I can do."

Just then, Miranda came in.

"Are you coming with me to Pemberton Lloyd's Cabbage Castle?"

She laughed. "No, thanks. I'm going to my final wedding dress fitting today. Sorry, you're on your own."

"Okay, see you later."

***

After Gus left, Miranda went outside onto the veranda to put on her boots, but no matter how hard she pushed, her foot wouldn't fit in. She turned it upside down and knocked it against the wall. Two frogs plopped out.

"Urgh!"

"What's wrong?" Gretchen called.

"Frogs in my boots! I hate it when they hide there."

"You're lucky it wasn't a scorpion. You should always shake them out first before you put them on."

"Yeah, I forgot."

Gretchen yelled, "See you later. Good luck with your dress-fitting."

"Thanks!"

***

Later that afternoon, Miranda arrived home before Gus.

Gretchen said, "How did it go?"

"Good, thanks. She's an excellent seamstress."

"I told you she was good."

Miranda glanced over her shoulder and shivered. "It looks like we're in for a thunderstorm, Gretchen. Seeing it's so quiet, go home early before the downpour starts."

"Thanks. I will." Gretchen gathered her stuff and left.

Moments later Gus came home, slamming the door behind him. "I reckon we're in for a big storm."

"Yes, that's why I sent Gretchen home early. It's too dangerous to drive in the pelting rain."

Gus smiled. "Thanks. I would have said the same."

"So, what was the problem with the Cabbage Castle Koi?"

"He wants to extend his ponds, but he has a lack of filtration. I explained to him what he needs to do. He'll have to get a builder in to help him."

"Good, I'm glad it wasn't a bad call. Now, what would you like for dinner tonight?"

"Anything pleases," Gus replied.

As Miranda entered the kitchen, the sky grew dark, thunder rumbled, and large raindrops fell. She reached to turn on the stove, but a flash of lightning followed by a huge crackling sound stopped her. "Eeh!" she yelped. "Let me put shoes on before I touch anything electrical."

Just then, the lights went out.

"Oh, darn! I can't cook dinner."

Gus shrugged. "No worries. Let's eat out."

"Driving in the rain is dangerous, and it's Friday night; I doubt we'll get a booking at the Magoebaskloof Hotel."

"I'll drive slowly. Let me phone before the lines go down." Moments later, Gus hung up.

"And?" Miranda said. "Get a booking?"

"No, they're full."

"That's a pity."

He smiled. "No worries. We're going to the Tzaneen Royal Hotel."

She wrinkled her nose. "I've heard it's a bit of a dive."

He sighed. "I need food, and I'm no snob. Should we go or not?"

She smiled. "Yeah. Why not? The electricity might be off until tomorrow morning. Let's go.

<u>CHAPTER FORTY-NINE</u>

Bullseye

On arrival at the Tzaneen Royal Hotel, a waiter dressed in a white, crisp, cotton uniform led them to a table for two in the dimly lit dining room and drew back their chairs.

"Thanks," Gus said as they sat.

The waiter inclined his head causing the black tassel on the top of his fez hat to swing forward as he presented the menu.

"It doesn't look too bad," Gus remarked.

Miranda smiled. "It's better than staying home in darkness and eating bread."

The waiter carried a silver platter with warm bread rolls, placing one on each side plate with tongs, and asked, "Sir, ready to order?"

Gus patted his belly. "Yeah!"

"What will it be?"

"Mutton stew for two, thanks."

He nodded and removed the menu. Another waiter appeared and poured a wine sample.

Gus tipped the glass back and smacked his lips. "Great stuff. A glass each, thank you."

The waiter poured Miranda's before serving Gus.

Gus held up his glass. "Cheers, Miranda, my beautiful bride to be."

"Cheers, my handsome prince."

While they drank and chatted, their waiter returned bearing their steaming hot plates of stew.

The strong-smelling aroma wafted across the table. "Mmm! Delicious," Gus said as the plates were placed.

"Thank you." Miranda smiled.

"Enjoy your meal." The waiter left to serve others.

Classical music played softly in the background.

Halfway through her meal, Miranda stopped eating. She threw down her knife and fork and gagged into the starched cotton napkin.

Concerned, Gus asked, "Are you okay?"

She shook her head.

His eyes widened. "Are you choking?"

Again, she shook her head.

"What's wrong?"

She pushed her chair back, pointing to her plate.

He peered closer and gasped. "Waiter! Waiter! Come here *now*! What the hell is this?"

Everyone stopped eating and gawked.

Embarrassed, Miranda felt her face flush.

The waiter hurried over and bowed. "Yes, sir?"

Angrily, Gus pointed to the offending sheep anus, stewed to perfection, with its perfectly placed poo pellet spot in the middle, not unlike a bullseye. The waiter stooped to examine the target of consternation. Immediately, he recognised their cause for concern and removed the offending platter while promising to bring another.

Miranda shuddered. "No, thank you. Don't bring me anymore; it's all been cooked in the same pot."

The headwaiter rushed over to deal with the fuss. After a heated discussion between him and Gus, they reached a conclusion. Gus didn't have to pay for their meals, and as further compensation, they were each offered one free drink in the bar.

Gus sighed. "Okay, mate. That'll do, thanks. But I tell you what--we won't be eating here again."

Gus took Miranda's arm as they walked through to the smoky bar and got seated.

Miranda shivered. "That was the most disgusting thing I've encountered in a restaurant."

Gus grimaced. "Horrid. Let's try not to think of it while we enjoy our drinks. Hopefully, by the time we get home, the power will be back on." He held her hand and rubbed it affectionately. "Now what would you like?"

"A glass of white wine, please."

"Okay, I'll have a beer. At least, we know they both come out of bottles and should be safe."

She giggled. "It'll be a good story to tell our kids one day."

The barman served their drinks as rowdy men entered. Miranda lowered her head, murmuring, "Oh, no...."

"What?"

"That's Piet van der Skiet and his gang. They're drunk."

Gus steered Miranda gently by the elbow. "Come. Let's go and sit in that dark corner over there. Hopefully, he won't see us. We'll sneak out the door when we're done."

No sooner had they got seated when Gus heard Piet's voice behind him boom, "Well, well. Look who we have here. Miranda the slut and her dog!"

Gus clenched his fists, pushed his chair back and rose to his full height. "Don't you call my fiancée a slut! Apologise at once."

"Stuff you!" Piet slurred. "I don't apologise to bitches and dogs."

Gus's jaw muscles tensed. "Listen here, you little Chihuahua--if anyone's a bitch-dog--it's you."

Piet belched. "You callin' me a whaaat? A shoo-wow-wow bitch-dog?"

"Apologise to Miranda."

Piet's rasping, raucous laugh filled the room. "You can't make me, *dog*."

Gus drew a deep breath and roared, "You're the only dog around here! You're nothing but a *stoepkakker*."

Piet's iron fist lashed out. Gus ducked, the glancing blow swiping the side of his face. Piet underestimated the strength of Gus's cattle pregnancy-testing arm as it reacted faster than Piet's drunken brain calculated. Gus shot one solid punch to the point of Piet's defiant, up-tilted jaw, sending the stoepkakker-Chihuahua reeling across the bar room. Piet's head made a sickening thud as it hit the floor. His body lay dead still. People gasped, screamed and fled as they pushed chairs over in panic.

"Let's go," Gus said.

Miranda grabbed her handbag and ran.

They were leaving the hotel foyer when the distinctive sound of a cocking gun clicked behind them. "Stop! Put your hands in the air. You're under arrest."

Gus turned to look.

"Freeze! Police!" yelled the uniformed policeman as his partner clicked steel handcuffs onto Gus's wrists. "Come with us."

CHAPTER FIFTY

Justice

One of Piet's friends pointed at Gus and yelled, "Yeah! He started the fight."

"Bullshit!" Miranda interjected. "You're a lying snake!"

Another of Piet's friends shouted, "Call an ambulance! Piet's not breathing! He's dead!"

Cold fear trickled down inside Miranda's body; starting at her scalp, trickling into her heart with ice-like tendrils and then into her bowels. *Dead? Oh, no. God, help us!*

Two policemen frog-marched Gus away.

Momentarily, torn between loyalty and obligation, Miranda wasn't sure which way to turn. She wished to follow Gus, but Piet wasn't breathing. She knew how to do CPR. Piet's friends were too stupid and drunk. They were running around squawking like the flightless chickens. Obligation won--she fled to help Piet.

When she arrived at the bar, Piet was in a sitting position, groaning and clutching his head. Enraged, she spun on his friends. "You bunch of vipers! I thought you said he wasn't breathing?"

One guy laughed. "Well, he wasn't."

"Rot! I don't believe you. You're troublemakers."

Piet latched onto Miranda's arm. His grip was like an iron cuff.

"Let me go!" she yelled.

"You're my girl. You want me."

"Urgh! *Never*. You're disgusting. I swear you're mad. Let go!"

He leered into her face, still clutching her arm as he rose to stand. As he stood, his grip softened, and his eyes rolled back, then he staggered and fell over.

She checked his pulse and respiration; they were okay. Then she hauled him onto his side, placing him in a recovery position. Vomit spewed from his mouth. His friends rushed backwards, holding their noses. Miranda continued to hold Piet's head sideways, maintaining his clear airway. *Maybe he has a brain injury.*

Tzaneen, being a small town, had a hospital and police station nearby. Within minutes the paramedics arrived bearing a stretcher. Miranda stepped back as they briefly assessed their patient before carting him off. They would do the best they could.

The headwaiter thanked her for taking control of the situation. She asked the barman, "Did you see who started the fight?"

Piet's friends stared at him, waiting for his reply.

Miranda glimpsed the fear in his eyes as he shrugged. "I don't know. I was busy."

Piet's friends smiled.

Miranda turned to the headwaiter. "Take me to your manager."

"Yes, madam. Come this way."

Behind closed doors, Miranda spoke with the hotel manager and discovered the van der Skiets were supposedly banned from the hotel for previous barroom brawling.

"Why were they here?" Miranda asked.

"Our barman's new and probably didn't recognise them."

Miranda pursed her lips. "It seems to me your barman felt too intimidated to say *who* caused the fight. Please, bring him here into your private office and ask him."

Afterwards, the barman confessed he had seen Piet throw the first punch. Armed with that information, Miranda informed the manager of her recent bum meal.

Embarrassment clouded his face. "I'm sorry to hear about your unfortunate experience. We must cut costs where possible. Sometimes we buy cheap meat from people who slaughter for us. Stew pieces are the scraps collected and swept into a bag. It seems that part went unnoticed."

Miranda's eyes bored into his with a cold stare way beyond her years. "Hotels are supposed to buy meat through abattoirs--not from outside sources."

His body visibly stiffened but he remained quiet.

"As compensation," she said, "Come with me now to the police station. I want your barman to make a statement that clears Gus Bullock's name."

"But we're very busy tonight...."

Miranda's eyes narrowed. "If you don't do as I say, I swear tonight will be this hotel's last night--ever! I'll do everything within my power to make sure it closes. I'll report you to the health department and to the Hotel Board. You'll lose everything when my disgusting dining experience story hits national headlines."

His eyes told her she had him by the throat.

"Come," she said.

He called his barman, and they walked to the police station. On arrival, she saw Gus sitting at a   policeman's desk and writing a statement. He looked up with pen poised. "How's Piet?"

"Last seen alive and heading to the hospital."

"One of his friends is in the next room," Gus said, "and is laying an assault charge against me."

"I've brought two witnesses to help clear your name." Miranda introduced the hotel staff.

The thickset policeman sat as he listened to their stories.

She left them to it and went to the front desk to ask if she might phone the hospital.

"No," said the official, pointing out the door. "There's a public phone on the street."

Miranda found the booth and inserted coins into the slot and dialled. After being put through and getting the information sought, she returned with ground-breaking news. "Sorry to interrupt, but I just phoned the hospital. They say Piet's okay. He passed out because he's drunker than a sailor gone overboard."

The large policeman tore up papers as he rose and fetched Piet's friend. Holding him by the scruff, he asked the barman, "Is this the man who stole the rum bottle?"

Wide-eyed, the barman nodded. "Yes, Sir."

The policeman snapped handcuffs on Rum-thief and said, "You're under arrest. I'm charging you with drunk and disorderly behaviour, theft and false testimony. Tonight, you sleep here--in the holding cell." Then he turned to Gus. "I apologise for the misunderstanding. You're free to go."

Miranda smiled. "Thank you, Sir."

A genial grin spread across the officer's face. "Is Karl Kaalvoet Mostert your father?"

"Yes, Sir."

"I know him!" He chuckled. "We went to school together. He's a good man."

"True, Sir." Relieved, she held Gus's hand. "Come. Tomorrow, we have an early start."

CHAPTER FIFTY-ONE

The Promise

The following morning, Gus rose early before the day became too hot, and did 120 cattle pregnancy tests. On his return, he sat down to an early lunch of cheese, sardines on toast and a salad that Miranda had prepared.

Miranda eyed him. "You look pensive."

He finished eating and pushed his chair back. "After last night's altercation with Piet, I've come to realise it's time for us to leave Africa."

Wide-eyed, she stared. Although he'd promised to return to Australia at some stage, so far it had all been talk.

"Are you ready to start a new life?"

"Yes! A million times--yes."

He smiled. "I'm not sure what I did to deserve your affections. You could've chosen to marry someone else in a better financial position."

"I love you for just being yourself. There's no way I'd marry a boring accountant or lawyer--they're too soft. I admire the work you do. You're strong and funny. Above all, I love you because you're kind."

"What about Piet, the hunter?"

She rolled her eyes. "Are you kidding? Piet's doomed to stay the eternal idiot. He's nothing but a rough drunkard with the potential to turn into a wife-beater." She grimaced. "I'm glad the police are on to him. I'd like nothing better than never to see him again."

"I've shared your sentiment for a while," Gus said. "That's why I applied for a job in Queensland, Australia. I have the chance to buy into a mixed veterinary practice. The good news is they want me soon."

Her eyes lit up. "How soon?"

"Five weeks from today."

She jumped up and hugged him. "Our wedding's in three weeks' time. Two weeks for a honeymoon and then we're off to Aussie!"

"Yeah, that's right. Are you ready to leave your pets behind?"

Her face tensed. "*Please*, can't they come?"

"Six months quarantine, plus transport. I can't afford it. The money is best put towards our future home and business."

She cuddled Wingnut. "I can't leave Wingy behind!"

"And I can't afford to take her. Look, I'm sorry, Miranda. But these are big-girl decisions. You have a few weeks to find homes for our pets--including your horse."

Fighting tears, she bit her lower lip and turned away.

He stood behind and wrapped his arms around her waist. "I'm sorry, I know these are tough decisions."

Tears slid from her eyes in silent anguish before a solitary sniff escaped.

He rocked her body gently while kissing the top of her head. "It's not too late to change your mind."

Her body shuddered. "I must speak to my father."

***

Three weeks had passed since the barroom fight, and Piet had made a good recovery. Piet's friend withdrew his false charge against Gus. When the police took a closer look at Piet, a stack of other crimes were revealed. Piet had managed to clock up several assault charges, while his friends' poaching crimes were revealed. Now under police scrutiny, Piet and his friends had no choice but to stay away from Gus and Miranda and conduct themselves with care.

When Karl Kaalvoet heard of Piet's and his friends' plight, he said, "You know, it reminds me of an old African proverb. *If the sun were to shine at night, people would see that it's not only the hyena that's evil.*"

Miranda sighed. "Oh, Dad, I hope you don't think I'm evil for leaving you and moving to Australia."

"My child, you're not evil. You're a young woman and must plan your life. You've chosen the way you wish to live, and I'll always love you."

"I love you too Dad." She hugged him.

He held her by the shoulders and looked in her eyes. "Something's troubling you. What's up?"

She swallowed. "Gus can't afford to take any of my pets to Australia. It'll break my heart."

"No, it won't--you mustn't let it. I'm surprised you never thought about this sooner. Are you sure you wish to marry him?"

"Oh, yes, Dad. He's the only man for me."

He cleared his throat. "Then you have chosen well."

"If only he were much richer, then I could take my pets--especially little Wingnut."

As he smiled, his leathery skin wrinkled. "Poverty is no crime, only laziness."

"He's certainly not lazy!"

"I know, and in him, I see the start of a prosperous man."

"I hope so."

"Life's a calculated gamble," said her father. "Prosperity's not about having a big bank balance. People can be prosperous in health, love and with family too. Remember, money is just a tool that buys material items. It can't buy love. If a person has no love, they have nothing."

"You're right, Dad. That's why I want you to live with us once we're settled in Australia. Will you come?"

"Maybe, but not just yet. First, you two need time to sort out your new life."

She frowned. "I still haven't found homes for our pets."

"Two people already phoned about buying your horse. So, Ruby's sure to get a good home. I'll keep Fat Chops and Spy. Soon Gretchen will be moving in with all her cats."

"What about Wingnut?"

He smiled. "That's part of the surprise I had planned for your wedding day, but seeing you're anxious, I'll tell you now. I'm paying for Wingnut's expenses; she's going with you."

Miranda flung her arms around his neck. "Thanks, Dad! Tell me, what's the other part of your surprise?"

"I've booked you and Gus into a private game lodge for your Honeymoon."

"Wow! Gus'll love that. Thank you, Daddy!"

"There's more...."

"What?"

"You and Gus have proved your ability to handle money. I'm impressed, you've managed to plan a big wedding on a budget. So, at the end of it, I promise to pay the bills. I want you to start your new venture with as little debt as possible."

"Wow! And wow again, Dad. How can I ever repay you?"

"With your love and respect. Please, remember me when I'm old; that's all I ask."

"I promise I will, Dad."

CHAPTER FIFTY-TWO

Haenertsburg Chapel

Soft rain blessed the morning of Gus and Miranda's wedding. Locals claimed the rain was a blessing from God and their union would be fruitful. By midday, the mist cleared allowing sufficient warm sunshine through to brighten their special day. Their wedding was scheduled for 4:00 pm at the quaint, little Haenertsburg village church. The whole community was abuzz with excitement as they gathered in droves to attend the service in anticipation of a great social celebration. Miranda arrived fashionably late by a few minutes; just long enough to ensure all guests were seated.

As she approached the church, arm-in-arm with her father, she became aware of the strains of gentle piano music and cheerful chatter. An usher lifted his arm and signalled to the pianist at the front to commence playing. Old aunty Margaret played the first bars of Mendelssohn's Wedding March as everyone rose to their feet in hushed silence and craned their necks to see the bride's entry.

Karl Kaalvoet smiled. Miranda reminded him of his late wife; if only she had lived to see her daughter marry. His eyes took in Miranda's soft, simple, sleeveless, cotton dress; adorned with its small, pale pink bows that gathered the soft fabric into scallops above the floor-length hemline. A coronet, made from pink and white rosebuds entwined with fine greenery, and gypsophila flowers held her wispy, light veil in place as it flowed down her back. He whispered in her ear, "You look lovely. Are you ready?"

Miranda nodded. As they took the first two steps forward, a man pulled the bell rope. The first, lofty bell-toll rang out across the valley with jubilance. As she entered the church, she became aware of foot scuffles and stifled cries. Something was amiss. Her eyes darted sideways in furtive panic as she saw a couple of women with hands clutched over their mouths, cowering against their husbands. An elderly man touched Miranda's arm, leaned in and whispered, "Don't worry. A bat just fell out of the bell tower and flapped around. A guy caught it. Everything's under control."

A wave of relief flooded through her veins. She continued to move sedately down the aisle as she noted Gus's radiant smile and approval as she came to stand by his side.

The black-robed minister signalled the congregation to be seated. Afterwards, he proceeded to announce the wedding banns in a dry, monotonous monologue, "Therefore, if anybody should know of any reason that these two people should not be joined together in holy matrimony, they are now to declare it."

An awkward silence ensued as everyone paused with baited breath. How could there be any objection? Right then, Piet van der Skiet's voice roared, "I do! Objection, minister, BUT ...."

Piet never finished his sentence. Karl Kaalvoet's police officer friend clamped his meaty hand over Piet's mouth and said, "Pardon, minister. He's drunk as a skunk! And, under arrest. Please continue."

Piet was dragged out, kicking and struggling, by three burly men while mirthful snickers rippled through the congregation.

The minister said, "Never, in my 42 years as a minister, has anyone ever responded to marriage banns at the altar in such a manner." He paused thoughtfully. "Would anyone else like to object? We have more policemen available and willing to perform their duty."

Another ripple of mirth.

Soon, the congregation settled and listened respectfully to the couple's religious vows exchanged before God. Finally, the minister said, "I now pronounce you man and wife." He turned to Gus. "You may kiss the bride."

Gus and Miranda kissed for an embarrassingly long time until a guy shouted, "Hey, save it for later!" Everyone bellowed with laughter. The old pianist pounded her keyboard to life as the newlyweds walked joyously down the aisle under clouds of dried rose-petal confetti and whoops of joy.

***

Their wedding was a huge success, thanks to the local community's efforts and gigantic attendance. Steve Prinsloo, Gus's boss from Phalaborwa, had come along. So too had David Swanepoel, the army vet from Metz Hospital. A reunion of friends and memories surrounded the couple. A kind lady had volunteered to decorate the venue hall with flowers. Another four had organised the setting of the banquette hall. The men had hunted impala for the pot, and other farmers had donated vegetables. Best of all was the two-tiered fruitcake, adorned with beautiful, intricate white icing. Shouts of applause rang out as the wedding cake was cut and shared. Champagne was served, and toasts were made. Once the speeches were over, Gus and Miranda opened the dance floor with the first dance. Next, she threw her bouquet; a happy young girl caught it.

Gus turned to Miranda. "You look stunning!"

"Thank you. You look pretty tasty yourself."

Eventually, it was time to leave. Miranda and Gus climbed into their car amidst well-wishers as they headed to a wooden hut in a nearby nature reserve for their first honeymoon night together.

Gus turned to Miranda. "I put our bags in the boot. Are you set to go?"

She beamed. "You bet!"

They leaned out the car window, waving goodbye to friends as they headed off to their overnight accommodation.

"Thankfully, it's not too far to go," Gus said as they drove 18 km down a dirt road heading towards the small reserve. But when they arrived, the gate was locked. Gus hooted. Nothing. No nightwatchman, no access.

"Oh, no!" Miranda wailed. "Now we're screwed. And not in the way I hoped."

"Calm down," Gus said. "It's no good upsetting yourself on our wedding night. I'll think of something."

<u>CHAPTER FIFTY-THREE</u>

Beauty and the Beast

Their car's headlights continued to shine on the high, locked gate, highlighting the heavy-duty chain and sturdy padlock. They waited for another five minutes, but nobody came to their rescue.

Gus shrugged. "I guess we'll have to return to the reception hall and ask if anyone can help."

"You're kidding? We can't return to our wedding party--nobody does that."

"We don't have a choice unless you're prepared to sleep in the car."

Miranda groaned. "Oh, no. This is awkward. Embarrassing, to say the least."

Gus manipulated the car and headed back the way they had come. On arrival at the town hall, many people had left, some were clearing up while a few men sat around in various groups joking and laughing.

Curious onlookers gathered as soon as their car pulled up. Frik Bezuidenhout shouted, "Hey, what brings you back? Is everything all right?"

"No, mate," Gus said. "You're just the man we need to see. We're locked out. It appears the night watchman's gone feral."

Frik chortled. "I had a feeling the old basket might sneak off." He delved deep into his trouser pocket and produced a key. "Here, take this. It's a spare. I told him to wait, but I guess the lure of beer and women called him home. Sorry for the inconvenience. Tomorrow morning, leave the key in the cottage kitchen, and I'll collect it."

Gus grinned. "Thanks, mate. Tonight, you're my hero."

"Think nothing of it. Now go and do what married people do."

Gretchen rushed forward, calling, "Wait! Miranda forgot her handbag and purse. Your holiday bookings are inside."

"Thanks, Gretchen." Miranda smiled. "You saved the day."

Gus eyed Miranda's bag. "Luckily we came back. We'll need that."

A cheery crowd waved goodbye as the honeymooners departed for the second time.

***

Later, when they reached their cottage, they collapsed on the bed into each other's arms.

"Wow, that was stressful," Miranda said. "I'm glad we've got tonight's bed sorted."

"Let me ease your mind," Gus offered. "And while I'm at it, I'll ease your clothes off too."

She giggled. "Oh, I'm so lucky to have you all to myself."

"Funny you should say that. I was thinking the same about you!"

A passionate night ensued. Afterwards, they fell asleep, secure in each other's new commitment. The next morning, they rose to the sounds of chirping birds and squabbling vervet monkeys high in the surrounding trees. Warm sunshine streamed in as they drew back the curtains.

Miranda stood stark naked, with hands on hips, before Gus and asked, "Well, what do you think?" She smiled coquettishly.

"I'm an exceptionally lucky man."

She shook her head. "No, that's old news. Look again."

His eyes locked onto her shapely breasts. "You're the world's most beautiful woman."

"No." She sighed. "Look again."

His hungry eyes traversed her body with ardent approval. "I love you. What more can I say?"

"Urgh!" she moaned. "Men are all the same. Once you see tits, you stop thinking. Can't you see anything else?"

Gus looked baffled. "See what?"

"My pussy!"

He grinned. "Yeah, I see it. Beautiful."

"No, Dummy. Look again! I shaved my muff into a heart shape especially for you--and you didn't notice!"

He floundered for consolation. "Oh, yes. Now I see. Thank you, Miranda. What a lovely gesture."

Clearly unimpressed, she rolled her eyes. "All men are the same."

"*Whoa!* I don't like that. It sounds like fighting talk. We should be making love and not war."

"Whatever. I'm annoyed because you didn't see it--I had to tell you."

He blushed. "I'm sorry. I never meant to offend you. Next time, I swear I'll notice."

"There won't be a next time! I won't do it again."

He looked hurt. "Okay, I understand. But I must add something here."

"What?"

"If you think all men are the same and unobservant, then I will counter it by saying 'ditto', woman. You are no different."

"What! Are you crazy? Don't you dare...."

"Sssh!" Gus put his finger to her lips. "Hush, my little hot-head. It's your turn to look at *me*." He pirouetted on one muscular leg, looking no better than a clumsy gorilla ballerina. He stopped turning with his hairy back towards her.

Her eyes widened. There, right in the middle of his hairy back, a pattern had been shaved. Now she noted the large heart-shape with the letter 'M' in the middle. She felt a hot wave of humiliation. "Oh, Gus. I'm sorry! Honestly, I don't know what to say...."

"Try: *thank you*; or, *I'm sorry*; or, *I love you too*."

She laughed until tears ran. "Now, we're even."

"Yeah, and don't you forget it." He wagged his finger playfully in her face. "Come on, let's get out of here. I can't wait to see that private game lodge."

***

Two and a half hours later, they arrived at Nguni Tree Haven Safari Lodge. As they climbed out the car to walk to reception, a tame cheetah sauntered by, panting in the heat. Gus whipped out his camera and snapped a shot.

A deep, male voice laughed. "Welcome, Gus and Miranda, to our game lodge. Photography is the only kind of shooting we allow here. My name's Kevin, and I'll be your tour guide."

"Pleased to meet you."

"Come, follow me to your room."

"Wow, this is amazing!" Miranda said as soon as they entered their room, which was high up on stilts amidst treetops. "What a spectacular view."

Kevin smiled. "This is the best room we have--the most luxurious. Enjoy your stay."

Gus grinned. "Thanks, mate. We sure will."

"By the way," Kevin said. "Everything has been prepaid. Feel free to eat and drink all you wish. All our amenities are available at no extra charge. We have guided game tours twice a day. Our afternoon one starts at 3:30 pm. Feel free to meet at the zebra-striped Landrover."

"Thanks!"

After he left, Gus said, "Your father is generous. He's been so good to us."

"I know. He's a real sweetie."

***

The afternoon game drive delivered opportunities for memorable photographs from the back of the open-air Landrover. First, they drove through a herd of buffalo. Then they spotted a lone rhino with a large horn, but he looked twitchy, so the driver decided to move on. Next, they ventured near a herd of elephants with young at a waterhole. They quietly photographed the big beasts' playful antics as they witnessed them spraying each other while wallowing in the water.

On the way back to the lodge, the driver stopped and pointed to a lion kill. Gus craned his neck. "Oh, wow! That looks fresh."

"Yes," Kevin said. "I'll drive closer."

Miranda's heart pounded in her chest. They were close enough to smell fresh blood. A male lion stopped eating long enough to look up and roar. Gus snapped a photo that later revealed the lion's big teeth and blood-stained chin.

"I hope they don't turn on us," Miranda said. "I don't feel safe sitting in this open-air Landrover."

"If they charge or come too close, I'll drive off," Kevin said.

"Have you had any close shaves with tourists?" Miranda asked.

"A few, but so far, all have survived."

***

Later, when they returned to their tree-top accommodation, they found their cottage had been ransacked, and a foul-smelling turd was left on the floor as a token of appreciation for the free pickings.

"Oh, this is disgusting!" Miranda shook her head. "I would've thought security was better than this at such a smart lodge.

Gus poked his head out the window and laughed. "Ah! Look, there go the culprits."

Miranda looked and saw a troop of baboons down below with their laundry spread out on the lawn. "Oh, you're kidding! That one's got my favourite bra on its head!"

Gus snapped a photo of the rascal, then said, "I must say, you look better in it."

She delivered a playful slap to his arm and laughed. "Thank you."

Kevin helped get their clothes back, but everything had to be re-laundered. "Next time," he warned, "when you go out, ensure your windows and doors are closed so they can't get in. They won't try their luck when you're inside the cottage."

That night, they dined in a thatched shelter overlooking part of the Olifants River, at a table set for two. A waiter came and lit a mosquito-repellent citrus oil candle for them. Miranda touched the delicate rosebud on the table and said, "I love pink roses."

Gus's eyes smiled warmly towards her. "I know, that's why I asked them to put one here."

"Oh, you're so thoughtful. Thank you."

"This is the most wonderful experience of my life," Gus said, holding her hand. He observed many animals coming to drink from the river, as was their early morning and evening ritual. Hippos floated peacefully while impala, kudu and wildebeest drank.

Amazed, Miranda gasped. "Look there! Far over to the left of that thorn tree--see the leopard?"

"Yeah." Gus watched the sleek animal lap water before slinking off quietly back into the bush.

"They tend to be nocturnal, so that was a lucky sight."

***

The following morning, the two lovers awoke to the feeling of warm air blowing over their faces. Gus cocked an eye, just in time to see a giraffe with its head through their window, stealing apples off their dresser.

He whispered in Miranda's ear. "Sssh. Wake up slowly. A giraffe's stealing apples from our bowl."

She peered out from beneath the sheets and giggled.

The long-necked animal turned to gaze at her before withdrawing its head back out the window where it continued to munch the foliage around their window.

***

The following day, Kevin took them to visit the white lions of Timbavati and some tourist shops that were rich in African curios.

As their Honeymoon rolled on, each day brought forth some new, small adventure. Cooling off in the crystal-clear stone swimming pool was another luxurious option when it was too hot for game drives. Their stay at the game lodge passed sooner than they thought possible, but a new adventure lay ahead--their journey to Australia.

***

On the morning of their departure, Karl and Gretchen drove them to the Johannesburg Airport. They walked together to the international departures section where they kissed and hugged farewell. Old Karl withdrew a handkerchief from his pocket and wiped his eyes before hugging Miranda firmly to his chest. "Good-bye, my child, till we meet again."

Tears sprang to her eyes too, catching her by surprise. "Thank you, Dad. You've done so much for us. We can never repay you."

"One more thing," Karl said. "I have this for you." He handed Miranda an envelope. "Promise me not to open it until you are on the plane."

"Okay, Dad." She said, taking the crisp white envelope and placing it safely in her handbag.

A loud woman's voice pierced the airwaves from loudspeakers above the noisy crowds. "Calling all passengers for flight JB4719, Johannesburg to Brisbane. Please clear your boarding passes now."

Gus looked up at the overhead board. "That's us. We've got to go through." He shook Karl's hand warmly. "Bye, Dad. Till we meet again."

Miranda turned from her father with tears streaming as Gus put his arm around her and escorted her through the Departures Gate.

***

Once all passengers were on board the plane, the air hostess welcomed everyone and then proceeded to demonstrate emergency procedures. All seatbelts were fastened. Soon, their plane taxied down the runway, turned south and powered up as it took off into the azure sky.

Ten minutes later, Gus turned to Miranda and asked, "What's in that envelope?"

She pulled it out of her bag, and they read it together.

> *My dearest, Miranda and Gus*
> *Best wishes on your new venture and life together. I've bought you a farm in Queensland; my lawyer will forward you the papers.*
> *Miranda, I'm glad you managed to tie that wild Australian Dingo-man down. My gift to you is a well-bred and trained Australian Stock Horse. He'll be delivered to your farm as soon as you're ready. I've enclosed contact details.*
> *And, Gretchen and I are planning to visit you next year after we're married.*
> *See you soon: God willing.*
> *Love*
> *Dad*

Gus said, "You know, I really like your father. I hope he and Gretchen come to live with us."

"Me too." She touched Gus's hand. "I'm so glad we tied the knot. I love you, Dingo-darlin'!"

Gus smiled.

"And I can't wait to practice making babies."

His eyes widened. "Who said anything about *babies*?"

"I did. Because I've finally tied my Dingo down, mate."

THE END

Epilogue:

Old cars were without air-conditioning. They were the days before GPS and mobile phones. Locating farms and sick animals could be a test of wits--especially with language barriers and people who confused left turns with right.

Strange horse facts: Horses cannot vomit. Horses don't eat wire or nails although cattle can and often do. A horse's lips are as sensitive as human fingers; they tend to feel their food as they eat.

These stories date back to a time before the introduction of affordable sonar pregnancy testing on cattle farms in rural South Africa. Over the past 40 years, veterinary equipment and medicines have improved and become more attainable. Back then, a full day's work for a young, fit vet might include manual rectal examinations of 300 to 400 cows. Time efficiency depended on the ability of a farmer to organise his crew effectively. For the vet, the short-term complications of a day in the sun were: gritty eyes (from dust), dehydration, sunburn, a green arm and a stiff shoulder. Long-term side-effects often included: skin cancer, back stiffness and exposure to brucellosis.

However, with the advancement of modern equipment and easier procedures, veterinary has become more accessible and appealing to women. In modern times it has become a female-dominated profession.

<u>REVIEWS</u>

Please, leave a review; but don't complain about the use of UK
English, or compare this with James Herriot,
or you'll appear to be a moron--you were warned!
BEWARE OF THE DOG.
Try not to hurt its feelings; it gets snappy when I'm attacked.

Thanks for reading.

Eat, sleep and breed well.

Stoepkakker Friend

-X-

ABOUT THE AUTHOR

Nicole O'Connor was born in Zimbabwe in 1965. After living in Africa for five generations she and her family moved to New Zealand. She studied nursing at B.G. Alexander College of Nursing in Johannesburg, South Africa, and qualified with distinction. Horses and art are her favoured interests. She is a keen animal lover and found the love of her life when she met her top-dog veterinary surgeon husband. Together they have two grown sons and a houseful of happy pets.

Her other book titles include:

HOTEL GIRLS-- Amazon: Book, Kindle & Audible
https://www.amazon.com/Hotel-Girls-Nicole-OConnor-ebook/dp/B00OI77OPU/
Genre: romance / coming-of-age / humorous twisted romance (*contains some sex with minimal swear words)

THE EVOLUTION OF SYLVIA GRAVES
Amazon: Book & Kindle
Genre: romance / coming-of-age (*contains some sex and swear words)

WEBSITE:

www.bestbookchoice.com

FACEBOOK:

https://www.facebook.com/BestBookChoice/

AMAZON AUTHOR PAGE:

https://www.amazon.com/Nicole-Ann-OConnor/e/B00OPNUWCO/ref=ntt_dp_epwbk_0